EMPRESS IN DISGUISE

EMPRESS IN DISGUISE

EMPRESS IN DISGUISE BOOK 1

ZOEY GONG

AMANDA ROBERTS

Red Empress Publishing
www.RedEmpressPublishing.com

Cover by Cherith Vaughan
CoversbyCherith.com

PREFACE

In one of the girls' schools in Peking there was a beautiful child, the daughter of a Manchu woman whose husband was dead. One day this widow came to the principal of the school and said: "A summons has come from the court for the girls of our clan to appear before the officials that a certain number may be chosen and sent into the palace as serving girls." "When is she to appear?" inquired the teacher. "On the sixteenth," answered the mother. "I suppose you are anxious that she should be one of the fortunate ones," said the teacher, "though I should be sorry to lose her from the school." "On the contrary," said the mother, "I should be distressed if she were chosen, and have come to consult with you as to whether we might not hire a substitute." The teacher expressed surprise and asked her why. "When our daughters are taken into the palace," answered the mother, "they are dead to us until they are twenty-five, when they are allowed to return home. If they are incompetent or dull they are often severely punished. They may contract disease and die, and their death is not even announced to us; while if they prove themselves efficient and win the approval of the authorities they are retained in the palace and we may never see them or hear from them again."

Court Life in China
Isaac Taylor Headland

ALSO BY ZOEY GONG

Contemporary Romance

The New Year Boyfriend

The Animal Companions Series

A Girl and Her Elephant

A Girl and Her Panda

A Girl and Her Tiger

Empress in Disguise Trilogy

Empress in Disguise

Empress in Hiding

Empress in Danger

ALSO BY AMANDA ROBERTS

Fiction Novels

Threads of Silk

The Man in the Dragon Mask

The Qing Dynasty Mysteries

Murder in the Forbidden City

Murder in the British Quarter

Murder at the Peking Opera

The Touching Time Series

The Child's Curse

The Emperor's Seal

The Empress's Dagger

The Slave's Necklace

Empress in Disguise Trilogy

Empress in Disguise

Empress in Hiding

Empress in Danger

Nonfiction

The Crazy Dumplings Cookbook

Crazy Dumplings II: Even Dumplinger

1

———

"*D*aiyu! Daiyu!" my sister, Junli, says as she jumps up and down and pulls on my arm. "What's it say? What's it say?" We are two of dozens of people crowded around a palace official who is nailing a piece of paper to the community board in the marketplace.

"I don't know," I say, not only because I can't see over the crowd, but because I can't read. I wait for the official to make an announcement, but as soon as he finishes his task, he elbows us out of the way and moves on. I can see he has a whole stack of papers to put up. Everyone moves in front of the sign, and I know I'm not the only one who can't read it. Still, it must be important if it is from the Forbidden City.

"What's it say?" Junli asks again.

"Excuse me, uncle," I say to a kindly looking man standing next to me. "What does the sign say?"

"Probably nothing that concerns you," he says as he squints. "Looks like there is going to be a selection ceremony for new consorts for the emperor. Manchu consorts." The man spits as he turns and walks away. I see two men talking animatedly about the announcement, and I hear one of them shout a loud curse on the imperial family.

"What's he talking about?" Junli asks. I grab her arm and pull her away from the crowd. No wonder the man putting up the sign left in such a hurry. He didn't want to be around for any fights that might break out because of it.

"The emperor is looking for a new wife," I explain simply and quickly to Junli. Actually, he'll probably take dozens of women into his court as concubines, but I don't want to explain this to a six-year-old. "But only from among the Manchu, of course."

"Oh," Junli replies. As young as she is, even she is aware of the bitter division between the mostly Han Chinese people and the ruling Manchu elite. Two hundred years ago, the Manchu were a bunch of horse-riding, barbarian nomads living north of the wall. They invaded our country during a moment of weakness and now rule us all.

"It would be nice to be an empress," Junli says absently. "Or a princess, wouldn't it, Daiyu? Then I'd live in the Forbidden City and wear the prettiest clothes."

I raise my eyes to the large, imposing, red-brick wall of the Forbidden City that looms over our poor neighborhood.

"I shouldn't think so," I say. "It looks like a prison. You know why it's called the Forbidden City, right?"

"No."

"Because once a woman enters, she is forbidden from *ever* leaving!"

"No!" Junli says. "That's not true."

"It is," I insist. "The women are all locked inside a beautiful garden. There are luscious plants, plenty of fruits and vegetables, and they wear beautiful clothes. But it's a trap."

"What kind of trap?" I have her hooked now.

"A spider's trap! Rawr!" I hook my fingers into claws and

snarl. Junli squeals and runs away from me. We dodge between other market-goers, around a beggar, and down a long row of food stalls. The smoke and steam of the grills and bamboo baskets make my mouth water.

"Hey, hey!" a man says when I make the mistake of catching his eye and slowing to a walk. "Steamed pork bun! Very cheap! Very delicious!"

I shake my head and walk away, my stomach growling. I only have enough money for a jin of rice and a measure of pork to feed my whole family. I can't waste any of it on myself. But when I look back to the road, I don't see my sister.

"Junli?" I call out, and already I can feel myself panicking. "Junli!" I rush down the road, nearly toppling over a woman with bound feet.

"Watch out!" she scolds.

"Sorry!" I shake a man's sleeve. "Have you seen a little girl?" He shrugs and turns away. I should never have let her out of my sight! It's so easy for a child to get snatched. A pretty little girl could fetch enough money at a brothel to feed a family for a month.

"Junli!" I scream.

"I'm right here," she says, appearing at my side from seemingly nowhere. She's holding a stick of fried meat, chomping away happily.

"Where did you get that?"

She points to a nearby vendor. "He dropped it on the ground, so he said I could have it."

The man gives a small smile and wave. I take Junli by the arm and drag her away. I know the man meant well, no sense in letting the food go to waste, but the idea that my sister had no qualms about eating food dropped in the dirt, such was her hunger, makes me sick.

We finally make it to the market stall of a woman I know well. "Good morning, laoma," I say.

"Welcome, little sister," she says.

I hand her two coins and a metal container from a slouch bag that hangs from my shoulder. "Rice and pork." She nods and takes the container from me, measuring out the rice and then pouring it into the container. My face falls when I pick the container up.

"It feels a bit light," I say. She points up to the sky.

"There's a drought. The farmer brought me much less than usual, so I had to raise the price. The governor of Peking has refused to help supplement the meager harvest."

"What about the emperor?" I ask.

The woman scoffs and then laughs. "You think he cares about us? He'll soon have a hundred more mouths to feed after the selection process."

It doesn't seem fair that one man should have enough money to feed a hundred wives while my father can barely afford to feed his only one and his five children. I weigh the container in my hands again. "This isn't enough for my family, you know that."

"Sorry," she says with a shrug. I'm struck dumb. I don't have more money, but I can't return home with so little food. I'm about to cry when the woman takes pity on me and opens my container, dropping in another small scoop of rice. It still isn't enough, but it's the best she can do. At least she gives me the usual amount of pork. I take my purchases and slip them into my bag as I walk away.

"Hey, you cheated my wife!" I hear a man growl at the woman.

"I'll tell you what I told her—" the woman says, going on to tell him the same story she told me. I take some solace in the fact that she must not have been lying if she was charging everyone more money. It wouldn't be good business to cheat repeat customers. Still, I'm not sure what I'm going to do. Our food is already not enough for everyone. Mama looks so thin, I think the new baby at her breast might be sucking her very essence from her.

"Look, Daiyu," Junli says, shaking my arm and pointing ahead. An opera troupe has set up in the middle of a market road. They are all dressed in colorful costumes, though only one man is singing. The rest of the troupe are playing instruments, an erhu, a flute, and a drum. A dwarf with a monkey goes around the crowd with an upturned hat, asking for donations. I wish I had money to give them.

The opera is a popular one, if a little vulgar. It's called *Drunken Beauty,* and while there are some other characters early on, the majority of the opera is sung by one person. An imperial concubine, in a bid to get the attention of the emperor since she is merely one of three thousand concubines, has invited the emperor to meet her for a drink at the One Hundred Flower Pavilion. However, through a mix-up, the emperor doesn't show up, so the concubine drinks the wine alone. Through the show, the concubine becomes increasingly drunk, which leads to a series of hilarious songs and antics and even some impressive acrobatics, depending on the skill of the performer. This young man seems to be focusing more on his singing, which is quite lyrical.

The dwarf stops in front of Junli and lets her pet the monkey. She touches his fur and then runs back to me laughing.

"Did you see? Did you see?" she asks me.

"I saw. Go on, watch the show." She goes back to the front of the crowd where a few children have gathered. I look around at the people, most of whom are familiar to me. People from the same neighborhood who have lived around me my whole life. People in the same situation as my own family, trying to survive on less and less money each year while the families grow ever larger. I shield my eyes from the growing sun and dust that is blown about on a meager breeze. Aside from the great red wall, all of Peking seems to be various shades of brown. The drought has been more intense than I realized.

I look away from the singer as the sun reflects from his headdress right into my eyes and I see a shoe vendor. I almost turn away—I could never afford a pair of new shoes —but then a thought strikes me and I wander over.

"New shoes, miss?" the man asks. "Lucky red shoes sure to fit your lotus feet."

"I don't have lotus feet," I say. The man looks down at my unbound feet and then sniffs. "I have a few pairs for big-footed girls."

"No," I say, "I was wondering if you are buying." I reach down and slip my shoes off. It's summer, so I don't really need them when the roads are dry. I hope I can get enough for them to buy food to last my family a few days. I can scrape together enough supplies between now and winter to sew myself another pair, I hope.

The man holds his hand out. "Let me see."

I hand him the shoes and a small amount of sadness takes me over as I look at the delicate flowers Mama embroidered on them for me.

"Fair quality, but rather used," the man mumbles. I shrug. I don't know how long I've worn them, since at least last summer, but they've held up well. He reaches into his waistband and pulls out two small coins. I laugh.

"You expect me to go barefoot for so little?" I reach for the shoes to pull them back.

"Fine, fine, little sister," the man says, pulling out two more coins. I hesitate, wondering if I could get more, but I know I can buy enough rice for a week with what he's offering. I nod and quickly grab the coins. I return to the opera and clutch Junli's shoulder.

"Aww," she moans at having to leave.

"Come on, Mama needs us." As I move away, the dwarf slips through the crowd in front of me, holding his hat up expectantly. I feel a small pang of guilt as I hold tightly to the coins in my hand. I know the troupe isn't performing for free, but in expectation that people will give at least a small amount of money in exchange for the entertainment. But I have six hungry mouths waiting for me, not counting my own, so I push my guilt aside along with the dwarf as I drag Junli with me back to the food stall.

As we pass the sign announcing the new concubine selection, I'm reminded just how unfair it is that a bunch of barbarians should have so much while the rest of us have so little. I don't even have a pair of shoes to wear while the emperor will be able to dress a hundred women in multitudes of fine silk garments.

I turn to the big, red wall and spit on the ground. I know no one inside will ever know the insult I just sent their way, but it makes me feel a little better.

2

"I wish you hadn't sold your shoes," Mama says that evening as I fry up some of the meat to add to the children's bowls of rice, bowls that are full for the first time in weeks. I add some meat to the last bowl and hand it to Mama. She shakes her head.

"No, you eat it," she says.

"I ate earlier, while you were sleeping."

She hesitates, and I think she knows I'm lying, but she's far more hungry than I am. She's so thin, she appears to be nothing more than bones covered by tight skin. The baby sucks at her breast constantly and yet still cries in hunger.

"Please," I say, near to tears.

She takes the bowl and eats eagerly, though I can see the tears in her eyes as well. I know it hurts her to take food from me, but if one of us is going to die of hunger, it will be her first, and then the baby. I can go on with less food for a while. I've done it before. I know that I just bought more rice than we have been able to afford in weeks, but we need it to last as long as possible.

"Is there any more?" my sister Mingming asks.

"Not tonight," I say. "But there will be more tomorrow."

The door to our one-room house opens and Baba walks in. His eyes go wide when he sees the children all eating.

"What is happening?" he asks. I fill a bowl with rice and pork and hand it to him.

"I found a little extra money," I say, "and was able to buy more rice than usual. Here, eat."

He takes the bowl and practically pours it into his mouth, the food gone in only a minute. When he's done, he sighs in satisfaction.

"What did you have to do to get it?" he asks me accusingly when he hands the bowl back.

I can't help but be hurt by his words and look away as I rinse the bowl in a small pail of water.

"I sold my shoes," I say. I don't have to look at him to see the shame on his face, I can feel it keenly enough. He grunts and walks over to the bed, sitting next to Mama as he takes off his own shoes and stretches out.

"Here," he says. I turn and he flips a coin at me. "That's all I was able to earn today."

Mama tisks her tongue and looks away. She earns more money than Baba does through her embroidery work than he does through day-laboring. Still, altogether, it's not enough to feed a family of six, not counting the baby. Mama hands the baby to Baba and totters over on her bound feet to sit by the open window, pulling her embroidery basket next to her. She needs to get as much work done as possible while there is still light. The baby whines as Baba rocks it.

"Dong Fa told me that he sold his second daughter to a brothel last week," Baba says.

"What?" I ask with alarm. The Dong family lives at the end of the alley, and we've known them most of my life. Their second daughter can't be more than eight years old.

"And the baby he sold to a family whose son died," he goes on rather absently as he continues to rock his own tiny baby. I look at Mama and see that she is not working, but staring at her hands intently. "She is to be a ghost bride when she is old enough."

A ghost bride. A fate worse than death according to some. Even though the boy is dead, the girl will be considered his wife and must serve her in-laws as any dutiful daughter-in-law would for the rest her life—but without the comfort of a husband and children of her own. She'll spend her life as nothing more than a slave.

I'm not sure why Baba has brought this up except to hint that one of the children will have to be sold if we are to survive. I look at my sisters, Mingming, who is twelve, Junli, who is six, and Huanji, only three, and fear grips my heart at the idea of any of them being forced into a brothel. Of course, the madam would assure Baba that they wouldn't be given to customers until they were old enough, but we all know that that isn't true. There is no shortage of wicked men who will pay for the company of a girl too young to understand what is happening to her.

"I will find a position," I say, standing up from my bucket. "I can find a place as a maid to a rich family. Or I can go to Suchou and get a job at the embroidery factories."

"No!" Baba says, placing the baby aside and standing to face me. He's terribly thin, much like Mama, but he is at least a head taller than I am. "If we do that, you'll never be able to marry. It's been hard enough to find a husband for you with your big, ugly feet."

I curl my toes under and move my pantlegs to try and hide my feet. I glance at Mama and her tiny bound feet. It was unconventional for Mama to not bind my feet. In fact, I don't know any families with girls with unbound feet, no matter how poor. It's nearly impossible to find a husband for a girl with unbound feet. But Mama couldn't do it to us.

Mama says that she nearly died after her feet were bound due to an infection, and her younger sister did, in fact, die. So she was too afraid to bind our feet, and Baba couldn't do it, so instead, we are a family of big-footed girls. Some people have even mistaken us for Manchu girls at times since the Manchu do not follow the tradition of foot-binding.

In some ways, I'm grateful that my feet were not bound. It's a life of constant pain, and the daily ritual of having to wash and wrap the feet is painful and tiring. But I know that the chance of me marrying, of any of us marrying, is very small.

"You know I'm not going to marry no matter what," I say. "My feet aren't bound and I have no dowry. I only have sisters, so no one will believe I can bear sons. The matchmaker has never knocked on our door because she knows we are all lost causes."

"Then what good are you?" Baba asks, his voice straining. I know he wants to yell, be angry, but tears prick the corners of his eyes. He feels like a failure, I know it. "I should just sell you and be done with it!" he says, turning away from me. "All of you!"

There's no point in arguing with him. It's the same fight week after week. Baba has said for years that he should sell us, but he never does. He loves us too much, to his own detriment.

"Come on," I say to the other girls, motioning toward the door. I pick up the pail of dirty water and follow them into the hutong, the alley where we live. I toss the water away and then follow the girls as we walk toward the water pump, one shared by the whole neighborhood.

We pass a building that has been converted into a public house and I see Dong Fa inside, drinking. I feel sick. To think he just sold two of his children and is wasting the money on getting drunk. He at least could have used it on food for his remaining family. But as we reach the water pump, which is very near the Dong house, my heart thumps hard and I drop the bucket.

Dong Fa's wife is dead. She's laid out in front of the house, covered by a white cloth. I only now notice that a few people have gathered around to stare and gossip.

"What happened?" I ask a person standing next to me.

"Hung herself," the woman says, shaking her head. "You heard what happened to her daughters? She couldn't stand the pain of it."

Tears escape my eyes and I think I will be sick. Not for the Dong family, but for my own. I know that Baba has no real wish to sell us, no matter what he says, but will it come down to that or dying of starvation? Mama is already so thin, and the baby sickly. I do not believe it will survive the winter.

"Daiyu?" Mingming says, tugging my sleeve. "What's wrong?"

"Go back," I tell her. "Take the little ones home."

"Why?" she asks, concern on her face. "Where are you going?"

"Just go," I tell her, pushing her away. I don't wait for her to try and talk me out of it before I walk away. I have to do something. I can't let my family die or my little, innocent sisters be sold away.

I start walking, and the sun begins to set. I won't get far before dark, but I have to hope it's far enough.

I pass several brothels, red lanterns lit outside and women with obscene amounts of paint on their faces calling enticingly to passing men to join them inside. But I walk on. If I'm going to sell myself to a brothel, it's going to have to be worth the money. These places wouldn't pay enough to save my family.

I keep walking and walking, walking until my feet hurt and the sky is a deep blue. It won't be safe for me to be out at night in an unknown place, so I have to hurry. I start to cross a street and hear a horse whinny and a man cry out. I fall back and realize that I walked right in front of a horse pulling a carriage. The horse rears up as the man grabs the reins and tries to steady it.

"I'm sorry!" I say, my heart in my nose and my knees shaking so hard I'm not sure I can keep walking.

The door to the carriage flies open and a finely dressed woman steps out. I know she is Manchu as soon as I see that she is wearing shoes with thick platforms. The Manchu might not bind their feet, but they still wear ridiculous shoes that make it difficult to walk.

"What's going on?" the woman screeches. "I nearly fell and broke my neck!"

"Sorry, mistress," the man says, getting the horse under control. "This idiot girl tried to kill herself by throwing herself in front of the horse."

"I didn't!" I say to the woman. "It was an accident. I'm sorry."

The woman looks at me as if she has seen a ghost. "Who...who are you?"

I look at the man and then see that a few people have gathered around to watch what is going on.

"No one," I say.

The woman steps forward much more quickly than I would have thought capable on her precarious shoes and grabs my arm. "Who are you?"

"No one!" I say again as I try to pull away, but she has a terrible grip on me.

"Tell me, girl, now!" she orders.

"Let me go!" I yell and I push her away. She loses her balance and falls back. A man from the crowd steps forward to catch her. As the woman stands back up, she gives me a hard look and I know she's going to grab me again. I turn and push my way through the crowd.

"Stop her!" I hear the woman call. "Stop that girl!" But thankfully no one does, and in a moment I'm through the crowd and running back toward home.

Was she going to have me arrested for accidentally stepping in front of her carriage? I can't wait around to find out. I don't like the way she was looking at me. Was she angry? Afraid? I can't be sure.

It's late and growing dark and the woman might hire men to find me, so I must abandon my plans to sell myself tonight. There's always tomorrow.

3

———

"No, don't!" I yell as Huanji tries to splash me with some of her wash water as I serve up bowls of congee for breakfast. She laughs and splashes me even more.

"Leave your sister alone," Mama says with a chuckle as she bounces the baby on her knee. "Look, Daiyu, she's smiling!" I take Mama a bowl and see that, indeed, the baby is smiling and cooing, not crying for once.

"She's so cute," I say. "What are we going to call her?" We've just been calling her "baby" so far.

"I don't know," Mama says as she tries to juggle the baby and her bowl. Baba comes over and takes the baby, holding her up in the air.

"She's a strong one," he says, and I can see the pride in his eyes. One night of sleeping with full bellies seems to have done everyone some good. I haven't seen so many smiling faces in this house since... Well, I can't remember when.

"Where are you going to look for work today?" Mama asks Baba.

"I think I might walk to the riverfront," he says. "There is always cargo that needs unloading."

"It's so far," Mama says, concerned. "You wouldn't make it back today. Are you sure you're up for it?"

"I have a lot of energy today," he says. "Besides, we need more money to keep us together. More than I can find around here. You have enough food for the week, so I'll stay at the wharf for a few days. When I get back, maybe we should think about moving closer to the river so I wouldn't have to travel so far to find decent-paying work."

I'm not sure if this is a good idea or not. Dock work is brutal, and I doubt Baba would live to be an old man if he decided to try and do it every day. The area is also dirty and stinks of fish. We would have more money, though, so it's a difficult decision.

"The emperor is holding the consort selection soon," I say. "There could be work building more rooms and palaces in the Forbidden City soon."

Baba scoffs. "Consort selection. Ridiculous. How many women does one man need?"

"I'd like to be a consort," Junli says as she twirls around. "I'd have beautiful dresses and servants and so much food! I'd send most of it back here to you, Mama, so you'd never be hungry."

"Such a thoughtful girl," Mama says, squeezing Junli's chin. "But I'd never see you. Could you live your life without ever seeing your loving Mama again?"

"I'd come back!" Junli exclaims, her eyes wide. "I'd never leave you, Mama!"

Mama holds Junli close. "Well, there's no need to worry. The emperor will only marry Manchu girls, so you are quite safe."

There's a heavy pounding on the door that immediately

raises the tiny hairs on my arms as I remember the accident I nearly caused last night. Did the woman find me? Did I really do something so terrible?

"Hong Laoye!" a voice booms, asking for my father. "Open up!"

Baba looks at Mama, who is holding the baby protectively. She shakes her head, and Baba holds a finger to his mouth to tell us all to be quiet. It can never be good news when someone you don't know bangs on your door. I wonder for a moment if it has nothing to do with me, but is a debt collector.

There is another bang and demand for Baba to open the door. This time, the baby cries. Mama tries to shush it, but it is too late.

"Open the door," I hear a woman say, and it sounds just like the woman from last night. I look around futilely for somewhere to hide or a way to escape the single room dwelling.

Baba sighs in resignation and opens the door. "Yes?" he asks, folding his hands together and bowing respectfully.

I can't see outside with the bright morning sunlight shining into the dark room, but I see the shape of a man move aside and a smaller figure steps forward, nudging Baba out of the way as she steps into our home without invitation.

I can see her more clearly now than I could the night before. She is still wearing the pot-bottom shoes of a Manchu, which makes her appear taller than any of us. Her floor-length robe is heavily embroidered, and her head-dress is studded with so many jewels and decorations I wonder how she can hold her head up. She is undoubtedly a wealthy woman.

She holds her chin up as her eyes sweep around the

room. She frowns as though there is a putrid smell, and I suppose we do stink compared to her since we have no more than a single basin to wash in and no perfumed soaps to use.

"My lady?" Baba asks, confused when the woman doesn't speak.

Finally, her eyes land on me and I instantly fall to my knees and bow my head.

"Forgive me, my lady," I cry into my hands. "I'm sorry. I should have watched where I was going. I'm sorry if I caused you any upset."

"What is going on?" Baba asks, stepping between myself and the woman. "Who are you? What do you want with my daughter?"

"Calm yourself," the woman says. "I had to make sure your daughter didn't run away again. Thankfully she wasn't too difficult to identify."

"Who *are* you?" Baba asks again.

The woman smiles. "Someone who is about to change your life."

~

*M*ingming pours tea into teacups with chipped edges, but the strange woman, who is sitting primly on a rough-hewn chair, accepts the cup graciously.

"My name is Ula-Nara Mingxia, of the Bordered Blue Banner clan," she says proudly. It means little to me which Manchu clan she belongs to. What is she doing in our house?

"My husband was a general in the imperial army, but he died some time ago," she says. "Quite young. We had only one daughter before he had to lead a campaign against foreign invaders. He never returned home."

"I am sorry to hear that," Mama says as she nurses the baby. Mingxia looks at the baby longingly. I'm suddenly alarmed, afraid that she is going to want to buy the baby for herself. But why?

"My daughter is the most precious thing in the world to me," the woman says, turning her gaze from the baby to my mother. She reaches out and places a hand on Mama's arm. "You can understand that, can't you? The need to do whatever it takes to protect your children."

"Of course," Mama says cautiously.

Mingxia gives a small smile. "I knew it. After all, you have five! And you haven't sold any of them! They must mean a great deal to you. Which is why I know you will understand me and want to help me."

"Help you?" Baba says. "How can we help you?"

"I suppose you have heard that the emperor will be holding a selection for consorts soon," she says.

Baba nods. "It has nothing to do with us."

"But it does to me and my daughter," the woman says. "She is sixteen and required by law to appear during the selection." She looks at me. "How old are you, girl?"

I look at Baba, and he nods for me to answer.

"Fifteen."

The woman smiles. "And you are unmarried, obviously. Is she promised to be married?" she asks my father.

"No," he says, embarrassed. "She... Her feet are unbound and we have no money for a dowry."

Mingxia laughs. "Well, you might be outcasts among your own people for abandoning such a barbaric practice, but it just might be what saves your lives."

"What are you talking about?" Baba asks, growing irritated. "You come into my home, insult my family, my people. Yet you want my help for some reason I cannot understand. What do you want?"

Mingxia stands—which we all do as well—and motions to the man who arrived with her, who is now standing guard at the door so we won't be disturbed.

"Bring her," she says. The man nods and steps out. I walk over to the window and peek through the cracks in the shutters. The man goes to a finely decorated rickshaw. The street is too narrow for a carriage such as the one she was riding in last night. The man helps a woman out of the rickshaw and down to the street. I can't see what she looks like because she is wearing a thick veil. The man leads the woman inside and Mingxia takes her hand.

"Go ahead," Mingxia instructs the other woman, and she lifts her veil. We all gasp when we see her face.

It's me!

"Wha...what?" I ask, unsure of what I'm looking at. She appears slightly taller than me, but that is because of her pot-bottom shoes. Her skin is also a lighter shade than mine; I suppose she hasn't spent much time outside the way I have. But aside from that and her fine clothes, it's as if I am looking at myself in a pool of water. The longer I stare, the more differences I see. Her nose is slightly upturned, and she has a noticeable freckle on her right jaw. Her cheeks are also rounder since she probably has never gone to bed hungry in her life.

The longer I look at the girl, the more reassured I feel that this is a mere coincidence and not a trick of witchcraft.

"How strange," Baba says. "How can two girls who are not even the same race look so similar?"

"This is my daughter, Lihua," Mingxia says, wrapping her arm around the girl's shoulders. "Isn't she beautiful?"

"Of course," Mama says. "She looks just like Daiyu, who I always thought was a beauty. If I'd had the strength of character to bind her feet, I'm sure we could have made a good match for her."

Mingxia snorts. "What, to another poor day-laborer? A fishmonger? Is that truly what you would have wanted for your eldest daughter?"

"It's honest work," Baba says. "What would you eat in your fancy palace if not for people willing to fish and slaughter pigs?"

"You misunderstand me," Mingxia says. "I simply mean that it is a blessing from Heaven that you did not bind the poor girl's feet."

"Why?" Mama asks. "How? What do you want from us?"

"I want your daughter to take Lihua's place at the emperor's selection for new consorts."

My jaw drops and when I look to Mama and Baba, their faces show just as much shock.

"No," Mama says. "It's impossible. We are not Manchu."

Mingxia waves the objection away. "What does it matter if they look alike? No one would know the difference."

"But...why?" I ask, looking at Lihua. "Don't you consider it an honor to be chosen as a consort? You could be the mother of the next emperor."

"I will never see my daughter again if she is chosen!" Mingxia says before Lihua can answer. "She's all I have in the world! Please, will you help us?"

"No!" Baba says without hesitation, and I nearly cry. I know he loves me, loves all of us. "Why should we help a spoiled, entitled Manchu woman like you?"

"Because I can pay," Mingxia says. She reaches into one of the bilious sleeves of her robe and pulls out a small silk purse. I expect her to open it and offer Baba a few coins, but I nearly faint when she holds the whole bag out to him.

"Take it," she says. Baba doesn't. He looks to Mama, who shakes her head.

"No," he says. "I don't trust you. Don't know you."

"Look," Mingxia says, opening the bag to show the gleaming gold coins. I hear Mama mutter something under her breath. It's even more money than I thought. Not cheap copper coins—gold. More money than I could ever count.

"This is only the beginning," Mingxia says, and I start to understand that she is desperate. Just how much is she willing to offer? "I can bring you more if you agree. Just say yes."

Mama and Baba look at each other, each afraid to speak. Of course, part of me wishes they would say no, but they would be foolish not to consider the offer. They would be fools not to accept. But could they live with themselves if they said yes? Will we all starve to death if we say no?

I can't let them carry the burden of having to make the choice. Wasn't I about to sell myself to a brothel only last night? It cannot have been mere chance that I stepped in front of the carriage of a girl who looks exactly like me and I didn't go through with my plan. The ancestors must have some hand in this.

Baba runs his hand over his mouth and chin. He knows he must give an answer. He looks at me.

"Daiyu," he says, his eyes tearing. It is killing him that he feels he must say yes, and I can't bear it. I step away from him toward Mingxia.

"I'll do it," I say. "I'll take Lihua's place at the consort selection."

"Paise Heaven!" Mingxia cries as she hugs Lihua to her. She then pulls me to her and hugs me tightly. When she lets go, she holds my face in both of her hands. "You won't regret this, my darling."

As I pull away and look at my family with watery eyes, I know she must be right. They will live—we all will live, and none of us will have to be sold. It has to be the right choice.

There is no other.

4

"Are you sure?" Baba asks.

Of course I'm not sure! I don't even know what I'm agreeing to. I just know that I can't let my family starve when I could save them.

"No!" Mama says, but Baba ignores her, speaking to Mingxia.

"What exactly are you proposing?"

"I'm sure it's nothing much," she says. "She probably won't get picked. Her skin is dark and she lacks the refinement of a true Manchu. She would only need to stand in for Lihua at the selection, and when she is rejected, she can come back home. She would only be gone for a day at the most, I'm sure of it!"

"If you really thought your daughter didn't stand a chance of being picked, you wouldn't be here," Baba says.

"The odds of Lihua or Daiyu being picked is very small. There will be hundreds of families descending on the capitol in the next few weeks ahead of the selection. Daiyu is one girl out of those hundreds. She's not trained, not educated." My cheeks flush red. "It is not an insult, dear, simply the truth, is it not?" I nod. "Exactly. She can't play an instrument or recite poems. It's a near impossibility that she would be picked. My daughter, though, is a highly trained lady of quality. The emperor would surely want her for himself."

"Then why doesn't Lihua just play stupid?" Mingming asks, crossing her arms. "Fail on purpose."

Mingxia laughs. "Can the elegant swan pretend to be an ugly goose? Can the chrysanthemum appear as a vile weed? If Lihua tried to act the fool she would surely be caught and punished for trying to deceive the emperor."

I'm alarmed at this. "But what if *I'm* caught deceiving the emperor?" Mingxia presses her lips together, not wanting to say.

"The penalty would be death," Baba says. "It would be treason. We would *all* be held responsible."

Mama holds the baby tight with one arm and puts her other one around Junli. "No!" she says, and this time Baba doesn't ignore her. "It's too dangerous!"

Baba looks at me, not as convinced as Mama that I shouldn't do it. I suppose, if I am caught, I can just tell the emperor that I am an orphan, and that was why I agreed. No one ever need know about my family. If I died, at least they would be safe and well taken care of thanks to Mingxia's money. Besides, I already said I would do it.

"I'll do it," I say again.

"Daiyu—" Baba says, placing his hands on my shoulders. "You don't have to do this. We can find another way."

"No," I say. "I *want* to do this. I want to make sure that none of us never go hungry again."

"It's dangerous—"

"I'll be careful," I say. "I'll keep my head down and not attract attention. Lihua and I may look similar, but she's far more beautiful, more elegant than I am. I'd never be picked, I think Ula-Nara Furen is right about that." I see Mingxia smiling, holding her daughter tight.

"But if you are, we would never see you again," Mama says.

My eyes water at the thought, but I do my best to keep them from falling. I can't let my parents know just how terrified I am or they won't let me go. "I won't be. I promise."

"So, we are in agreement?" Mingxia says, and I can tell she is eager for us to strike a bargain.

"Yes—"

"No!" I say, cutting Baba off. I pick up the purse of coins. "This is payment for me attending the selection only. If I am picked, you must give my parents another bag of equal value—"

"I think that's fair," Mingxia says.

"I wasn't finished," I say. "*And* any gifts sent to your house by the emperor for the purchase of your 'daughter'." It is customary for a groom's family to send gifts of animals, silks, furs, and other items to his wife's family the day of the wedding, even when wedding a concubine. The emperor must surely send handsome gifts to the families of his consorts as well.

Mingxia nods. "Done."

I try to hide that my hands are shaking as I close the purse and hand it to Baba. His eyes are wet and he holds tightly to my hand. "I always knew you were a good girl, Daiyu. But I had no idea just how selfless you could be. How did a worthless man such as I am ever raise such a dutiful daughter?"

"You have endured hard, backbreaking work every day of your life to provide for us," I say. "You and Mama have both given us your all. I can do no less for you."

"Come, Daiyu," Mingxia says and she and Lihua walk toward the door.

"What?" I ask.

"You must come home with me, now. We need to get you cleaned up, find some clothes that will fit you. You can't attend the selection looking like a pauper."

I look down at my simple, stained robe and wrap my arms around myself, suddenly feeling as if I am not wearing anything at all.

"There are some things I must teach you. How to stand, how to walk, how to comport yourself."

"Comport?"

"Oh, Heaven," Mingxia says, rubbing her forehead. "See? We have a lot of work to do if we are to pass you off as the daughter of a Manchu lord. I suppose you don't know about Manchu morning rituals?"

I shake my head.

"Or how to greet an emperor or empress?"

I shake my head again.

"Exactly. The selection is some time away, but we need to get to work as soon as possible."

I nod slowly. "Yes, I see. May I have a moment with my family?"

"I suppose," she says. "But only a moment. I'll be waiting in the rickshaw." She, Lihua, and their servant all stepped out of the house, and I feel as if I can take a breath for the first time since the man banged on our door.

"Daiyu, you can still say no," Mama says.

"No," I tell her. "I cannot. I have accepted her money and she has agreed to my terms. I must keep my word."

Mama bursts into tears, and I realize that she has been barely holding herself together this whole time. She sways and Baba and I help lead her to the bed before she falls. I hand the baby to Mingming, but I see Mingming is crying as well. Junli is comforting Huanji, and I'm now on the verge of tears myself. I feel my determination wavering and wonder if I've made a terrible decision. Yes, we need the money, but the risks are so great.

I think about what I told Junli just the other day about women in the Forbidden City never being able to leave. I wasn't exaggerating. If I am chosen, I'll be living in a prison. I am giving up any chance of freedom, any chance at a full life if I do this.

But my family will live. And they will live *well*. The money in that purse alone will keep them from ever going hungry. And it will provide dowries for my sisters. They will be able to marry men with far better positions. Merchants, perhaps, instead of laborers or fishermen.

Six lives in exchange for one. My life for that of my family—and of future generations to come.

"I must do this, Mama," I say, my confidence returning. I think Mama can see it in my eyes. She pulls me to her and holds me tight.

"If you are chosen, this is the last time I will ever see you."

"And if I am not chosen, I'll be back in a few weeks," I say.

"What Heaven wills," she says and I nod. Whatever happens is never truly in our own hands, but that of the gods. I force myself to release her and stand. If I don't leave now, I might not be able to. I turn to my sisters.

"You are the oldest now," I tell Mingming. "You must take care of the others."

"I will," she says, trying to not cry.

"Don't go, Daiyu!" Junli says, wrapping her arms around my legs.

"I must," I say, prying myself away and kneeling down in front of her. "We will see each other again, I promise." She wraps her arms around my neck and hugs me with all the strength her little arms possess. It takes all my strength to remove her.

"Be a good little girl," I say to Huanji, who is only three so must not have any idea what is going on. She nods but says nothing as she clings to Junli.

I stand and face the last person I must say goodbye to. Baba grips my shoulders, his eyes rimmed red. I think he wants to say something but will lose his composure if he does. I nod, feeling much the same way. He pulls me tightly to him and I lay my head on his shoulder and don't fight the tears that I cannot hold back. I feel his shoulders shake and know that he is crying as well.

Finally, I feel his grip loosen and I pull back. I have a sudden terrible thought at the memory of the Dong Fa drinking in the tavern after selling his daughters.

"Use the money wisely," I tell him. "Don't waste it. If I'm not chosen, we won't get any more. This must last us for a very long time."

He nods. "I know. Don't worry about that." I nod and press my lips. I'm sure there is more I should say, something profound, but I don't know what.

"The mistress bids you to come, now," the man says, sticking his head back through the doorway.

"I'm coming," I say. Baba releases me and I move to the door.

"Don't you have a bag?" the man asks. I think for a minute, wondering if there is anything I need to take with me, but other than the clothes I'm wearing, I cannot think of anything. I shake my head. The man groans and steps back outside.

I take one last look at the tiny one room that has housed my family for the whole of my life. The walls we cover with paper in the winter to keep us warm. The window with a broken shutter. The bin we use to wash dishes, clothes, and ourselves. The chipped cups and splintered chairs. The one large bed and few patched-together quilts. It's not much, but it was all we needed.

I look one last time at each member of my family. "I'll see you again," I repeat. "I promise." Before they respond and my resolve shatters completely, I turn and run to the rickshaw.

"About time," Mingxia says in annoyance. She and Lihua crowed together as I climb up beside them.

Lihua tisks as she tries to scoot far enough away that she doesn't touch me. "She's going to get my dress dirty," she whines to her mother.

"Shut your mouth," Mingxia says. "It's a small price to pay for your freedom. Go on," she orders the rickshaw driver, a thin man who is only wearing pants and flimsy shoes.

Mingxia holds up an umbrella to protect her and Lihua from the sun, but I'm too far away to get any benefit from it. I'm wondering where the servant is going to sit when the driver begins to pull and the servant trots along beside us.

We move slowly down the alley, as it's not very wide and is thronged with people, many of whom stop and stare at us as we pass. When we finally reach the end of the alley, we turn onto a wider street and the rickshaw puller starts to run. How such a small man has such strength, I have no idea. I've never ridden in a rickshaw before. Never had the money or the need. I rarely ventured much farther than our neighborhood. But as the wind begins to whip through my hair, I feel as though I am flying.

5

The rickshaw zooms along streets broad and crowded. More than once I see a man or woman jump back to avoid getting their feet crushed under the large wheels, followed by the shaking of an angry fist and the yell of a curse. It's a bit funny, actually. How can they not see such a large contraption coming right at them? Though, I suppose they don't expect for us to come upon them so quickly.

After only a couple of blocks, we've traveled farther from my home than I've ever been, and I see a part of Peking I've never seen before. We are riding up the eastern wall of the Forbidden City, but it is so far away, I can barely see the golden tops of the wall.

The sights and sounds are not so different from my own hutong at first. Crowds of people bustle about, many carrying wares for sale—clothes, cooking pots, rat traps. Everything is dry and dusty. Children—some clothed, some not—chase each other perilously close to the road. Women sit in the doorways of their homes, washing clothes and gossiping with neighbors.

Slowly, though, I notice that the crowds start to thin out, the people dress a little nicer, and walls begin to line the road. Other than a few servants rushing about—many still dressed more finely than me—the streets are surprisingly empty by the time our rickshaw comes to a stop.

All along both sides of the road are tall gray walls about three times my height, with doors of varying colors—red, green, and black—every so often. The door we have stopped in front of is green.

Mingxia reaches across her daughter and grabs my arm. "Remember," she says, staring at me intently, "tell no one why you are really here. Do you understand?"

"Yes, of course," I say, trying not to wince as her nails dig into my skin.

"Promise me," she says, giving me a small shake.

"I promise!" I say. She hesitates, as if she isn't sure she can trust me. Or perhaps she is doubting the whole idea. I know I am. Either way, she finally nods and her man helps each of us out of the rickshaw to the ground.

We step through the door and down a short hall. There is an opening to the left to a small courtyard along with several small rooms. We come to a wall carved with dragons and have to turn left to enter through another door, this one red. Through the door, we find ourselves in a large court-yard and I gasp.

There is a small waterfall spilling into a pond stocked with red and yellow fish. Winding paths are lined with green grass and small flowering bushes. There are even a few small trees for shade, and plenty of stone benches to sit and enjoy the peaceful scene. I've never seen such a green space in all my life.

"Where are we?" I ask, thinking this must be a palace,

and I'm suddenly afraid. Who could they have taken me to see?

Mingxia looks at me for a moment before responding, "Our home."

"You live here?" I ask. "Just the two of you?"

Lihua shrugs. "The servants have rooms somewhere."

I then notice a woman sweeping a walkway. A man is tending the garden. Another woman is pounding corn into meal.

"How many servants do you have?" I ask.

"Who can keep count?" Mingxia says. "Come along."

I have to shake my head in disbelief. I didn't know that there were people in Peking who lived like this. I knew that we were very poor compared to most people. But the richest people I knew still lived in small houses with only a servant or two at most. I had heard that there were men rich enough to have several wives and dozens of children, but I had never considered what their lives must look like compared to mine. I had assumed that most of Peking looked very similar to my own neighborhood. There were the poor who lived in hutongs and the imperial family in the Forbidden City. I had never bothered to imaging life in between. Why should I? Even if I had married, my life would not have looked much different from the way I had grown up.

We go to the west of the courtyard, where the woman was pounding meal. "Ah Lam!" Mingxia yells, and a woman who looks to be about the same age as Mingxia, though more plainly dressed, appears.

"My lady?" the woman says.

"This is Daiyu," Mingxia says. "She's going to be staying with us for a little while. She is to be a companion for my daughter. Isn't that right, Daiyu?" She gives me a pointed look.

"Yes," I say, trying to force a smile. "A companion." So, Mingxia intends to keep the plan even from her own servants. Considering how similarly Lihua and I look, I'm not sure this will be possible, but I don't dare say or do anything that might upset Mingxia.

"Clean her up," Mingxia commands. "Find her some proper clothes and prepare a room for her in the north wing."

"Yes, my lady," the woman says with a bend of her knees and a nod of her head.

"This is Ah Lam, the housekeeper. She will take care of you. I will see you at dinner," Mingxia says to me as she wanders off. Lihua gives me one more long look down at me before tossing her head and following her mother.

"So, you are to be a companion for the spoiled brat," Ah Lam says, shocking me. "Lucky you." She turns and goes back inside and I follow her into a long kitchen.

I see several women working, sweating over a kettle of boiling rice and a wok of frying meats among other activities. My mouth starts to water as I smell the food cooking and see the shelves of vegetables, rice, and flour. A whole side of pork hangs from the ceiling, along with several chickens, ducks, and fish that have either been dried or smoked.

I'm torn between wanting to be polite and feeling a ravening hunger tear at my insides. When I see a steam basket of baozi—meat buns—sitting on a table, probably left over from breakfast, I cannot control myself. I grab one of the buns and take a bite, quickly working my way through the chewy dough and nearly crying when I taste the savory meat. I eat so quickly, I'm panting for breath when I'm through—and the other two buns on the table are still calling to me.

I see Ah Lam standing next to me. I wipe my mouth with the back of my hand and begin apologizing profusely for my behavior.

"So, you are a lady's companion, are you?" she asks, and I know she doesn't believe for a moment that I am who Mingxia claimed. I say nothing. It would insult both of us for me to continue to lie, but neither would I betray the promise I made to Mingxia in the rickshaw.

The woman gives a small nod toward the last two baozi. "Go ahead," she says, and I don't argue.

When I'm finished, I look around and see that Ah Lam has placed a large bucket in the middle of the room. She has several smaller buckets filled with water beside her as well.

"Come on," she says, "step in."

I tentatively do as she says.

"Not even any shoes," Ah Lam says with a tisk as she shakes her head. "Where did she scrounge you up?" she mutters to herself. "All right, off with your clothes."

I wrap my arms around myself. Of course, I was used to washing in front of my family, but these women are strangers. I take a breath and look at the wall as I begin to unwrap my shirt. As soon as I'm naked, Ah Lam dumps one of the buckets of cold water over my head and I shriek. I usually just use a rag and dip that into the water, I don't dump the water onto myself.

Ah Lam then works her hands into a lather and runs them through my hair, scrubbing my scalp. "Calm down, I'm not killing you. Just the lice and fleas you've undoubtedly got."

I clench my teeth as she washes my hair and body and

then dumps another bucket of water over my head. She then hands me a large cloth to dry off with and orders me out of the tub. I reach down to get my clothes off the ground, but Ah Lam grabs them first and tosses them into a nearby cooking fire.

"Hey! Those were mine!"

"You won't be needing those rags anymore, dear," Ah Lam says, not unkindly. "I have some of the young miss's cast-off clothes for you." She then kicks a pair of soft-soled slippers to me and wraps me in a sheet.

"Follow me."

As I shuffle behind her back to the courtyard toward the main door, I notice that a few more people have appeared—more maids and a couple of men who look like they do more laborious tasks—and are watching me, whispering behind their hands. They must all be wondering who I am and why I am here. I doubt any of them believe for a moment that I am to be a companion for Lihua.

We go back to the carved dragon wall and to the side walkway I saw just inside the main door. The courtyard here is open to the sky and there is a long wall of doors for small rooms. I see a maid exit one of the rooms, pulling the door closed behind her, and she stops and watches me with a gaped mouth. I realize that these must be the servants' rooms.

Ah Lam opens the very last door and I follow her inside. The room is dark and dusty, having not been used for some time. There is a plain wooden bed, a couple of blankets, and a small stove for heating coal in the colder months. There is a very small window carved into the gray brick wall that lets in a little light and allows me to see into the alley.

"I'll fetch a broom so we can sweep this out," Ah Lam says as she dusts her hands off. "And I'll bring you the clothes in a trunk so you can keep them clean. Once you are dressed, try not to sit on anything in here."

I give a small smile and nod, but I'm holding back tears. No one has been unkind to me—quite the opposite in fact—but everything is so different. I have nothing, not even my own clothes, and I know no one. I'm sure Mingxia will never allow me to contact my family while I am living here. The best I can hope for is that I will be sent away on the first day of the selection and be allowed to return home—to my *real* home, not this strange place.

Ah Lam starts to pass by me to leave the room, but she stops and looks at me, gently chuffing me under the chin.

"It will be all right," she says. "The mistress might seem tough, but whatever she promised you, she will stand by her word."

I give a small smile and nod, but a lump in my throat keeps me from speaking. Ah Lam then leaves me alone to find me some clothes to wear. I hold the sheet tightly, feeling oddly chilled despite the summer heat.

Even though I know the house is filled with people, and that there are other houses all along the alley, it seems so very quiet here to me. Nothing like the loud, busy street where I spent my whole life.

I have to stand on my tiptoes to see out the small window. It is carved from the bricks that make up the wall, but slats were left in place so that no one could crawl in or out of the house.

I feel like I'm in a cage.

6

When Ah Lam drapes the long Manchu robe —qipao—around my shoulders, I nearly collapse from the weight of it. From my neck to the floor, the gown is dark blue and heavily embroidered with light blue clouds and white birds. The neck and hems are embroidered in a simple repeating pattern. As I run my fingers over the embroidery, I marvel that the gown is a "cast-off" from Lihua. It's finer than anything I've ever seen, much less worn. Even the opera performers I saw from time to time did not have gowns this lovely.

"Sit," Ah Lam instructs, pointing to the crate she'd had brought in by one of the male servants. It was full of not only gowns, but pot-bottom shoes and liangbatou head-dresses as well. Using a comb, Ah Lam brushes and parts my hair. She wraps each section around a piece of wood called a bian fang, twisting and plaiting the excess tightly in the back. It's painful, but I say nothing. I can't help but wince occasionally, though.

"There, let me have a look at you," Ah Lam says. When I stand up and turn to face her, she gasps.

I touch my face and then the dress. "Is something wrong?"

"I...I did not notice it before, but you look just like Miss Lihua," she says, and my cheeks go hot. "Who *are* you? Why are you here?"

I shake my head. "I can't tell you."

Ah Lam tisks and chews her thumb. "This is because of the selection for consorts, isn't it?" she says. I say nothing. "I knew the mistress was upset when she heard that Lihua had to attend, but I never thought she'd do something so drastic."

What can I say? If Ah Lam was able to figure out what Mingxia and I had agreed to, other people are sure to follow.

"You...you won't tell anyone, will you?" I ask quietly. She looks at me for a long minute before shaking her head.

"Of course not," she says. "Though I will talk to the mistress about it. Perhaps she can be persuaded to drop the deception. You realize that if you are caught, we could all be put to death?"

"I know."

"You *know*? And you still agreed? What does the mistress have hanging over you?"

I shrug. "Nothing. I agreed willingly to save my family."

Ah Lam sighs. "They must be very poor indeed. This drought... It has been a difficult time for everyone."

I scoff. "Not everyone. I saw your stores of food in the kitchen. That food could feed my family for months."

She opens her mouth to say something, but then seems to think better of it.

"And not for the emperor," I go on. "We are starving and what does he do? Hold a selection to take a hundred wives.

Any man who can feed a hundred wives has far too much money."

"The emperor is no mere man," Ah Lam says. "He is the Son of Heaven. The father of his people."

"He is *not* my father," I say. "My father would die for us."

"You don't understand because you are not Manchu," Ah Lam says. "But you better learn—and fast. If you go into the Forbidden City and even *think* a bad thought about the emperor, you'll find yourself a head shorter."

My hand goes to my neck and I shudder. I've never seen a person executed, but I have heard about it. Every few months it seems, a scaffold is built outside the walls of the Forbidden City and a spectacle is made of the deaths. People travel miles to watch. There are vendors, acrobats, singers. It's like a temple fair, except someone—usually several someones—dies at the end.

"You have a lot to learn, girl, whoever you are."

"My name is Daiyu," I say. "I didn't lie about that."

Ah Lam chuckles as she nudges me to sit on the trunk again. "Well, your name will be Lihua soon enough, so you better get used to that as well."

She picks up one of my feet and helps me roll up a silk stocking, securing it at my thigh with a ribbon. She then places a shoe on my foot with a pot-bottom platform. She then does the same for the other foot. She takes my hands and pulls me to standing.

I wobble and would fall down if not for Ah Lam holding onto me. The shoes are heavy, which keep me firmly planted to the ground.

"Okay, walk," she says when I find my balance. I think she must be crazy, but then I realize that if I am to appear as a Manchu lady, I am going to have to walk like one. I pick up one foot and drag the platform across the ground as I try to step forward.

"Ai-yo!" Ah Lam says, wincing. "Not like that! Pick your foot *up* when you walk."

"I'm trying," I say, bending my knee as I lift my foot into the air.

"Not like a horse!" she says. "Stop! Here." She helps me sit again and takes the shoes off of me before stepping into them herself. She pulls her robe up so I can clearly see her feet.

"Like this." She walks so that she lifts the right shoe in front of her, takes a small step, and then puts the foot down slightly crossed to the left. She then lifts her right shoe, swings it forward, and then places it down slightly crossed to the right. In this way, she walks around the room in small, flowing steps.

"I'll trip over myself if I put one foot in front of the other like that," I say.

"Well, you better learn how to do it," Ah Lam says as she removes the shoes and puts them back on me. She once again pulls me to standing and holds both of my hands as she leads me around the room. My gown that once dragged the floor is now elevated just enough that it no longer touches the ground, but it still prevents me from seeing my feet. I look down anyway, trying to make sure I am doing the steps right.

"Lift your chin," Ah Lam says. "You are a lady, not a peasant."

I raise my head and look at Ah Lam's face.

"Higher," she says. "Don't look at me. I'm only a servant."

I raise my head and look up to the ceiling as I concentrate on my steps. I see a few spiders I didn't notice before and tremble. I'll have to thoroughly sweep the room before sleeping tonight.

~

When I enter the dining room that evening, I'm shaking. I've spent the whole afternoon walking around my room, trying to find a balance between elegance and not falling on my face. My legs are quite tired from the weight of the shoes. Thankfully the qipao was a dark color because I ended up on my knees more often than not.

I don't raise my chin as I enter the room. Mingxia and Lihua are not my equals, so I keep my neck bent and my eyes downcast as I approach. When I can see them from the edges of my sight, I pull my hands together and hold them out, forming a circle with my arms. Then, I bend my knees, lowering myself as much as I can without toppling over. Ah Lam told me that this was the proper way for a lady to greet a superior. I hope she was right because I can't see the expression on Mingxia's face. Is she pleased? Disappointed? I hope she replies soon because I am not sure I can hold this position much longer, my legs quivering beneath me.

I hear the rustle of silk and realize that Mingxia has approached me.

"Stand up," she says. "Let me have a look at you."

I do as she says, returning to my upright position, but still I keep my chin and eyes down. She seems a bit annoyed by this and grips my chin, lifting it so that I must look at her.

There are tears in her eyes. "You look perfect." She then turns to her daughter, who looks far less pleased. "See, Lihua, I told you. It is sure to work."

Lihua presses her lips and crosses her arms. "She doesn't look like me at all! She still looks like the dirty girl we found in that dreadful hovel."

I look down at the gown, afraid that Ah Lam and I did not get all the dust off of it from my many tumbles today, but I don't see anything.

"Nonsense," Mingxia says. "She is certainly not a beautiful as you. She lacks the...natural refinement of a true Manchu bannerwoman, perhaps. But she certainly has the potential to pass as you, don't you think?"

Lihua sighs. "Fine. I suppose."

"Of course, you do," Mingxia says to me as she holds my hands tightly and smiles. "This will work. I promise."

I nod. I hope she's right. I have to believe she is. If she's wrong, I will lose my life.

Mingxia then leads me over to the round table and helps me take a seat on one of the lacquered stools. In my silk robe, the seat is slippery and I have to keep my back rigid to keep from sliding off.

Ah Lam then enters the room carrying a bowl of steaming rice, followed by a maid carrying two dishes of food. It already looks like so much food to me, but another maid brings still more food. My stomach growls loudly since I haven't eaten since the steamed buns that morning, but I try to restrain myself so I can follow Mingxia's lead. But she does nothing, and she and her daughter look at me expectantly.

"I'm sorry," I whisper. "What should I do?"

"Serve the rice, stupid," Lihua snaps. I look to Mingxia, who nods. I grab one of the bowls and scoop rice into it with a wooden ladle, then I offer it to Mingxia. She doesn't take it, so I place it on the table in front of her. She gives an approving nod. I then prepare a bowl for Lihua and place it in front of her. I sit back down with my hands in my lap.

"And yourself," Mingxia says. My hands are shaking as I try to prepare a bowl for myself, but I drop the ladle on the ground. I hear Lihua tisk and sigh in annoyance.

"We are never going to eat," she mumbles. I reach for the ladle, but forget my shoes and start to slip off the seat.

Ah Lam grabs my arm. "I got it." She reaches down and picks up the ladle for me, but she doesn't hand it to me. Instead, she disappears for a moment before returning with a clean one. She then serves the rice to me.

"Well, we got there in the end, didn't we?" Mingxia says. She picks up her chopsticks and chooses a piece of pork from a bowl of simmering spices. "Go on," she tells me.

I hesitate as I watch Lihua pick up her own chopsticks and begin to eat, afraid I'm going to do something else wrong. Once they are no longer looking at me, I begin to eat, picking at my food carefully so I don't drop any on my qipao.

"We have very little time to prepare you," Mingxia says. "The emperor has not set a date for the selection yet, but we should receive the details soon. In the meantime, you must learn as much as possible about being a Manchu woman."

I nod. "Yes, my lady."

Mingxia sighs. "There is a difference between a servant and a lady," she says. "Raise your head. Look at me." I lift my eyes. "Sit up straight." I hadn't noticed that I had started to slump. "Put your bowl down and bring the food to your mouth with the chopsticks. Don't shovel the food into your mouth like a horse at a trough."

I feel my stomach clench and my appetite flees. I had done well when I first entered the room, but when I am not focused, I fall back into my old habits. I don't know how I can do this. One mistake and the emperor is sure to see right through me. "She's going to get us all killed," Lihua hisses.

"Lihua!" Mingxia scolds. "Don't say such a thing."

"It's true!" she says. "She can't even eat properly. How is she going to learn anything? She'll have to recite the lineage, learn to play an instrument, quote poetry."

"What?" I ask. "What is she talking about? I thought I only needed to *look* the part."

Mingxia seems flustered for the first time. "Well, looking like a Manchu lady is the most important aspect. But...yes, there is much you need to learn if you are to truly present yourself as a lady to the emperor. As Lihua."

"But, why?" I ask. "I'm supposed to fail, right? If I can't do all those things, I will be sent home."

"If you don't do them as well as the other girls you may be sent home," Mingxia says. "But if you can't do them at all they will know something is wrong. All refined young ladies can play music, paint lovely pictures, or recite poems. Lihua can do all those things. She's quite accomplished."

"But she's been learning her whole life," I say. "I have only weeks."

"Which is why you must work very hard," Mingxia says. "Every moment must be used in training."

I'm beginning to seriously doubt my decision. I look at Lihua and see her sitting tall, looking down her nose at me without an ounce of effort while my back is aching terribly and my shoulders are still slightly hunched over.

"We will begin in earnest tomorrow," Mingxia says as she stands. "It has been an exhausting day for all of us. Sleep well and I will see you before breakfast for morning greetings." Lihua stands and follows her mother. I nod even though I have no idea what she is talking about. *Morning greetings?*

"Manchu children greet their parents every morning," Ah Lam says as she and the other maids start to clear away the nearly full bowls of food. I hope the food doesn't go to waste. Perhaps the servants eat it. "I'll tell you what to say in the morning."

"Thank you," I say, but I'm beginning to wonder what the point of it all is. It's impossible. I'll never be able to pass for a Manchu lady.

"Lihua sings like a bullfrog," Ah Lam says as she sits next to me with a bowl of food she's kept behind for herself. She pushes a small bowl of meat toward me. She must have noticed that I hardly ate anything. With Mingxia and Lihua gone, my appetite seems to return.

"I'm sure that's not true," I say as I take a bite.

"Oh, it is," Ah Lam says. "When she starts to sing, I know it is time for me to go to the market for the shopping."

I chuckle and take a few more bites. "You are just trying to make me feel better."

Ah Lam shakes her head. "That girl might have the airs of a lady, a pretty face, but she's not as accomplished as she likes to think. Her talents are mediocre at best."

I shake my head. "It doesn't matter. She's still better than me. I've never even held a paintbrush before. And reciting poetry? I can't read!"

"You could," Ah Lam says, "if you'd had a teacher."

I shake my head. "There's not enough time—"

"You know what hard work is, don't you?" Ah Lam asks. "Lihua doesn't. Everything has been given to her since the day she was born. Spoiled. She's not clever by half, and she'd never be able to cope if she suddenly lost everything. But you—you know how to survive."

I begin to understand what Ah Lam is saying. Lihua may have been raised with every advantage, but she didn't make use of it, while I had to struggle for every single meal I ate.

"Your life is on the line," Ah Lam said. "The lives of your family. You aren't going to give up now, are you? You haven't even started yet."

I sigh. Ah Lam is right. I do have time to at least try. When the day of the selection comes, if I'm still not good enough, Lihua can go to the selection. We don't have to go through with this.

"Thank you," I say. "I don't know why you are being so nice to me."

"When the mistress gets an idea in her head, she doesn't easily let go," Ah Lam says as she stands and removes the last few dishes from the table. "And she's much easier to live with if she thinks she's getting her own way. Just do as she says, and we'll all get through this. The selection is only one day, right?"

"Right," I say.

Ah Lam gives my hand a squeeze. "I'll be back to help you walk back to your room." She gets up and clears away the last of the dishes, taking them to the kitchen.

I exhale. One day. It will only be for one day. I can pretend to be someone else for one day.

Can't I?

7

———

"Fitful and falling, autumn moonlight fills clumps of chrysanthemums."

Mingxia nods as I recite a poem that I have been practicing.

"Lonely and desolate, the circling wall endures the west wind.

Night lengthens, the lamp oil runs out: I am blocked from my studies."

Lihua is here too, at a table a little behind her mother, and she fingers a horse-hair writing brush, clearly bored. She's supposed to be working on her calligraphy, but instead she watches me, making faces to make me forget my lines. I try to ignore her, to focus on Mingxia, who nods happily, or Ah Lam, who mouths words to me when I am unsure. But Lihua is hard to ignore.

"My malaise lifts, the window is still: I set aside my needlework.

Stirred by the wind, chilled crows flock and scatter.

Shriveled by the frost, worm-eaten leaves are half-transparent."

It is not only the words I must remember, but slight movements of my hands, a tilt to my head, to add emotion to the recitation.

"Slanting sunlight is chill and cold—evening in the deserted village.

I...I...stand..."

Lihua sticks out her tongue, crosses her eyes, and waves her hands by her head like the ears of an elephant. I forget my line. I look to Ah Lam, but I can't make out what she's mouthing to me.

"I...stand...with the wild geese..."

"Stop," Mingxia says, standing. "What is this? What is happening? Why are you stuttering like a fool? Why are you slumping?"

"I'm sorry, my lady," I say. "I forgot my next line and became flustered."

"What have I told you?" Mingxia says. "You must never lose control of yourself. That might be acceptable for a Chinese girl, but never a Manchu lady. Your dignity is the most important aspect of your character and bearing."

"Yes, my lady," I say, dropping my chin to my chest in embarrassment, which I remember is the wrong thing to do a moment too late as Mingxia grips my chin and holds my head up.

"Never forget who you are," she says. "The daughter of the bannermen who rode across the steppes on wild horses. Who overcame cold and starvation and wild beasts to become the greatest military force the world has ever seen! Men who overthrew the Ming empire to become emperors of the largest country in the world. To ascend from mere nomads to become the Son of Heaven."

I understand that she is proud of her heritage, but it is not *my* heritage. To me, the Manchu are nothing more than imposters. A bunch of wild, butter-eating, horse-riding barbarians who invaded China in a moment of weakness and made us their slaves.

For me to have to pretend to be Manchu, to wear their formless robes and ridiculous shoes, to have to act as though they are superior to true Chinese is a terrible indignity. If my family didn't need the money so badly, I never would have agreed to this. But I have agreed. I have taken Mingxia's money. So I know I must do my best to play the part I've taken on. I remember the opera performers who used to put on shows in my neighborhood, how the man playing the part of the consort did so with such grace, such elegance, even though he wasn't a woman at all. I have to be as convincing in my own performance if I am to have even a chance of pulling this off and not losing my head.

I lift my chin, straighten my back, and smile. "Of course, my lady. Forgive me."

Mingxia smiles and releases my chin. "There. Beautiful. Remember, if you forget a line, maintain your dignity above all things. Do not stop, or cower, or beg forgiveness. Continue on. Either make up the words until you remember or bow to signal the end of the performance."

Bowing in my pot-bottom shoes is not a skill I have yet mastered. To balance while I bend my knees, lower my body, and incline my head is quite a feat, and something I must continue to practice when I'm not being trained in something else.

"My lady." A maid appears and bows before Mingxia. "It is time to leave if we are to arrive at the princess's palace in time." Even though Mingxia spends as much time as possible training me, her social obligations have not come to an end. She is still expected to attend all matter of casual visits, birthday parties, ancestor celebrations, weddings...

The list goes on. She must keep up the appearance that everything within her household is completely normal and that she is honored that her daughter will be appearing at the consort selection.

"Of course," she says. "Daiyu, keep practicing while I am gone."

"Shall I go with you?" Lihua asks.

"No," Mingxia says, which does surprise me. My understanding is that under normal circumstances, Lihua would attend her mother on such calls. But it seems that Mingxia wishes people to forget she even has a daughter. Lihua has rarely left the house since my arrival.

"Help Daiyu with her training," Mingxia says. "She needs to practice her erhu."

The disappointment is evident on Lihua's face, but she does not argue with her mother.

The maid escorts Mingxia out of the house, and several more of her maids and servants attend her as well. I can hear the horse that leads the procession whinnying outside and the braying of the donkey that will draw the cart. One would think the empress herself was passing by, judging by the number of attendants that must travel with Mingxia wherever she goes. But I have learned that this is quite normal for a lady of high rank, whether Manchu or Chinese. Often, when in my room practicing, I can see the processions pass by my window as they travel down the street. I never saw such a procession back in my own hutong. No well-bred lady would ever have reason to pass through there.

As soon as Mingxia leaves, Lihua pulls a novel from one of her long sleeves and begins to read, completely ignoring me. When Lihua isn't ignoring me, she's sending dirty looks my way or trying to sabotage my training. I've tried to ignore her. Under normal circumstances, girls like us would never meet. But I'm here to help her...aren't I? Shouldn't she want me to succeed? If I fail, if they learn that I am not really Lihua, won't her life in be danger as well?

"Lihua," I ask, sitting across from her, "why don't you want me to succeed?"

"I don't know what you are talking about," she says as a maid brings us a piping hot pot of fresh tea and a selection of snacks. Lihua picks absent-mindedly at the nuts while I eat a sweet cake. I've never had such wonderful treats before. When all this is over, I have to admit that I will certainly miss the food.

"I can't help but think that despite all the trouble and money your mother has gone through to spare you from the selection, you aren't glad of it," I try again.

"Perhaps you aren't as stupid as you look," she says, still not looking at me.

"Why?" I ask. "Mingxia is doing all this for *you*."

"I never asked her to," Lihua finally says, slamming her book on the table and glaring at me. "I wouldn't mind having a chance at becoming empress."

"Wait," I say, rubbing my forehead, "you *want* to go to the section? Why haven't you told your mother."

"I have," Lihua says. "But she won't hear of it. I'm the only child she has and if I am chosen, then, yes, she'll never see me again."

"Then why do you want to go? Wouldn't you hate to leave your mother?"

"I have to marry eventually. No matter who I marry, I will have to leave my mother's home and go to that of my husband and his dreadful family. There's no way around it."

I realize she has a point. It is the same in Chinese families as well. It's why daughters are often not as prized as sons. A son will stay with his family for life; a daughter will leave. Some families don't want the expense of raising, dressing, and educating a daughter, not to mention raising a dowry, only to send her away after a few years to never see her again. Daughters, according to some fathers, are a waste of resources.

Unless you are a Manchu girl of just the right age to be selected as a consort for the emperor. Instead, the emperor will pay the family handsomely for their daughter. In fact, I am a little confused by Mingxia's decision. If Lihua must marry someone, would she not want her daughter to marry the best man possible? Who could be superior to the emperor?

"So, that is why you are making things difficult for me?" I ask. "You are hoping I will fall so far short that Mingxia will have to send you instead if she doesn't want to risk her life?"

"Exactly," Lihua says, a smug smile on her face. "Isn't it an excellent plan? If you fail, I can go to the selection and you can go home. Everyone is happy."

"Except Mingxia," I say. Lihua waves away my concern.

"She'll accept it. What else can she do?"

It is a tempting idea. I don't *want* to go to the selection. I don't want to risk my life for these spoiled Manchu women. But what will Mingxia do to me if I fail? To my family? I'm sure they have already spent some of the money. They had to buy food at the very least. They probably bought clothes, blankets, cooking tools. They may have even bought a better house. If I fail and Mingxia demands the money back, we would never be able to pay it back. I would be the ruin of my family.

I shake my head. "I'm sorry, but I can't."

"Why?" Lihua asks, her smile fleeing and tears rimming

her eyes. "You don't want to go to the selection. You want to go home."

"I can't betray the trust your mother has put in me," I say. "If I try my best and still am not good enough, I will have to live with the consequences, but at least I will know that I didn't give up. If I fail on purpose... I don't know what will happen, but it will all be my fault."

Lihua stares at me for a moment, her face blank, as if she can't understand what I'm saying. Her face then turns into a snarl and before I can react, she grabs the teapot from the table. I barely have time to lift my arm and protect myself as she smashes the porcelain pot against me. I scream as I fall back from my seat, the tea still hot, though thankfully no longer scalding.

Lihua rounds the table, lunging at me like a fearsome tiger, her hands like claws as she lands on me.

"You stupid, stupid girl!" Lihua screams. "I hate you! You're stealing my life!"

She's stronger than me and weighs more, so I can't fight back. I can't even push her off me. All I can do is try to protect my face from her scratches, though I feel a sharp pain in one of my arms.

"My lady!" someone says.

"Stop this!" another voice cries. There's then a variety of voices and I cannot make out what they are saying. All I know is that Lihua's weight is lifted off of me enough that I'm able to scurry away. I feel someone grip my shoulders and help me stand as I stumble out of my shoes.

I cling tightly to the woman, who I realize is Ah Lam, as I watch two other servants hold onto Lihua. Ah Lam then pushes me behind her as she storms up to Lihua.

"Stop this," Ah Lam says. "Your mother would be

disgusted by your behavior. There is nothing dignified about the way you are acting."

"Let me go!" Lihua yells and the servants do as she orders. I stay huddled behind Ah Lam. Lihua storms off, somehow still wearing her pot-bottom shoes, and grabs her book before retreating to her quarters. Only after she is out of sight am I able to breathe.

"What happened?" Ah Lam asks.

"She wants me to fail," I say, wiping away tears with my sleeve. "She wants to go to the selection." I wince as my sleeve rubs against my arm. I look and see a long scratch that is oozing blood.

"Ai yo!" Ah Lam says. "Come, we must clean it and treat it immediately. If you have any marks on your body, you'll be sent away immediately."

I wonder for a moment if it might be better to let the wound fester. If I could be sent home for such a little thing, Mingxia could hardly count it against me. Still, I see that my gown is filthy, and I have no idea where my shoes are. My hair must look a fright. I cannot let Mingxia see me like this.

Back in my room, Ah Lam helps me change and tends to my injury. My right ankle is also sore and I realize I must have twisted it in the fight.

"Lihua is a spoiled thing," Ah Lam says, "used to getting her way. It must have sent her into a rage when you did not automatically agree to her request."

"She has only herself to think about," I mutter. "I have my whole family to consider. I can't fail Mingxia or my family."

"I'm sure you won't," Ah Lam says.

"I am sure I will," I say. "I can't remember poems. I still can't paint or play music. I can't even remember to hold my head up. They are going to know I'm not Manchu as soon as I step out of the cart at the Forbidden City."

"You are doing better than you give yourself credit for," Ah Lam says as she spreads a stinging ointment on the scratch. "I would never know you came from the streets to look at you now."

"But I'm still not good enough to pass for a Manchu lady," I say. Perhaps Lihua is right. I'll fail no matter how hard I try.

"You are more of a lady than that little upstart has ever been," Ah Lam says, chucking me under the chin. I disagree, but I don't tell her that.

"Stay here and rest," she says as she gathers up the ruined clothes. "And don't let Lihua upset you. Soon enough, you'll either be in the palace or back at your own home and you'll never have to see her again."

I give her a thankful smile. I suppose that is one good thing about being chosen—Lihua being out of my life forever.

8

———

I can't sleep, and I'm sure no one else in the house is either. It is the night before the emperor's consort selection, and Mingxia has not wavered in her decision to send me in her daughter's place.

I heard Mingxia and Lihua arguing until well into the night, though I could not understand all that was said. For the past few weeks, Lihua continued to make my life miserable, and I know Mingxia was aware of it. She purchased a balm from the apothecary to heal the scratch on my arm, and any other injuries that came along. Eventually, Mingxia had to banish Lihua to her room to keep her from leaving any marks that might still linger on my body when the consort selection came.

The house is silent now, but it won't be for long. Everyone is supposed to rise at the hour of the tiger to help me wash and dress, still many hours before dawn. The preparation will take hours, then Mingxia will escort me to the palace, which I am told will take several hours as well. The girls have been ordered to arrive at the palace by the hour of the horse, so soon, the streets around the palace will be thronged with donkey carts as hundreds of girls try to arrive at the palace at the same time.

"Heaven help me," I whisper out my window into the dark night. The moon is high in the sky, but it does little to illuminate the alley outside. I've done all I can to try and learn to be a Manchu lady. Mingxia had a new gown made just for me so I wouldn't stand out in an ill-fitting robe. I've memorized poems, learned to walk slowly and gracefully on pot-bottom shoes, and I can even sing a couple of popular Manchu songs. But if I should be challenged to do more—to play an instrument, dance, or recite my family history, I'm sure to give myself away. I have to hope that I will be dismissed long before I would be asked to do anything of that sort.

I wonder what my family is doing. If they are well. If they know that in a few hours I must report to the Forbidden City. News about the Manchu rarely ever reaches our neighborhood. Why would we care what the rich and powerful invaders are doing? It is strange that a palace official even put a flier about the consort selection up in our neighborhood. There are no Manchu there. Well, I suppose there could be some. After all, I am about to be a Han Chinese within the Forbidden City. Some people always end up where they shouldn't be.

There is a knock, and Ah Lam opens the door carrying a candle. "It is time," she says solemnly. The light from the candle casts shadows on her face and accentuates the creases of worry that run around her brow and mouth. Early on she tried to talk Mingxia out of the plan as well, but it came to nothing. I think that Mingxia must have gotten quite angry with her. I saw a red mark on Ah Lam's cheek one day; she never spoke against my training again.

I nod and follow her from the room. I am to dress in

Mingxia's chambers to keep from getting myself or my clothes dirty.

When Ah Lam opens the door to Mingxia's rooms, I see Mingxia and Lihua waiting for me. I start when I see that Lihua is dressed in the simple clothes of a maid. Her hair is tightly pinned behind her head and she wears no paint on her face. For the first time, I realize that Lihua and I do look alike. I didn't realize the difference a little paint and a new set of clothes could make.

Ah Lam takes me to a side room where a large brass basin full of water is set up. She instructs me to get inside and sit down. The hot water feels wonderful on my skin and seeps down to my bones. It is summer, but the evenings can still get chilled. The water warms me all the way through in a way I didn't know was possible. I've never had a hot bath before.

I dip under the water to wet my hair and Ah Lam uses a perfumed soap to wash my hair, scrubbing my scalp with her nails. It is painful, but I do my best not to wince or even utter a sound. I know she has to get me as clean as possible.

She then uses a rough, horse-hair brush to scrub my skin until it turns pink. She rubs me with thick, creamy milk before rinsing me clean. She says the milk will make my skin whiter so I look less like a peasant, but I doubt it will work. You cannot undo a lifetime in the sun with one wash.

When I finally get out of the tub, Ah Lam rubs my whole body with scented oil. Then, I sit to have my hair prepared. I am surprised when Ah Lam stands back and Mingxia takes her place behind me. Mingxia runs a comb through my long hair one hundred times. She wraps my hair tightly around the flat bianfang, pinning it in place so that not a single hair can fall out of place. She then attaches the heavy, fan-shaped liangbatou headdress. She attaches pink silk flowers to the headdress, along with butterfly-shaped hairpins and additional jewels and pearls. To one side, she attaches a long pink tassel studded with seed pearls that make a slight rattling when shaken. It is there to remind me to stand still enough that I don't make a sound.

Mingxia then prepares my face. She uses a light rice powder to make my skin brighter, then she lines my eyes with kohl and paints my lips with a red stain.

Finally, it is time to dress. I look out the window and see that the sky is beginning to lighten. We are running out of time. Ah Lam helps me into a long silk shift that feels cool against my skin. Then she and Mingxia help me step into the long, light blue qipao. The collar, sleeves, and hem are embroidered with an ornate pink pattern. It is clasped at my neck and down across my shoulder. The sleeves are bilious and hang long past my hands.

As Ah Lam helps me put on my pot-bottom shoes, I think Mingxis might cry. Her eyes water and she looks at me with a pride I have until now only seen her express at Lihua.

"You're a vision," Ah Lam says.

I know I must look beautiful. Look like an elegant lady. Look like someone else. But I avoid looking in the mirror. Once I am back home, I don't want to remember myself this way.

"Come," Mingxia says, and she motions toward the door. I take a deep breath and step forward, one foot carefully crossing in front of the other, my chin held high. Indeed, the headdress is so heavy that if I were to tilt my head, I would surely fall over.

We walk through Mingxia's garden estate and out the door. The one thing I am glad of this day is that I will never see this house—never see Lihua—again. I am not exactly sure how Mingxia and Lihua plan to convince other people that she is a mere maid, but that is not my concern.

The donkey cart is waiting for us, along with a male servant to help me inside. I glance down the road and see donkey carts outside two other houses. The streets will soon be strewn with carts carrying precious cargo. The servant helps me step into the cart, where I then sit cross-legged on a bed of satin pillows.

"We will wait here for your return," Mingxia says. "Once you are dismissed, you must come back here. You will then change back into the clothes of a maid and will return home."

"Yes, my lady," I say since I am unable to nod my head. I had hoped I would not have to come back to this place, but I suppose the ruse must continue for a moment even after I am sent away.

She looks at me for a long moment, as if she wishes to say something else. She takes my hand and gives it a tight squeeze.

"Good luck, my girl," she says.

"I will not disappoint you," I say with a confidence I don't truly feel. How can I? I am a fraud. I could never be a Manchu lady. A rich spoiled girl who never had to worry about anything. I have worked hard. I have gone to bed hungry. I have been spat upon by those who thought they were my betters. I can never forget all the things that made me the girl I am today. I am sure my true identity will show in my eyes. But what else can I do? I will play the part I've been assigned and then return to my home. My people. My family.

Mingxia nods and releases me, stepping back as the servant closes the door. I catch one last glimpse of Ah Lam wiping her eyes. A moment later, the cart jerks forward and I have to grab onto the cushion I am sitting on to keep from toppling over. After a moment, the cart finds its stride and I am able to sit up straight again.

I peek through one of the curtained windows at the city, now bright with sunshine. We pass through the complicated maze of alleys toward the Forbidden City. Every few minutes, there is another house with a donkey cart outside of it. I see other girls dressed very similarly to myself climbing into them or standing nearby while they say goodbye to their families.

For some families, it is a celebration. There is laughter and cheering. The popping of firecrackers. The waving of flags and streamers. For others, it is a funeral. There is much weeping and I see more than one girl begging not to be sent away.

I feel a kinship with the sad girls. We all pray that we will not be chosen, but rejected early. This way we will not dishonor our families, but neither will we have to endure life as a prisoner.

I wonder if there are any other girls out there like me. Girls plucked from poor families to take the places of cherished daughters so that they are not lost forever. I suppose it is not likely, but Mingxia can hardly be the first or only parent to attempt such a scheme. I wonder if I will know such a girl if I see one.

The cart comes to a stop, and I wait for the door to open, but it does not. The cart jerks forward, then stops again. I realize we must have found the line of carts at the east gate of the Forbidden City where the girls are to be dropped off. I have no way of seeing in front of us, so I cannot begin to guess how long it will take us to reach the gate—or how many more times I must be jerked about in the cart like a ragdoll.

Thankfully, it is only about half a dozen stops before the door opens and a hand reaches in for me. I step out as gracefully I can—which isn't very—and my breath falls out of me as I look up at the red wall towering before me. I have lived within the shadow of the Forbidden City my whole life, but never have I been this close to it. There is no sky, no earth—only red.

"My lady?"

I blink and see that a man in a plain black robe is waiting for me. I give a smile, then I remember I must be more demure and smile less.

"Please." He motions toward the gate where another man in a black robe is waiting at a table. The cart I arrived in clatters away and another one takes its place. I look down the road and there are carts as far as I can see.

"Name?" the man at the table asks me.

"Ula Nara Lihua, of the Bordered Blue Banner Clan."

The man flips through a stack of papers, pulling one out.

"Date of birth?"

"The tenth day of the eighth month in the eighth year of the Yongzheng Emperor."

The man nods as he uses a brush to mark something on the paper, which he then hands to me.

"Suyin!" he calls and a plainly dressed woman near the table gives a slight curtsey before coming to my side and offering me her arm.

It is actually rare for a Manchu lady to go anywhere without her maid to help her walk. However, for the consort selection, the girls are not allowed to bring anyone with them but are assigned maids, servants, and slaves that have been chosen by imperial officials. I suppose this girl is to be my maid for the day. If I am chosen, will she remain with me? No, I must not think that way. I won't be chosen. I will return to my family.

"Hand that paper to the astrologer inside," the man at the table tells me. "Next!"

I have passed the first test. No one seemed to have the slightest suspicion I was not who I claimed to be. I turn to walk to the gate and my right foot catches on the ground. I nearly stumble, and would have fallen if not for the girl at my side.

"Thank you," I say to her and immediately regret it. Lihua would never thank a maid. My hands are shaking and I am afraid to look around and see if anyone is staring at me.

"Do not worry, my lady," the maid, a young girl, perhaps no older than my sister Mingming, says. She squeezes both of my hands and gives me a reassuring smile. "You need not be afraid. I will help you."

I give a small nod and stand up straight again, balancing the weight on my head with my neck. I take a step and this time do not stumble. I place one foot in front of the other as we walk through the gate into the palace.

9

———

As we walk through the gate, I'm struck by the beauty of the place. I could never have imagined what the inside of a palace looked like, but it certainly wasn't a place of so much color.

The city of Peking might be gray and brown, but I am now standing in a glorious park, imminently more striking than even Mingxia's courtyard.

Paths wind around flower beds with clusters of blooms in every color. Some of the walkways are open so that you can see the sky—which seems a little bluer here—but others are covered to offer protection from the sun. Some of the coverings are trellises from which beautiful white and purple blooms dangle. A curved bridge provides a path over a clear stream where I can see orange, red, and gold koi. I spy a turtle sitting on a rock in the sunshine, and out of the corner of my eye see a frog leap and disappear into the water. There are open-air pagodas that would be perfect for gathering and chatting with friends, or perhaps doing embroidery in the light of day so it is less taxing on the eyes than indoor lighting.

But the most beautiful sight of all is the hundreds of ladies who, like me, are being escorted by a maid down the path, over the bridge, and through another large gate. Each girl—for some cannot be older than thirteen—wears a different color robe and holds her head high to balance the ornately decorated liangbatou upon her head. Compared to so many elegant young ladies, I surely will not stand out.

I still have no desire to be chosen. This place is beautiful, but it is still a cage. And I have no wish to pretend to be Manchu for the rest of my life. But I feel slightly guilty at the fact that I am grateful to be here. A girl such as me should never be allowed to see the inside of the Forbidden City. It is a sight I will surely never forget.

We are lead through a gate with three doors and come to a large screen wall carved with nine dragons, each one a different shade of red, gold, and blue. From there, we are escorted to the left and through another gate. This one opens up to a large, baren courtyard. There is only a flat, stone ground. No trees, no flowers, no winding paths. There are hundreds of girls already here, if not a thousand, all arranged in long lines facing a large building.

"Paper," a voice says. I look to my left and a man is holding his hand out to me. He is dressed similarly to the other men I have seen, except his robe is blue instead of black. I then remember I was supposed to hand the paper with my birthdate on it to an astrologer.

He glances at the paper and then nods. "Line up."

I mutter some sort of thanks as my maid—I think the man at the gate called her Suyin—leads me to one of the lines and then releases my hand. I feel a surge of panic that she might abandon me and grab her wrist.

"Don't worry," Suyin says. "I will wait with the other maids." She nods to the very back of the courtyard where there is a little shade next to the wall where hundreds of plainly dressed women are standing. "I will come back for you when I am needed."

I nod and reluctantly release her arm. She smiles and then trots off to join the others. I can't say anything and have been practically struck dumb by the grandeur of everything around me. I don't belong here. Not someone has plain and poor as me.

A girl and her maid walk up behind me to wait in line.

"I'm so nervous," the young lady says.

"Don't be," her maid replies. "You are sure to be chosen."

"I hope you are right."

The maid then leaves her lady the same way mine did, probably eager to get out of the sun, which I only now feel beating down on me. I feel a little woozy as the heavy robe threatens to pull me down. But I do my best to maintain my balance.

"What's your name?" the girl behind me asks.

"Da—Lihua," I say. "Ula Nara Lihua."

"I'm Ayan Gioro Yanmei," she says. "From Canton."

I try to remember if I know anything about Canton and come up with nothing. Would a Manchu girl know where Canton is? Is it an important place? Is it very near to here? Very far? She waits for a reply expectantly.

"I have a home here in Peking," I say, recalling what I know about Lihua's past. "But I grew up in Mongolia. My father was a general."

"Was?" she asks.

"He passed when I was young."

"I'm sorry to hear that."

I give a small smile and shrug, unsure of how to reply. I don't have any feelings on the matter, and it seemed that

Lihua didn't either. I don't think she remembered him at all.

"Quiet!" I see a stern-faced woman glaring at me. I give a small bend of my knees and neck.

"I'm sorry."

"Ula Nara Lihua," she says, looking at my paper. "Your birth chart is very much in line with that of the emperor. Very auspicious. You advance."

I'm shocked into silence for a moment, but thankfully, it seems the woman doesn't expect a reply as she moves on to Yanmei.

The woman humphs and grips Yanmei by the chin, turning her face right and left. "Your birth chart is not very auspicious, but you are pretty enough. Advance."

Yanmei exhales in relief as the woman moves on. "Oh, thank Heaven," she mutters.

"Dismissed," the woman says to the girl behind Yanmei. The girl bursts into tears as her maid rushes up and takes her hand. I look around and see that there is a matronly woman working her way down every line, telling which girls to stay and which ones to leave. I only now notice that hundreds of girls—most of them—are being dismissed, some crying as they walk back out the gate, some obviously relieved.

I cannot believe that so many girls are being sent away while I am being told to stay. I had hoped to sent away in the first round. I should be heading home now! My heart is heavy with worry that I have even progressed this far.

The woman who told me to stay didn't mention anything about my appearance, only my—Lihua's—birth chart. I wonder for a moment if Mingxia knew that Lihua's birth chart was auspicious enough to have her advance. If it was likely that I would be chosen based on that alone, she would have told me, right? But she never said a word. She insisted that I *wouldn't* be chosen.

But the more I think about it, the more angry I become. Mingxia is not a stupid woman. She knew that Lihua would advance. That was why she hired a stand-in, hired me, to take Lihua's place. She lied about the probability of me being chosen because she needed me to agree. I was a fool to ever trust that woman. She wouldn't have had any qualms about lying to me, deceiving me. I'm nothing to her. Just another worthless Chinese she could walk over with her stupid shoes and use to her own advantage.

"What's wrong?" Yanmei asks me. "Are you not glad?"

"No," I spit, and the shock on Yanmei's face reminds me to be more cautious. "I mean...I would prefer not to be chosen. I will miss my family."

"I understand," Yanmei says. "My mother cried so much this morning, it was hard to leave." Her eyes water a little, but she blinks it away.

"Line up!" a woman shouts and all the maids who are still present come rushing forward to help us move forward, toward the giant building, filling in the empty spots left by the girls who were dismissed. There are still maybe a hundred girls left.

"The emperor approaches!" a voice calls out, and everyone—lady, maid, eunuch—drops into a bow. The ladies are allowed to remain upright, though crouched over their precarious shoes. Everyone else goes down on their knees, their foreheads to the ground in a kowtow. Thankfully my maid is able to help me crouch before she kowtows.

I am supposed to keep my chin to my chest, but I cannot help but raise my eyes and try to catch sight of the emperor. I see a group of men gather on what I now realize is a balcony on the front of the building before us. I cannot see him clearly, he is too far away, but his yellow robe—he is the only man allowed to wear imperial yellow—shines brightly. He waves to us, even though we shouldn't be able to see him with our heads bowed, and then he disappears again.

"Stand!" a woman orders, and we do so. "Each row should follow their assigned supervisor for the physical examinations."

The supervisors appear to be matronly maids, much like the one who has been barking orders at us this whole time. We are all led out of the courtyard where we are then separated, each line of girls taken to a different building.

One at a time, we are then taken behind a screen where we are ordered to undress and stand naked on a small pedestal. It is terribly humiliating, and I try to cover myself with my hands, but each of my arms is pulled away, examined by a different woman, while still others inspect my legs, my feet, my breasts, my behind. They poke and prod and run their rough hands over me and I'm about to burst into tears when I'm finally told to step down and put my clothes back on. Thankfully, my maid is there to help me. But my heart sinks when I am told that I am to advance to the next portion of the selection process.

As soon as we leave the examination room, I find a bench and collapse onto it and give way to tears.

"My lady!" Suyin says, sitting next to me. "What's wrong? Didn't you hear? You will advance! You were not dismissed."

"That's why I'm crying!" I say. "I hate this place. I feel so humiliated."

"But why?" she asks. "Everyone must be examined.

There is no shame in it. I had to be examined before I could even be selected as a maid."

"Really?" She nods. I take a deep breath and wipe my tears away. I wish I could tell her the truth. That I'm not only embarrassed, but distressed that once again I have been advanced to the next level. This is going terribly. I should already be on my way back home by now. But I am only one step closer to having to stay here forever.

"Come, my lady," Suyin says. "Let me repair your face."

I am so unused to wearing paints I didn't even think about how I must look after crying. Not to mention standing in the sun for so long. She leads me away from the door to the examination room—every few minutes a new girl emerges, many crying as they are led back toward the main courtyard, I assume to be sent away. I wonder just how many girls are going to be left after this portion.

We sit on another bench under a nearby tree where the air is cooler. She reaches into one of her sleeves and pulls out a small container of powder and a bit of cotton and then begins to dab the powder on my face.

"How did you know to bring that with you?" I ask her.

"One of the older maids told me," she says. "She went through the last selection process a few years ago."

"Your name is Suyin, right?."

She reaches back into her sleeve and pulls out a smaller pot and a brush and fixes the kohl around my eyes. "Yes."

"That's a nice name," I say. "Are you part of a clan or banner or something?"

"Probably," she says. "But I never paid it much mind. We were so poor, as soon as I heard the palace was in need of maids, I volunteered."

"You were poor?" I ask, and I am sure my question sounds terribly stupid. She thinks I'm Lihua, a spoiled rich girl. She has no idea that I'm Daiyu, someone so poor I've sold myself as well. But I am truly surprised. I thought all Manchu were wealthy.

She nods as she concentrates on painting my face. "But it's fine. I'll be able to take the wages I earn here and put away for a dowry so I can marry when I'm released from service."

"You can leave?" Everything she says surprises me more and more.

"Of course," she says. "I'm not a slave."

I find it almost insulting that a maid should have more freedom than a fine lady, but who am I to try and understand Manchu ways?

"There," she finally says. "Good as new."

"Thank you," I say, and I reach up to balance my liang-batou as I stretch my neck from side to side. It's so terribly stiff.

"Don't worry," Suyin says. "Next, you will see the emperor and his mother. That is the last part of the selection process."

My heart thumps hard in my chest. While I am glad to know that the end is in sight, I'm terrified of what the outcome will be. Will I be going home, or will I be shuttered within the walls of the Forbidden City forever?

"Lihua!" Yanmei comes over to me, a wide smile on her face. "I passed!"

"Congratulations," I say, and I wish I could be happier for her, but I would never wish for anyone to be a captive within the red walls.

"They say that we are to meet the emperor next," Yanmei says. "Are you ready?"

"I don't think I have a choice," I say.

Yanmei giggles, hiding her mouth behind her hand. "Oh, Lihua. You are so funny."

I give a small smile even though I wasn't joking. I've had very little choice in anything that has happened since I foolishly accepted Mingxia's money.

"Girls!" our supervisor snaps at us as she comes out of the examination room. "Why are you lingering here? You should be at the Hall of Imperial Peace!"

"Yes, ma'am," Yanmei and I say, and then our maids lead us away from the examination hall and through a series of gardens until we reach the Hall of Imperial Peace, which seems to be simply another large, open building.

Before climbing the steps to the hall, I hesitate. I look around and see no other girls. I am the last to arrive. Would anyone notice if I simply ran away? If I kicked off my shoes and caught up with the other girls who had been dismissed?

"My lady?" Suyin says, and I realize I'm only dreaming. I have no say in what happens next.

Only the emperor can decide my fate now.

10

"Who will I see inside?" I ask Suyin.

"The emperor, of course," my little maid tells me. "The empress, Empress Caihong."

"What is the emperor's name?" I ask. Suyin giggles, but then she realizes I'm not kidding.

"You don't know?"

"I...I'm just so flustered I can hardly remember my own name," I say. Suyin smiles, apparently believing me even though I'm not really lying. If I was asked to recite Lihua's family history right now, I'm sure I couldn't remember a thing.

"Emperor Guozhi, my lady," Suyin says. I nod and repeat the name over and over to myself.

"The person you need to impress the most is Emperor Guozhi's mother, the dowager empress," Suyin says. "Dowager Empress Fenfang."

"Why her?" I ask.

"Her word among the ladies is law," Suyin says. "Empress Caihong should be the head of the emperor's harem, but she isn't really, not until Fenfang dies. Fenfeng is the true head of the emperor's ladies. It is she who chooses the emperor's consorts."

"He doesn't choose his own wives?" I ask, a bit surprised. It is true in Chinese families as well that the mother-in-law is the head of the household. But this is no typical household. It is actually a bit humorous to me that the emperor—the supposed Son of Heaven—should still bow to his mother.

"Certainly not," Suyin says. "The emperor does not know the qualities of a capable wife. He would only pick the girls with pretty faces."

I think about all the girls who have already been sent home and those who have stayed. Wasn't Yanmei chosen to advance because she was pretty, even though she did not have an auspicious birth chart? And how many more were sent home because their bodies had a mark or a scratch? Would a freckle or scar make a woman less capable of bearing children? Even though my birth chart is auspicious, if I had been ugly would I have been sent away? I think I would have. I think this whole process is little more than a beauty contest.

"Come, my lady," Suyin says, tugging on my hand up the stairs. "The dowager empress will not be pleased with you for being so late."

Good, I think to myself. Hopefully it will be enough for her to send me away.

When I reach the top of the stairs, there is a large open room. I see dozens of girls kneeling on the floor with their heads bowed. I know I should keep my eyes down, but I cannot help but look ahead of them to the far side of the room. This could be my only chance to see the emperor.

In a large golden throne on a raised dais, I see a man slouched in his chair, as if he wished he was anywhere else.

It is the man who came to look at us from the balcony when we were in the courtyard, but I can see him more clearly now. He looks older than me, at least in his late twenties, possibly early thirties. He is not fat, but his cheeks are fleshy. He eats well. He wears a gleaming yellow robe and a long string of pearls around his neck. His hat is rimmed gold, but it is topped with red threads. He is clean-shaven and has gentle eyes.

To his right is a young woman, perhaps not even twenty years old. She has a high Manchu headdress ornamented with an enamel phoenix. This can only be Empress Caihong. I can instantly see why she is the empress, she is possibly the most beautiful woman I have seen in my life, with wide eyes, a narrow nose, and heart-shaped lips.

"About time you joined us, Ula Nara Lihua," says an older woman to the emperor's left—Dowager Empress Fenfang. She does not look cruel, but neither does she appear kind. Her features are soft with age and she wears no face paints. Her gown is a sedate green and her hair is wrapped tightly around a bianfang, but she wears no headdress.

I drop to my knees behind the nearest girl. "Forgive me, your...highness." I try to recall Mingxia's instruction on how to address various members of the royal family, but that was not a priority for me. I didn't think I would make it this far.

"Stand up," she orders me, and I do so, but this time I keep my eyes averted. "Turn around." Again I do as ordered. She nods approvingly and I take that as a sign to return to my place.

The empress dowager then speaks to the empress across the emperor, who seems to have little interest in the proceedings. On the left arm of the emperor's throne is a bowl. The empress dowager reaches inside and pulls out a small, flat piece of wood.

"Biangia Meifan," the dowager says. A girl several rows away from me stands up. The dowager hands the little card to the emperor, who drops the name into a bowl on his right side. I assume that means that this girl has been chosen as a consort. My heart starts to race as I realize that I have no way of sabotaging myself. The dowager will make her decision now.

A few more girls are stand, obscuring my view of the emperor. I look to my right and see that Yanmei has her hands pressed together and is praying fervently.

"Ayan Gioro Yanmei."

Yanmei chokes out a sob, but I can tell it is one of happiness. "May the emperor live ten thousand years!" she says as her maid comes over to help her stand.

I can see the dowager nodding with approval and I think that Yanmei will soon become one of the dowager's favorites.

"Ruburi Chunhua," the dowager says as continues to pull names from the bowl.

I have never been one of great faith, but if prayer worked for Yanmei, maybe it can work for me too.

Oh great, wise, merciful Heaven, I mutter to myself. *Please do not let me be chosen. Send me home. Ancestors, do not let me be taken from my family.*

The sound of woodchips being dropped into the bowl stop. I raise my head in hopes that the remaining of us are about to be dismissed.

"What do you think, my son?" the dowager asks. "Do any of these blooming flowers appeal to you?"

I lean to one side so I can see the emperor. He shifts to his other side, still not looking at any of us.

"I care not," he says.

"My son," the dowager says, a bit more firmly. "This has all been for you. Your empress and concubines have yet to give you a son."

The young empress tries to hide the pain that flashes across her eyes, but it is rather obvious.

"Then what is the point of bringing in more women?" the emperor asks.

"It will happen. I promise you," the empress says to her husband. "We must simply find the right vessel for your glorious seed."

The emperor gives her a sad half-smile before looking away again.

"Please, my son," the dowager says. "Look at the girls before you. They are the finest and most beautiful girls your kingdom has to offer. Surely some of them must appeal to you."

The emperor sighs and glances around the room, his eyes not landing on any girl in particular. He then places his hand in the bowl, stirs the woodchips around, and picks one at random. He hands it to his mother.

"Samala Qiao," the dowager reads. I let out a breath I didn't realize I was holding. This is true torture. How can the emperor leave such an important decision to mere chance?

Ula Nara Lihua," the dowager says as the emperor pulls another chip from the bowl and I exhale in relief again. Why won't the dowager release us instead of—

"My lady," Suyin whispers. I look up at her, confused why she is tugging on my arm to stand when we have not yet been dismissed.

I then realize that the emperor pulled Lihua's name from the bowl. *My* name.

"No," I whisper as Suyin pulls me up.

"Shh," she says gently.

"No," I mutter again. "No, he can't have chosen me."

A girl next to me who is still kneeling looks at me with pure anger in her eyes. She must be filled with jealousy that I was picked even though I don't want it.

"Please," Suyin whispers, her eyes pleading. I don't know what she is so scared of. It's me who is about to be imprisoned for the rest of my life.

"What's going on back there?" the dowager empress asks. She stands to get a better look. "Who is speaking?"

"I...I am," I say, raising my arm but keeping my eyes down. "Lihua. Umm...Ula...Ula Nara Lihua."

"What's wrong?"

Everything, I want to scream. *Please don't choose me!* But what would happen then? Has any girl ever rejected being chosen by the emperor? Would it instantly give me away as not a true Manchu that I do not find this a great honor? The knowledge sobers me. I don't want to be chosen, but neither do I want to be dead.

"Nothing," I say.

The dowager presses her lips disapprovingly before sitting again and turning to the emperor. "Are you sure you want that one?"

The emperor clears his throat and his eyes sweep over all of us, but I am not sure he ever actually sees me. "It matters not to me."

The dowager squeezes her hands together in obvious frustration. She then looks to the empress. "What say you?"

My heart races. Is it possible that I could still be dismissed and maintain my—Lihua's—dignity?

The empress picks up my chip from the bowl and then

says something to her maid, who hands the empress a piece of paper.

"Her chart is auspicious, Mother," she says. "*Very* auspicious." She hands the paper to the dowager, who looks it over.

The dowager nods. "Very well. Ula Nara Lihua stays."

I feel faint, and I am sure I would topple over if not for Suyin holding me up.

"Any more?" the dowager asks the emperor. He stands up quickly and leaves the room without another word. She looks at the empress, who only shakes her head.

"Very well," the dowager says, standing. "Thank you all for attending. If your name was not called, you will be escorted to the Hall of Literary Brilliance to await the return of your families to collect you. Please accept these gifts of thanks to your families for offering you to us this day."

As the girls shuffle out of the room, three eunuchs present the girls with gold ingots, a string of pearls, and a jewel hair ornament. How I wish I were among them. Not for the gifts, they mean nothing to me. But so I could return home to my family. I have already been separated from them for weeks with no contact. How I miss them and hope they are doing well. Are they full of good food and in a warm room? Or has the money already been wasted in frivolous purchases?

I shake my head. I can only hope that Mingxia holds to our agreement that whatever bride price is sent to her, she will send my family half. I now realize that I should have demanded all of it. After all, it was not *her* daughter that was sold.

Once all the girls are gone, we are once again arranged into straight rows in front of the dowager. "Congratulations, ladies," she says. "You are truly the most blessed among women."

"Thank you, empress mother," everyone says with a bow except for me. I follow the bow but have no idea what words to say.

"You must be tired," the young empress says. "Each of you will be assigned a palace and a eunuch servant. You may go to your new homes to rest and become comfortable here. Tomorrow morning, you will all be expected in the Palace of Longevity and Peace to pay your morning respects to the dowager empress and discuss the day's business."

"Thank you, empress," everyone says. At that, the empress and empress dowager leave the room, each escorted by half a dozen maids and servants. As soon as they are gone the room erupts into noisy conversation as the girls cheer, clap, and congratulate each other. I seem to be the only one who doesn't want to be here.

"We made it!" Yanmei says.

"So we did," I say, and I wish I could pretend to be joyous, but I cannot. I am angry with Mingxia for lying to me. Angry at myself for trusting her. Angry I didn't do more to be dismissed. I am now trapped here for the rest of my life.

For the rest of my days, Daiyu no longer exists. I am now Lihua—and I despise her.

                                 11
                              ───────────

I am the last one to leave the reception hall and
Suyin holds my hand as we walk through a maze
of courtyards and buildings.

"Isn't it wonderful?" Suyin says. "I am so glad you were
chosen, but I knew you would be, you are so beautiful."

I wrinkle my nose at that. I think anyone can be beautiful when dressed in expensive clothes and their face painted beyond recognition. I know I am not here on any merit of my own. I made it through the first part of the selection because of Lihua's birth date; I made it through the last part because my name was drawn from a bowl. All the girls in that room had the same chance as I did to be chosen.

But why did it have to be me?

"I am to be your maid from now on," Suyin prattles on. "I won't have to go back to scrubbing pots in the kitchen. It's a big step for me, and the extra money will help my family."

"Where are they?" I ask her, trying to distract myself from my melancholy thoughts.

"A long way from here," she says. "A small town about

two-hundred li to the west. My father is a servant for the governor of Zhili Province and my mother is a maid."

"How did you end up here?"

She glances at me curiously, as if I should know the answer, and I suppose any true Manchu girl would know. But I can't unask the question, so it hangs in the air between us.

"Every year a call goes out requesting girls to serve in the palace. I applied for three years before I was finally accepted. I was so disappointed when I ended up in the kitchen, but thankfully that didn't last long. I was one of the first girls to sign up to assist the women who were coming for the selection process. It's quite an honor."

"I'm sure it is," I say, and I realize that Suyin is quite ambitious for someone so young.

"Here we are," Suyin says, stopping in front of the door of a random building. I look around and, of course, I have no idea where I am. I am certain I would never find my way back to the audience hall, much less the gate I first entered. This place is so large and confusing, I don't see how anyone can know where anything is.

There is a eunuch in a blue robe standing by the door. He approaches and kneels before me.

"I am your humble servant, Jinhai. I will do my best to serve you, my lady."

Another servant. Already, this is too much. But I know there is nothing I can do about it.

"Thank you," I finally say, unsure of what else I should say instead.

Jinhai stands and leads Suyin and myself into the building. Inside, there is a short hallway, with latticed walls on each side, two openings in each lattice. I hear lots of chatter and laughing and realize that the building is divided into four rooms. As I walk down the hall, I see that the first two rooms are occupied. The girls in the rooms are excitedly looking at the furniture, bowls of bright fruit, and closets full of clothes.

Jinhai motions to back room on the left. "I am sorry, but this is your room."

"Why should you be sorry?" I ask.

"It is not very auspicious," he says. I'm not sure what to say to that, I have no idea how he came to such a conclusion. I walk past him into the room and am overwhelmed by how beautiful it is.

The walls are painted red and there is a large bed to one side with a heavy canopy. There are lacquered tables and chairs and a huge chest inlaid with shimmering mother-of-pearl. There are two large windows, each blocked by a redwood lattice. The lattice, I assume, is to keep anyone from climbing in or out, but they let in plenty of light, making the room bright and airy. I step to one of the windows and see a beautiful garden on the other side with a shade tree, a pond, and a concrete bench. There is a latch so that I can open the window if I wish.

"I don't know why it is inauspicious," I say. "It's lovely."

"I am glad you are pleased, my lady," Jinhai says.

I hear a burst of laughter from one of the other rooms and realize that there is little privacy here. There are no doors to the rooms, so anyone could walk in at any time, and conversations could easily carry. I will have to be careful of what I do and say even in my own room.

"Here is your chamber pot," Suyin says, pulling up a bed cloth to show me a large porcelain bowl. "And the bed will be heated when winter comes."

A heated bed? I try to keep my face from looking

surprised. I didn't know such a thing existed, but Lihua would surely know. She probably had one at home.

Suyin then walks over to the large chest and opens the doors. "And these are your clothes," she says. "A seamstress will come within the week to adjust them to your exact size."

At least ten robes, each made of silk in a different color and embroidered with different patterns, hang in the chest like a captured rainbow. Suyin pulls one out and holds it under my chin. It is so soft and the silk so bright it makes even the robe I am wearing that Mingxia gave me seem rough and dull by comparison.

I then think about the dozen girls who were selected today and how each one of them will have closets full of clothes just like this one and it makes me angry. These are more clothes than I would probably use in a lifetime, and I am just a lowly consort! How many gowns must the empress have? I simply don't understand how these women can have so much when I was raised with so little.

"Does it not please you?" Suyin asks, and I realize I must be making a terrible face.

"Of course it does," I say. "I am just a little overwhelmed."

"You must be tired!" Suyin says, putting the robe back into the chest and closing the doors. She then takes me by the hand and leads me to the bed. "You should rest. Jinhai and I have chores we should be doing anyway."

I sit down and reach to remove my shoes, but Suyin is quicker and does the job for me. She then climbs up on the bed behind me and begins removing the decorations from my headdress, then the pins to the headdress itself. When she removes the headdress, I let out an audible sigh of relief. My neck is terribly sore from holding the monstrosity up, and then I realize I am going to have to wear such contraptions every day for the rest of my life. Hopefully not headdresses that large, but still...

"Would you like something to eat or drink?" Suyin asks. "There is fresh fruit and I can brew you some tea. Or I can request something from the kitchen—"

"No!" I finally snap, and Suyin's eyes go large before she drops down in a crouch.

"I'm sorry, my lady!"

I sigh, realizing I've hurt her feelings, which makes me feel guilty, but I just want to be left alone. "No, I'm sorry. I'm just very tired."

"You must never apologize to a servant, my lady," Jinhai whispers to me. "You are never in the wrong!"

I open my mouth to argue with that. Such nonsense! But I don't wish to continue the conversation.

"Just...go," I say, and I feel a sourness in my stomach. I'm not the sort of person to give orders to others. I don't think that Suyin and Jinhai are lower than I am, but I don't know how else to have a moment to myself.

Suyin rises to her feet but keeps her head down as she backs toward the door. I notice that Jinhai backs away from me as well. So strange. Through the door I can see clear into the other room where another consort is trying on her new clothes, turning this way and that in front of a mirror to admire herself. I groan as I realize that I am still not alone. I crawl back on the bed—which is surprisingly soft—and lay my head on a pillow—a pillow!—and stare at the wall.

I can't sleep as my mind races. I hate this place. It's so large, a huge waste of space. And the opulence—it's so unnecessary! Who needs that many clothes? Who needs this many wives? I'll probably never even see the emperor. Never have a child of my own. This is the rest of my life—

me, alone, with only a maid for company and a closet full of dresses I'll never wear.

I punch the bed as tears start to escape my eyes. How could Mingxia do this to me? She knew Lihua would be chosen—she knew it! I was an idiot for trusting her, and now my life is lost. I'll never see my family again. I can never even inquire about their welfare without giving myself away. Why would a Manchu lady ever seek information about a poor Han family?

I must drift off eventually because I am awoken by the clattering of dishes. I sit up and see that several maids have brought in quite a large amount of food.

"What is going on?" I ask as I stretch and start to get off the bed. Suyin, of course, rushes to my side.

"Here," she says as she tries to put the pot-bottom shoes back on my feet.

"No," I say, pulling away. "I can't possibly put those back on today."

She bows and then goes to the closet where she pulls out a pair of silk slippers. I let her put them on me so I can find out why there is so much food in my room.

"Your supper, my lady," Jinhai says.

"What?" I ask. "There's far too much! There must be some mistake."

"No, my lady," he says. "This is the food allowance for a rank five concubine."

"A what?" I ask.

"A rank five concubine," he says. "That is the level you were assigned by the dowager empress."

"Rank five...out of how many?" I ask.

"Five," he says after a pause."

I shake my head. The lowest rank. I'm not even a consort, but a concubine. I'm not sure I know the difference, but consort at least sounded nicer. More like a wife. But I'm not. I'm a concubine, and my sole purpose is to give the emperor a son.

"I can't possibly eat all that," I finally say when the maids are finished delivering the food. "Tell them to send less in the future."

Jinhai and Suyin exchange a glance. "My lady," Suyin whispers, "you are not expected to eat it all yourself. When you are done eating, then your servants will eat. After that, you may offer the food as a gift to even lower servants."

"And then anything left can be given to your dog if you would like one," Jinhai adds, and Suyin nods.

"I'm sorry," I say as I take a seat. "I didn't realize it was for more people than myself."

"Don't apologize, my lady," Suyin says. "Over the next few days, Jinhai and I will help instruct you about how the court functions."

I motion to the empty chairs around the table. "Please, join me."

"We cannot!" Suyin says, horrified. "We cannot sit in your presence, and we certainly are not suitable company."

I groan to myself about all these silly rules. "Then why do I even have more than one chair?"

"You will make friends with the other ladies soon, I'm sure," Suyin says.

"Fine." I pick up a napkin, but Suyin takes it from me and lays it on my lap. I'm starting to feel like an invalid. Jinhai fills my bowl with rice and then offers me my chopsticks.

"You aren't going to chew it for me?" I ask, and his face drops in horror. I realize he thinks I am serious. "I was only joking." He gives an awkward laugh and steps back. I reach out and take a bit of food from the dish nearest to me along with a bite of rice.

It's delicious.

I thought the food at Mingxia's home was good, but this is completely different. It's wonderful. The meat is so tender it is like eating tofu, and the mix of spices dances across my tongue. I try another dish and find that it is just as amazing. By the end, I find that I have eaten far more than I thought possible and my stomach is bloated. I'll have to be careful that I don't end up fat.

Suyin and Jinhai then clear the dishes away and are gone for some time. I assume they are eating somewhere away from my presence. I take note that this would be at least a little time during the day to myself. Well, the evening, anyway. It is already dark outside, the room lit by several lanterns.

Other than think, I'm not sure what to do with myself. I hear low voices and step toward the door to my room. Across the hall, two ladies are chatting. I wonder if I should walk over, introduce myself, try to make friends. But when they see me watching them, they quickly shuffle to another part of the room where I can't see them. So much for that idea. I wonder where Yanmei is. She must be in another palace somewhere. Perhaps tomorrow I can seek her out. It would be nice to at least have someone to talk to.

I'm sitting in a chair, thinking, when Suyin and Jinhai come back. Jinhai has a small booklet and Suyin is carrying a stack of laundry.

"These are new undergarments," she explains. "Socks as well. Also silk rags for your moon phase. Do let me know when it comes so I can take extra care of you."

My face reddens at the idea of discussing such a topic

with a stranger, but I suppose there's no helping it. She'll be the person doing my laundry.

"Of course," I mutter.

"I need to go over the accounts with you, my lady," Jinhai says, laying the book before me. I have a sudden flash of panic. I can't read. The only accounts I've ever done is figuring out how much money I need for enough food to get my family through the day.

"Don't worry," Jinhai says. My unease must have been clear on my face. "I'll teach you what you need to know." I suppose it would be uncommon for any girl to have dealt with much money.

Jinhai points to a character at the top of the page. "This is your allowance from the emperor each month. And these are your expenses."

I feel sick when I realize I can't even read numbers. I have no idea how much money I have. And what does he mean "expenses"? Isn't everything provided for me?

"I'm sorry, I don't understand."

"Do not apologize," he says. "Everything in your room now, your clothes, your furniture, all that is a wedding gift from the emperor. And each season, you will be provided with new clothes, depending on your rank at the time. But any clothes more than that, you would buy yourself. Understand?"

"I think so," I say, though I still don't know how much money I actually have.

"The salary for your servants is to be paid out of your allowance."

"What?" I nearly shriek. "That's ridiculous. I don't even need servants."

Jinhai and Suyin look at each other, and I see a flash of fear across their faces. I suppose they are worried that they are about to lose their jobs. I remember how excited Suyin was when she told me she had been rescued from kitchen duty to serve me. I also realize that any Manchu lady of rank would have servants. Mingxia's home had a dozen at least. And I suppose I will need someone to help me dress and style my hair. And Jinhai seems very knowledgeable about how things are done around here. I have to keep reminding myself that this is my life now, and it is very different from the one I lived in the shadow of the Forbidden City. I might not have needed servants then, but I do now.

"I'm sorry," I say, rubbing my head. "I just didn't realize I would have expenses. I thought the emperor would provide everything."

"Don't apologize," he says. "I know this is all very new to you. Perhaps we should go over the rest of it tomorrow."

I nod. "That seems like a good idea." Suyin finishes her task and Jinhai stands near the door, and all of us look at each other in awkward silence.

"So...what should we do now?" It is evening, but far too early to go to sleep, especially since I had that nap.

"Oh, well, you can read or write," Suyin says, and my face falls. "Or you could play an instrument. I can bring you an erhu or pipa."

"I've always liked the erhu," I say, "but I'm not very good." I practiced a little when I was with Mingxia, but it sounded like a cat screeching.

"I can procure one for you," Suyin says. "And I can find a eunuch to teach you."

"That would be fun," I say.

"It would come out of your household income," Jinhai says.

"Oh." I'll need to find out how much money I have and

what things cost. But I don't know how to ask Jinhai for help without revealing just how uneducated I am.

"You can embroider," Suyin says. "Many of the consorts like to embroider gifts for the emperor."

"I suppose I'll have to buy the supplies," I say.

"Yes," Jinhai says, but then he lowers his voice. "But I can sell the pieces you make for you outside."

"Outside?"

"Outside the wall."

"You can leave the palace?" I ask, feeling excited. If he can leave, maybe I can too.

"Only with your permission, of course," he says. "And I can't go very far, or be out very long. I could never leave the city except when escorting you to Yuanming Yuan or Jehol."

I have no idea what those things are, but at least it means I won't be completely trapped inside the Forbidden City all of the time.

"But many ladies sell their embroidery outside to earn more money for their expenses."

"That is good to know," I say. "I can at least do that. It will be something to occupy my mind and my time."

"I'll purchase items for you tomorrow, my lady," Suyin says. "The embroidery office will be closed for the night."

"The embroidery office?" I ask and nearly laugh. Why would the Forbidden City have need for such a thing?

"Yes," Suyin says, confused. "The embroidery office has all the supplies you could need. They are the best quality, sent directly from Suchow. And the ladies who work there can perform any repairs that are needed to garments and shoes and such."

"Suchow," I say. "I always wanted to go there." I remember how I had told Mama and Baba I could try to find work there. But that life is behind me. Mingxia gave them more money for me than I ever would have earned as a seamstress. I wonder if she held up her end of the agreement and gave my parents whatever bride price the emperor paid for me. I look at Jinhai's accounting book and wonder if there would be a way to send more money to them. Or if I could ever trust Jinhai enough to send them a message. I suppose not. It would be too dangerous, too risky, no matter how long I live here. It is a secret I must always keep.

"I suppose there is nothing left to do for tonight, then," I say as I stand. "Might as well prepare for bed."

I find that I am glad I decided to go to bed early because, apparently, preparing for bed is a rather lengthy endeavor. First, Suyin helps me out of my clothes and into a light sleeping robe. I then must wash my face of all the paint and apply a variety of lotions and oils to make my skin white and supple. I'm told I can buy even more—better—face items for a price. Suyin then brushes my hair out one hundred times. She washes and massages my feet, and then does the same for my hands. I admit that such pampering is relaxing, but I still feel awkward having her do such things for me.

Finally, I crawl into bed. It is rather late I think, but I'm still not particularly tired. I am sure that Suyin and Jinhai are, though, so I lay in bed quietly, pretending to sleep until I can hear their soft snores. Suyin sleeps at the foot of my bed, and Jinhai sleeps on the floor near the door, apparently so that they are on hand should I need anything, but I don't know what I could possibly need while I am sleeping.

I am surprised by how quiet the Forbidden City is at night. Other than the hoot of an owl and chirrup of crickets, I don't hear another person. Occasionally I see a light pass the window, and I think it must be a guard patrolling the grounds. Somehow even he moves on silent feet.

I stare up at the canopy over my bed into the darkness, begging sleep to come, when I hear something. It's very faint at first, but the longer I listen, the clearer it becomes. I hear a sniffle and realize someone is crying. At first, I think it must be one of the other girls in the house, but then I realize it is much closer than that.

I sit up and see that Suyin is still sound asleep, her body rising and falling evenly. And it isn't Jinhai because it is certainly a female crying. I slip out of the bed carefully so as not to disturb Suyin and move toward the sound. It's coming in through the window, from the little courtyard I saw earlier.

I peek outside and can barely make out the form of a girl sitting on the bench, her white nightgown shining in the moonlight. I wonder for a second if I am seeing a ghost, a vision of a concubine who died of loneliness. But as she makes a snorting sound amid her crying, I know this is just a girl who is devastated to be here—just like me.

I go back to the bed and pick up my silk slippers and tiptoe toward the door. There is no one in the hall, and the front door of the palace itself is wide open. I slip outside and sit on the threshold as I put on my shoes, then I follow a path around the palace to where I know the courtyard must be.

"Who's there?" the girl asks, standing up in alarm when I step on some loose gravel.

"Shh!" I whisper. "I heard you crying. Are you all right?"

"Oh," she says, keeping her voice quiet as well. "Yes, of course. I shouldn't be out here." She starts to walk past me.

"Wait," I say. "You can stay. I wasn't able to sleep anyway, that's why I heard you."

She hesitates. "I'm sure we aren't supposed to be outside alone."

"There's a lot of things we aren't supposed to do," I say, and I can see a small smile form on her lips.

"There certainly are a lot of rules," she says, then we both laugh, covering our mouths so no one hears us.

"I'm Da—Lihua," I say.

"Wangli," she replies. "So, you live here? I'm in the next building down that way." She points down a path.

"Yes," I say, "with three other girls, and the servants of course. The other girls don't seem to like me very much."

"That's to be expected," Wangli says. "We are all in competition, are we not?"

I shrug. "It doesn't really matter to me."

She raises an eyebrow and I know I've misspoken. It's supposed to be my life's dream to give the emperor a son, isn't it?

"I guess you aren't very happy to be here either," I say. "Since, you know, you were crying."

"I was just missing my family," she says. "My mother, my brothers."

"You have brothers?"

"Yes, four of them," she says.

"Wow. I had four sisters."

"My brothers were always so protective of me. It's strange to be surrounded only by girls. And my mother..." She shakes her head. "She will be so alone now."

"My mother relied on me too," I say, and I want to slap myself for my stupidity. Lihua didn't have any sisters! I need to bite my tongue before I slip up and say something too revealing.

We hear the bang of a gong and a man cries out that is it now the hour of the tiger.

"We better get back inside before we are missed," Wangli says.

"Maybe we can meet tomorrow? We can have tea together or something."

"I'd like that," Wangli says. "It's good to have a friend, even if we are expected to be rivals."

I smirk. I want to tell her that she is welcome to the emperor if she wants him, but I don't want to overstep.

"Tomorrow, then."

She gives a little wave and then disappears from sight. I slip back inside the palace to my room, and then into my bed.

"Hmm?" Suyin raises her head sleepily.

"Nothing," I whisper. "Go back to sleep." It doesn't take long before she is quietly snoring again.

The stress and unease I felt earlier is a bit lighter now. I am glad to know that I'm not the only person less than happy to be here. And it will be good to have a friend. Hopefully between Wangli and Yanmei, I won't be as lonely as I feared.

12

———

The next morning I wake at eight and ten dishes of breakfast foods are brought in. After I take a bite of each—which was far more than I needed—a large copper tub is brought to my room. I see that the other girls in the house are brought copper tubs as well. A flurry of simply dressed servants then bring in several pails of water to fill the tub. Suyin—as small and young as she is—barks orders at them and I wonder just how many layers to the hierarchy of servants there are.

I climb into the tub and Suyin scrubs me from head to toe, spending extra time on my scalp and long hair. When I stand up from the water, she rubs scented oils on my skin. Thankfully Jinhai is not present. I know he is a eunuch, but he is also a man and I would not want him to see me naked.

Suyin wraps me in a silk robe and I sit on a chair at the dressing table as she gets to work on my hair, brushing it one hundred times and then combing more oils through it to make it sleek and smooth. She winds my hair tightly around a bian fang and then attaches a very small liang batou to the back of my head. Thankfully it is not very heavy. She then adorns the entire style in silk and jewel flowers.

Then she must paint my face, and I am already feeling exhausted. I can understand ladies spending so much time on their appearance for special occasions, but must I do this every day? It is already well past ten o'clock.

"Only the most basic of cosmetics have been supplied for you," Suyin explains as she mixes kohl with water and then paints a thin black line around my eyes. "You should purchase better ones."

"From my household allowance," I grumble. Living in the Forbidden City seems to be terribly expensive. I must find a way to learn numbers and math without giving away just how ignorant I am.

"Of course," Suyin says, apparently not hearing the bitterness in my voice. Finally, my face paint is complete and Suyin helps me dress. The silk qipao is not as heavy as I expected, the silk feeling cool and light against my skin. It is better quality than the gowns I was given by Mingxia, something I didn't think possible.

When I step into the pot-bottom shoes, I take a look at myself in the mirror. The image unnerves me because I hardly recognize the girl staring back. And yet this is who I am now. Every day for the rest of my life, I will look like this.

"You are so beautiful, my lady," Suyin says with pride, mistaking the reason why I stare.

"Thank you," I say, forcing a smile. I know the girl has worked hard to make me presentable, and I don't wish to insult her.

"Come," she says, offering me her arm. I see that the other girls in the house are also leaving.

"Where are we going?" I ask.

"To see the empress, of course," Suyin says. "It is time for the morning greetings."

"Of course," I say, having only a vague idea of what she means. I know that Lihua greeted her mother every morning, so I suppose we must pay the same honor to the empress.

It is nearly midday when I step out of the palace and into the sun. Jinhai is waiting for me by the door with an umbrella, which he holds over my head as we walk down the twisting maze of paths.

"Wangli!" I say with a wave when I see her step out of her palace. Wangli smiles and steps toward me so that we may walk together.

"How are you?" I ask her.

"Fine," she says. "I'm sure I only needed a good night's rest."

"Of course," I say. Before long, we make up only a small part of the large crowd of girls heading toward the same building and I feel a sinking sensation in my stomach. What am I to do when I arrive? Is this something I should already know? I don't realize my steps have slowed until Suyin ends up a step ahead of me.

"What is wrong, my lady?" she asks.

"Nothing," I say. "Only...I am very nervous."

"Lihua!" I see Yanmei waving at me and I wave back. She trots over to me, her smile large and the tassels dangling from her hair waving in the wind. How she can be so quick in her shoes, I'll never know. We greet each other with a hug.

"Can you believe it?" Yanmei asks. "Our first day as palace ladies. Isn't it grand?"

"I certainly never thought I would experience it," Wangli says dryly.

I introduce Wangli and Yanmei to each other.

"You are so lucky to live so close together!" Yanmei exclaims.

"I'm sure we can visit each other easily enough," I reply. I notice that there are other girls milling about in the courtyard, but I don't recognize them. "Who are they?"

Suyin looks over. "Some of the concubines who were already here before you arrived," she says. "They will not be happy that the emperor now has more ladies to choose from, but they were all elevated because of it, so they should be glad."

"They are all at least rank four or five concubines now," Yanmei's maid adds.

"You must bow to them when you pass them as your superiors," Suyin explains.

"And how should I greet the empress?" I ask, my heart racing as I see more ladies enter the audience hall.

Suyin offers me a kind smile. "There is no reason for concern. You will line up and perform your morning kowtow, then the empress will give her announcements and orders for the day."

"Well, first you will greet the empress," Wangli's maid explains. "Then the dowager empress."

"The dowager will be there?" Yanmei asks.

Her maid nods and then looks around as if to make sure no one is listening. I think the girl must be a gossip.

"The empress is supposed to be the head of the harem, of course," she says, her voice low. We all lean in to hear her better. "The dowager usually has no real power after her husband dies and her son and his wife become emperor and empress. She should be merely a figurehead, unless the emperor specifically asks for her advice."

"But the dowager hates the empress!" Wangli's maid

interjects. I think she was feeling left out. "She was an expensive bride, the most expensive there has ever been."

"Her bride price was more than all the other concubines combined," Yanmei's maid says. "She was a Mongolian princess."

I do find this a little interesting. I thought Mongolians were wild, savage people. They live north of the wall and ride horses across the great plains tending herds of yaks. Why the emperor would pay so much to marry a Mongolian, even a princess, I could never guess.

"Is that why the dowager despises her?" Wangli asks. "Simply because she was expensive?"

"She was expensive but has yet to give the emperor a son," Yanmei's maid says.

"Oh," Yanmei and Wangli say together with a nod of their heads.

Yanmei's maid opens her mouth to say more, but I see that the other ladies have all entered the audience hall.

"We should go," I say. "We can continue this conversation later."

They all seem terribly disappointed, and while the information is interesting, I cannot see how any of it matters to me. I'm a sixth-rank concubine and have no plans to change that. The farther I stay away from the center of the court, the better.

As we enter the audience hall, I am still nervous. I am sure that there is more to the morning greeting than bowing and smiling. There must be a specific way to bow and greet the empress and the dowager that the other girls will know from years of practice. I walk slowly so that others may enter ahead of me. I wish to be as far to the back as possible so I can mimic the other girls and be lost in the crowd.

When I enter the audience hall, I am struck by how

large it is. The empress sits at the back of the room on a golden throne upon a raised dais, and the dowager sits on an equally impressive throne at the same level. The empress is as elegant as I remember, her robe a deep golden color embroidered with flying cranes. Her headdress is much smaller than the one she wore yesterday, but it is still more ornate than anyone else's. It is like a golden filigree crown extending from one side of her head to the other. She has a slight smile on her face that makes her appear kind, approachable. I wonder if the reason her beauty is so striking is because of her Mongolian blood.

The dowager, on the other hand, looks stern. She wears no makeup, her gown black with gold embroidery. Her headdress is larger than that of the empress, but with few adornments.

To either side of the room are four long rows of chairs where many concubines—over fifty—are already seated.

"Good luck!" Suyin says as she gives both my hands a squeeze and then walks away.

"Where are you—" I then notice that all of the servant girls stand quietly against the back wall. The eunuchs all wait outside except for those that attend the empress and dowager.

The new concubines fall into three straight columns before the empress and the dowager. I end up in the middle column very near the back, which I hope is the perfect place to hide. I cannot help but look at the beautiful girls around me. In the row to my left, toward the front, I see Yanmei. To my right, very nearby, is Wangli.

"It is now time for the formal greeting by the new concubines," a eunuch at the front of the room, standing near the dais announces.

All of the girls bend down until they are sitting on their

knees, and I follow suit as best I can, though it is awkward in my ridiculous shoes. In unison, the girls then raise a handkerchief with their right hands, flicking it up over their shoulders and then back down again as though waving it dramatically. I remember that Suyin had tucked a handkerchief into one of my sleeves when she was dressing me and pull it out in time to take part in the third wave.

"May the empress live ten thousand years!" the girls all say, and I open and close my mouth, sure to remember the words for the next day. "May the empress mother live ten thousand years!"

"Rise and greet Lady An, rank three consort," the empress says, motioning to a woman sitting at the end of the row on our right. Lady An is not as beautiful as the empress, and her face seems tired, but she still smiles. We all turn and perform the same greeting as we did for the empress.

"Rise," the empress announces when we are done. "Take your seats."

I look behind us to see that several rows of chairs have appeared. As usual, I walk slowly, taking a seat to the back where I can disappear.

"The emperor has an eye for beauty," the dowager says. "I am sure each of you will bring him great delight in your turn." Everyone smiles but does not respond. "And plenty of sons."

I see several girls blush, and the empress frowns, turning her head aside for a moment before clearing her throat and resuming her usual, gentle face.

"I am looking forward to getting to know each you personally," the empress says, and my heart thumps hard in my chest. The eunuch standing near her hands her a red book. She reads four names from the book, thankfully not mine. Each of the girls stands when her name is read. "You four are invited to take the midday meal with me."

The girls gasp in surprise and then fall to their knees, praising the empress for her kindness.

I feel nauseous. If she plans to get to know all of us, eventually she will send for me. I might be able to fool servants and other concubines, but surely not the empress. She didn't get a good look at me at the selection, nor did I speak. I'll not be able to hide from her when we share a table.

"Lady Ula Nara Lihua," the empress says, and I think I will faint. *No, no, no!* She couldn't have meant me, could she? I see Wangli staring at me.

You! she mouths.

I slowly rise to my feet, but I can feel my knees shaking and fear I will topple over.

"Yes, your majesty."

"It says here that you can read. Is this true?"

My heart thumps so hard in my chest my vision turns black. I blink and open my mouth to speak but my tongue is dry as sand. *What do I do? What do I say?*

"Well?" the empress asks.

"N-n-no—" I start to whisper.

"Speak so you can be heard," the dowager barks.

"No!" I yell more loudly than I meant. I hear snickering and see several girls hiding their mouths behind their sleeves. "I mean no, your majesty," I say in a somewhat normal voice.

"What do you mean no?" the empress asks. Her voice is not unkind, but she clearly demands an answer. I try to remember anything Mingxia told me about Lihua's education.

"I...I had a tutor," I say. "But I was a very poor student."

"Then why does the introduction sent by your mother say you can read and write?" the empress asks.

"My mother..." I gulp. "My mother thought very highly of me. I am sure her praise is much exaggerated."

At this, most of the newer concubines burst into laughter they do not bother to hide.

The dowager claps her hands together once. "Silence! Such cackling is not becoming of a lady!"

The room is immediately quiet. The empress leans over and says something to the dowager from behind the red book.

"You may sit down, Lady Lihua," the empress then says.

My knees give way and I fall into my seat awkwardly. The girls around me who notice snicker again but quickly collect themselves. What does this mean for me? Have I already ruined everything? Will I be punished? Will I be found out? My stomach clenches and I fear I will vomit.

"Lady Euhmeh," the empress says, and a girl stands up who I recognize as one of my roommates.

"Yes, your majesty?"

"Can *you* read, as it says in your introduction?"

"Yes, your majesty."

"Good. You are to attend Lady An and help her with her duties managing the harem."

"Yes, your majesty." Eumeh gives a small bend of her knees and neck. I notice some of the other concubines—the ones that outrank us—grumbling or wrinkling their noses. Still, it is interesting that the empress asked if Eumeh and I could read and write and didn't take it for granted that we could. I thought most Manchu girls were literate, but perhaps I was mistaken.

"That is all for today," the empress says as she stands. We all stand as well, and then fall to our knees in front of our chairs, waving our handkerchiefs three times. The empress dowager then leaves the room, followed by the empress, and finally Lady An. All the remaining ladies are then joined by their maids and led out of the audience hall. Once I am back in the sunlight, I feel as though I can breathe again. At least for the moment. I am sure I have messed up somehow and that it will come back to haunt me.

"Lihua!" I turn and see Yanmei gliding toward me. "Are you all right? You look terribly pale."

I shake my head and try my best not to cry. "I did not expect to be called upon. I am so embarrassed."

Wangli and her maid join us, but she says nothing.

"Don't be!" Yanmei says, wrapping an arm around me. "I'm sure the empress is used to new concubines being nervous."

"But Mingxia... My mother misrepresented me," I say. "Should I be worried?"

"Of course not! Hardly any of us were given an education. She wouldn't have picked an attendant for Lady An from the new concubines if there was a higher ranking one who could have done the job."

I wipe the tears from my cheeks. "I suppose that is true." It must have been a rare thing indeed for Lihua to be as educated as she was. This sets me at ease somewhat.

"The household accounts have me nervous," Yanmei says. "I was a poor student and never had a head for numbers. I'm not sure how I shall manage it."

"You should ask your eunuch for help," Wangli says, and Yanmei raises an eyebrow. "They are all quite clever. They had to be educated to be selected for service here. If you need help with numbers or characters, he should be able to tutor you."

"I will do that, thank you," Yanmei replies. I tuck this information away, anxious to ask Jinhai about it when I return to my room.

"Is Lady An the only rank three consort?" Wangli asks, changing the subject, and I'm glad for the distraction. Yanmei and I shrug, but I can see that Suyin wishes to say something.

"What do you know?" I ask my maid.

"Lady An is the only rank three consort because she is the mother of the emperor's first daughter," she says. "The empress gave birth to another daughter the following year."

"I didn't know the emperor even had daughters," I say.

"They are of no consequence," Suyin says. "It is vital that the emperor have a son."

I nod, wondering at the irony of her statement. Considering the bride price that was paid for the empress, surely the emperor's own daughters would have some value to him.

"The position of rank two consort is being held for the girl lucky enough to birth a son," Suyin goes on.

Yanmei takes a deep breath and puts her hand to her chest. "If only I could be so fortunate."

"May the gods smile on all of us," Wangli says, but there is something not quite sincere about her words. Yanmei seems not to pick up on it, though.

"There were dozens of concubines before us," Yanmei says. "And we entered with dozens more. How are we ever to stand out?"

"I don't know," Wangli says. "Perhaps send the emperor a gift?"

Yanmei's eyes light up. "What a lovely idea! I should embroider a new handkerchief for him."

I see Suyin and Yanmei's maid share a glance I can't quite interpret.

"What shall we do now?" I ask. I have no idea how I am supposed to spend my time for the remainder of the day. I've been given no assignments. Shall I sit and stare at the wall?

"I'm famished," Yanmei says. "I was so nervous this morning, I could hardly eat."

"Your luncheon will be waiting for you upon your return, my lady," her maid tells her.

"That is good to know," Yanmei says. "It must be midday by now, if not later."

"It certainly takes a long time to dress," I say.

"I'm already rather tired," Wangli says. "I think I shall lie down for a bit."

"Perhaps after we eat and rest, we can meet again," I say. I know I must be careful about revealing too much about myself, but I can hardly abide the loneliness. I miss my sisters greatly, my heart hitching in my chest at the mere thought of them.

"There is a pretty pavilion near my palace," Yanmei says. "We can meet there at mid-afternoon?"

"I look forward to it," I say.

"As do I," Wangli agrees. At that, we give each other a smile and turn to head to our separate palaces. Our eunuchs, who had been standing back, now come to us with umbrellas to guard us from the sun.

"You seemed anxious to say something back there when Yanmei mentioned a gift for the emperor," I say to Suyin once we are out of earshot of the others.

"The emperor has plenty of handkerchiefs," she says.

"Then what do you suggest?" I ask her. Not that I am

interested in catching the emperor's eye, I am merely curious.

"Such gifts would only have meaning after the emperor learns your face and name," Suyin says. "The only way for that to happen is to be chosen to attend him in bed."

I can feel my face redden at that, but Suyin continues.

"It is the eunuchs in charge of household affairs who present the emperor with suitable company for a night."

"And how do they do that?" I ask, turning to Jinhai.

"It's rather complicated," he says. "But if you want any chance of being chosen, a gift must be made to the eunuchs in charge, not the emperor."

"Oh?"

"If you pay enough, the eunuch who presents the emperor with his choices will...*encourage* the emperor to pick your name."

"I see," I say. "And I suppose the price is quite high."

"Indeed," he says. "All of the girls will learn this eventually, and each will be sending a bribe in the hope that she will be chosen."

"But if everyone sends a bribe," I say, "then we would all end up on the same level again. How will the eunuch in charge make his choice?"

"Whoever gives him the most will be the winner."

"But...do we know how much the other girls paid?"

"No."

"So, you could pay your money and end up no closer to being chosen."

"Exactly," he says. "It is great risk. If you waste your money, you might lose all of it and not have enough for your household expenses."

"What happens then?" I ask.

Jinhai shrugs. "Your maids will be reassigned. You will

receive less food. You will not be able to afford new paints or clothes."

"So, I could end up living like a pauper even here," I say. "What a terrible waste of money."

"But the rewards could be so very great," Suyin says. "If you were to give the emperor a son, you would never want for anything ever again. The emperor would shower you with gold and silk. And then, one day, you would be the mother of the emperor!"

"Hmm." I can feel Suyin's excitement at the prospect. The higher I rise, the higher she would rise as well. I say nothing since I would hate to see her face when I tell her I have no plan to waste money on a chance to sleep with the emperor. No, I plan to live my life alone. I will keep my money and my terrible secret. And if I am not to be happy, I shall at least be comfortable.

13

─────────

or the next few weeks, life becomes very routine. I wake, eat, bathe, dress. We all greet the empress, the dowager, and Lady An. After the midday meal and rest, I join Yanmei and Wangli and we talk and work on our embroidery together. After the evening meal, Jinhai tutors me in math and explains the household accounts to me. It is difficult, but I think I am learning. It is simply taking what I already know about how to purchase or sell items and applying it to paper instead of memory.

Thinking of how I used to manage money for my family reminds me how much I miss them. I wish there was some way to see them. Of getting word to them. Of checking on their welfare. There must be a way out of the Forbidden City. My family lives in the very shadow of the palace wall. It would not take much time to slip out, see them, and return. But how could I escape? How would I slip away unnoticed in the first place? Suyin and Jinhai accompany me constantly and sleep in my room. I have been able to sneak out at night for a few minutes to myself, but any longer than that and surely I would be missed.

The weather is cooling as autumn creeps in, and I am able to convince Suyin to walk with me along the Forbidden City's wall in the evenings when the air is crisp. I notice that there are several old-growth trees along the wall, trees whose branches reach above the wall and shade the palaces and pavilions. There is one in particular that has a branch low enough that I would be able to grab it if I jumped. At least I think I could reach it. I have not had opportunity to try since it would be quite odd for me to try and climb a tree with my servants watching. I could easily climb the tree to ascend the wall and then drop down to the other side. It would be a long fall, but I do not think I would hurt myself.

But how to do it? How would I get away? What would I wear? How would I hide the evidence afterward?

"Suyin," I say one morning while bathing, "I have been thinking of taking up painting."

"Have you, my lady?" she asks as she runs a bar of scented soap over my arms and back.

"It never hurts to learn something new," I say. "And I have nothing but time."

"Indeed, my lady," she says. "I will inquire about a set of paints and brushes for you."

"Thank you," I say. "But it is rather a messy hobby, isn't it? I should hate to get paint on one of my beautiful gowns."

"I will drape a cloth around you," she says. "Not to worry."

"That might make it hard to move my arms, then, wouldn't it? I noticed that the maids who bring in the tub and water wear very practical, dark outfits. Perhaps you could procure me one to wear. That way I would not ruin my clothes, but I would not feel encumbered either."

Suyin pauses in her washing for a moment, and I think

she must realize that I am up to something. "It would be quite irregular."

"Well, no one need know," I say. "It would only be for painting. And as I improve, I am sure the maid outfit would no longer be required."

"I suppose, my lady," she says as she resumes washing me. "I will see what I can do."

stay up extra late so that Suyin and Jinhai will be exhausted when I finally allow them to go to sleep. Then, I lay in my bed with my eyes wide open, waiting for the night watchman with his lantern to pass by. I know this is stupid, dangerous, but I cannot help it. I am simply dying inside as I worry about my family. I just need to know that they are well. That Mingxia has paid them the bride price as promised. Then I can return to the Forbidden City secure in the knowledge that they are provided for.

It's after three o'clock in the morning, the hour of the tiger, when I finally see a light pass my window. I wait a little longer to make sure the guard is gone before I silently slide out from under my sheets. I then put several pillows in my place. I hope it will be enough that in the dark, should Suyin or Jinhai wake and look my way, it will appear as though I am still there. I grab my maid's uniform and tiptoe out of the room, down the hall, and out the door. This part I have practiced many times, so I am not surprised that no one else in the house stirs.

Once I am at the tree I decided would be my best way out of the palace, I slip off my sleeping garments and put on the maid's uniform. I fold the sleeping garments up and place them on the grass where they hopefully will not get dirty. Unfortunately, I must still wear my silk slippers. I thought about taking Suyin's or Jinhai's more practical slippers, but they are sure to be ruined and I do not want them to have to pay for my foolish outing. I braid my hair and secure it with a thin leather strip.

I stand under the lowest branch of the tree and jump. I miss, landing on my feet with a grunt. I put my hand to my mouth and crouch down, listening, afraid someone—especially the guards—might have heard me. After several minutes, I hear nothing, so I try again. This time, I grip the branch, but it is harder to pull myself up than I anticipated. I bite my lower lip to keep from groaning with the effort and use my feet against the trunk of the tree to pull myself up. When I finally climb upon the branch, I have to stop and catch my breath.

When I am ready, I am able to scale the next branch easily, and the one after that, and the one after that. Eventually, I am even with the outer wall of the Forbidden City! I scoot along a branch to reach the wall, but it grows so thin, I can feel it giving way beneath me. I grab the branch above me for support. I hear a noise and see that the guard is making another pass this way. I hold my breath and pray he doesn't find my sleeping garments. When he reaches my tree, he stops. He looks up, and I am sure I am about to be discovered, but then he looks away and keeps walking. My dark clothes must have done the trick.

I wait until he is long out of sight before I continue scooting along the branch to the wall, the branch beneath me growing ever weaker. Finally, I am within reach, but both of my hands are occupied, one gripping the branch below me, and the other holding the branch above. I will have to let go in order to grab the top of the wall.

I blow all the air out of my lungs, hoping to make myself

as light as possible. I should have peed before I started climbing, but it is too late for that. I release the branch above me and push off the lower branch with all my strength. I feel and hear the branch below me snap, but I manage to wrap both arms around the top of the wall.

"Hey!" someone yells.

"Did you hear that?"

"Where did it come from?"

The guards heard the snap as well! I use my feet to scurry up the wall until I can toss one leg over the top. I planned to sit atop the wall for a moment to prepare for my drop down the other side, but I did not plan on the tiles along the top of the wall to be so slippery! No sooner have I thrown my leg over than I am falling down the other side! I start to cry out, but stop myself. I hit the dirt ground below me hard, and all the breath in my lungs is knocked out of me and my vision goes black. I wonder for a moment if I've passed out, but then I realize that if I am thinking, I must not have. My vision clears and I can see that I am lying on the road that surrounds the Forbidden City. To my left is the large red wall. To my right is a maze of houses and hutongs. During the day there would be countless vendor carts here, but now, it is nearly deserted.

I push myself to my feet and my whole body aches. I look back to the top of the wall and wonder what I was thinking, planning to jump so far. If I'd landed on my feet, I surely would have broken my ankles. I shake my head at my stupidity and see a lamp from a guard patrolling the *outside* of the wall. I didn't even think about outside guards! If I'd fallen only minutes later, I surely would have been caught. I run away from the wall and down the nearest alley into the neighborhood along the wall.

I pass small homes with doors open, some lighted, some

completely dark. I see a well-lit public house where several men are drinking the night away. After a few minutes, I find myself on a wider avenue I recognize. I follow it, continuing to run. It's not safe on the streets for a girl at night, but I don't give anyone a chance to grab me. I know where I am and where I am going.

I turn left and then right, my heart singing at the familiarity of the streets. The houses, the people, the smells—home.

I finally find the narrow hutong where I grew up and stop for a moment to catch my breath. What will my family say when they see me? What will they think? Will they be happy? Or will they chide me for being foolish? I put one foot in front of the other as I walk toward my former home.

Perhaps...perhaps I will not return to the palace. If Mingxia paid my family what she promised, we would have more than enough money to live on. We could run away. Hide. Change our names, our history. The emperor would surely be angry. He would send for Mingxia and demand to know where her daughter is. Would he find the real Lihua? Mingxia and her family would surely be punished...but I don't care. As I stand outside the door of our little one-room house, I know there is nowhere I would rather be.

I tap softly, but there is no sound from inside. I don't want to wake the neighbors, so I tap again. When there is still no answer, I gently push the door open. There is very little light in the room, but a little moonlight shines in through the single window.

It is enough light to see that my family is gone.

Not only is my family gone, but everything we once owned, not that it was very much. The straw mattresses we slept on. The patchwork blankets. The chipped bowls and worn chopsticks. After living in a palace for the past few weeks, the room feels small. It never felt small before. It was a comfort to have my family close by.

I step back out of the room and into the narrow street. Where could they have gone? I have to believe that wherever they are, they are together. Hopefully they are warm and have full bellies. I don't notice I'm crying until I wipe a tear from my cheek. I am now truly alone in the world. Daiyu—and any trace of her—is gone. The Forbidden City is my home and the emperor is my husband. This is the only life I can live.

I hear a dog bark and realize I have been gone far too long. Suyin is sure to stir at some point. Hopefully the pillows will deceive her into believing I am still there, but I should still return as soon as possible.

I run down the alley back toward the Forbidden City, back to the place in the wall where I fell from the tree. From next to a house, I look left and right, checking for guards. When the coast is clear, I have a sickening realization.

I didn't plan on getting back inside!

I had been so focused on getting out, I didn't think about how I would return. It must be impossible to scale the wall from the outside, otherwise we wouldn't be safe on the inside. I'm such an idiot! What now? It would probably be better for me to just leave. I'm out, so why go back inside to a life I hate? But what would I do instead? I have no money, no food, no clothes, and nowhere to go. Mingxia would certainly not take me in.

If I was able to get out of the Forbidden City, perhaps I can find a way back inside. I shouldn't have been able to get out. So even though the wall should be secure from the outside, perhaps I can find a way through.

I look left and right again, checking for the guards. Then, my eyes scan the wall from top to bottom. I can see my tree peeking over the top, too high for me to ever reach. The wall appears smooth with nothing I could use for handholds. I rub my head as I try to think. Scaling the wall itself is surely impossible, so I must consider another way in.

The obvious way into the Forbidden City would be through the gates. But those are sure to be the most heavily guarded areas. I try to recall if there are any other openings in the wall.

The streams!

Countless streams wind through the Forbidden City, some quite wide, requiring expansive bridges to cross. The water must flow in and out somehow, somewhere. I try to recall where I have seen streams flowing through or under the wall.

I walk along the wall, trying to figure out where on the

other side my palace is. From there, I can orient myself and try to recall where the largest streams are. They must flow out of the Forbidden City to the canals dug around the city.

But this is not as easy as it seems. From here, I cannot tell where my palace is, and before I know it, I am at the end of the row. I gasp when I see the guards carrying their lanterns walking toward me. I turn and run back along the wall. Lights emerge from the other end as more guards complete their walk around the palace wall in that direction.

I'm about to run back to the hutongs when a small gate in the wall opens and a man steps out. I'm frozen in fear, and he looks at me with wide eyes, scanning me from head to foot.

"What are you—"

"Help me!" I whisper, grabbing his robe. He recoils at first, as though shocked I dared to touch him, but I don't give up. "Please, help me! I must get back into the Forbidden City!" I have no idea who he is. I have never seen him before. But since he is coming out of the palace, he must be a high-ranking eunuch.

"What?" he asks, still seeming to not understand my plight, but I do not have time to explain it.

"Please!" I hiss. "I'll be killed!"

The man looks around me, up and down the wall at the approaching guards. Perhaps I was a fool to say something, to ask for help. I should have kept running, left it all behind. He is more likely to turn me in than help me.

"Come on," he says, grabbing my arm and pulling me close to him, wrapping a protective arm around me. He leads me back through the gate.

"Sir?" I hear a male voice say, but the man who is helping me hides my face.

"Close the gate," the man orders without stopping.

"Yes, sir!" I hear the gate close and latch and feel some relief. But it is short-lived. In revealing myself to this stranger, I am sure I have put myself in great danger.

The man continues to hold me close, protecting my face from anyone catching a glimpse of who I am. Finally, we come to a stop and he releases me, pushing me against a wall. I open my eyes and glance around. I can see the empress's audience hall, so I can easily find my way home from here.

"Thank you," I say through heavy breaths.

"Who are you?" he asks.

I burst into tears. "I am so stupid! How could I be so stupid!" I hide my face in my hands and only want to sink to the ground and sleep forever. I should just kill myself and be done with it.

After a few moments, the man places his hand on my shoulder. "It's all right."

I stop crying enough to look up at him and see a kind face. He gives me a reassuring smile. It's a nice smile. He has nice eyes too. His nose is slim and there is a dimple in one of his cheeks. For a fleeting moment I think how unfortunate it is that he is a eunuch.

"My name is...Lihua," I say. "I'm a sixth-rank concubine."

His eyes go wide again and he drops his hand from my shoulder. "A concubine? I thought maybe you were a maid who got herself locked out. But...a concubine? How did you even get out?"

"I climbed a tree," I say. "Getting out was the easy part."

"The *easy* part?" he says incredulously. He stares at me for another minute, and then he starts to laugh. "You are... certainly not like any concubine I've met before."

"I'm sure the others are not as stupid as I am," I say. "I was able to get out, but I didn't plan for how to get back in."

"But why did you leave at all? If you were running away, why did you come back?"

"I wasn't running away," I say. "I just...missed my family."

"Oh," he says with a knowing nod. "I can see why that would be difficult for you."

We stand quietly for a moment. I am sure he has a hundred more questions for me, and I am waiting for him to demand a payment for saving my life.

"How were they?" he asks, and I'm so surprised by the question it takes me a moment to reply.

"Umm...gone. They were gone."

"Hmm," he says thoughtfully. "Well, I hope you see them again someday."

This man is so strange. I don't understand why he is being nice to me. Why he is comforting me. Another tear escapes my eye and I wipe my cheek.

"I should be getting back before I am missed," I say. "Thank you for helping me. If you ever need anything in return, do ask."

The man laughs, as if the idea that I could ever help him is preposterous, which I'm sure it is. "I'm just glad I was there to help. I shudder to think of what could have happened if you had been caught."

"I was foolish, I know. Stupid. I'll never do anything like that again, I promise."

He looks at me as if he wishes to say something else but cannot. I feel the same way. For some reason, I feel safe in his presence. As if I could unburden my heart to him. But I have already acted foolishly once tonight. I know better than to put myself at risk again.

"You should go," he finally says.

I nod and take a slow step away, half expecting him to change his mind and pull me back, making some sort of demand of me. But I take another step, and another. He doesn't stop me, but neither does he take his eyes off of me. I nearly trip when I reach the edge of a paved pathway. He chuckles and whatever spell he had cast over me is broken. I turn and rush away before I can change my own mind. When I reach my palace I have to stop and catch my breath. Blessed relief washes over me as I realize how close to death I came.

I start to go inside the palace, but then remember my clothes. I go back to the tree and remove my maid's clothes and silk slippers. I put on my sleeping robe and gather the other clothes together. I can't tell just how clean or dirty they are in the dark, but I can't take any chances. On my way back to my palace, I stop by a well and throw the clothes and shoes into it. The grass around the well is already forming dew as I silently sneak back to my palace.

By the time I reach my room, the sky is beginning to lighten, and I can see Suyin beginning to stir. I rush across the room and try to slip into bed, but she rubs her eyes and sits up.

"My lady?" she asks, still groggy. "Do you need something?"

"No," I whisper. "I was thirsty, but I am fine now. Go back to sleep."

"You rest," she says, growing more wakeful. "It is time for me to get up anyway." She climbs down from the bed and kicks Jinhai as she passes him to fill the kettle and place it over a small fire. Jinhai groans and rolls over to get a few more minutes of sleep.

I pull the blanket around me and face the wall, willing

my heart to stop beating so loudly. I should feel relieved. Victorious even. How many other girls have managed to sneak out and back into the Forbidden City without being caught?

Though I was caught, wasn't I? If I hadn't met that man, that eunuch, I would surely have been discovered. The emperor would never believe I had snuck out to see my family, especially since my only family is supposed to be Mingxia. He would think I had gone to see a man, a lover, and I would have been put to death.

I should have run away, I suppose, as soon as I realized that I had no way to get back into the Forbidden City. I have survived on very little for most of my life. Facing life on the streets without a coin to my name should have been very easy for me. But I panicked. Or perhaps I have become pampered and spoiled in my time here. I have so much food to eat, a soft bed, warm clothes. I have servants and friends. What more could I ask for?

I suppose one day, I might want more. A husband and children of my own. But for now, I have all I need and more than I could ever want. I must learn to be content in my new life. Forget my family. Forget Daiyu. Forget freedom. Does a fish born in a pond long for the sea? Certainly not. How can it long for something that it does not know exists? The world outside the red walls no longer exists for me.

I am a fish in a red pond.

15

———

*S*uyin quickly notices that my shoes and outfit are missing. I just shrug. She blames the girls in the laundry for either ruining the clothes and getting rid of them or stealing them.

"I'm sure whatever happened to them was an accident," I say. "Just let it go."

She presses her lips and looks away, folding my laundry angrily. I'm sure she will find *someone* to take the blame. I feel bad that some poor laundry maid is going to pay for my mistake, but I don't know what else I can do without revealing what I've done, so I sit quietly with my mouth shut.

"Greetings, most gracious ladies!" The chief eunuch for household affairs, Fiyanggu, steps into the entry hall and bends down on one knee. The other girls rush out to see what he has to say, but I linger near the door to my room. It is a rare thing for Fiyanggu to come to our palace in person instead of sending a messenger.

"Greetings, Fiyanggu," Chaoxing, one of the other concubines in our shared house, says. He might only be a eunuch and a servant, but he holds enough power that all of us know to be polite. "What have you come to tell us?"

He stands. "The emperor is hosting a birthday celebration for his brother tomorrow, and you are all to be in attendance."

The other girls all shriek and hop up and down in excitement. For those of us not summoned to the emperor's bed, we rarely have opportunity to see the emperor. I have seen him on occasion in the inner court, where we reside, but only from a distance. He is usually there to visit the empress or his mother, and he will walk with them in the garden. I have seen many concubines use such occasions to try and get the emperor's attention. They will trip and fall in his path or send their little dogs running to him. Sometimes the ruse works, and the emperor will be smitten by the pretty thing, inviting her to his bed not long after that. But most girls just end up looking foolish. Still, I think that Suyin and Jinhai have been disappointed that I have not tried to find a way into the emperor's good graces. I have not offered any bribes or tripped in his path. I understand why they are frustrated. They can only rise as high as I do—and I am content to stay where I am while they are much more ambitious.

"Tomorrow, after your morning greetings to the empress, you will all travel to the Summer Palace, Yuanming Yuan, for a great feast and entertainment," Fiyanggu explains.

Everyone—concubine and servant alike—dances and laughs with joy, and I have to join with them. The Summer Palace is west of Peking and is much larger than the Forbidden City, if you can believe it. It is said to be the most beautiful place in the world. Along the river, the palace has hundreds of palaces and endless acres of gardens. However, it is rather remote, far from the city, so the emperor must live at the Forbidden City most of the time to rule his empire.

"He sends you all a gift in honor of the prince." Fiyanggu waves his hand and four more eunuchs step forward, each carrying a small box, which they present to each of us. I scan their faces, looking for the young man who saved my life, but I don't see him. I have looked for him every day to no avail.

I open the box to find a blue cloisonne butterfly hairpin. I notice that the other girls have the same hairpin, but each is a different color.

"What is the significance of the butterfly?" I ask, and the other girls look at me as if it is a stupid question. But since we were all given butterflies, there must be some meaning to it.

"Very observant," Fiyanggu says. "The prince's mother was named Hudie, after the butterfly. She died when he was very young, so he honors her at every opportunity. He is quite fond of butterflies. The emperor wishes to surround his brother with butterflies at his birthday dinner."

"That is so kind," I say, and I think the emperor must love his brother very much. I am sure my husband is an interesting man who I will never have the chance to know better.

"The emperor is very close to his brother, Prince Honghui," Fiyanggu says. "It is a great honor for all of you to make his acquaintance."

The other girls sigh and get dreamy looks on their faces, and I suppose they must be dreaming that tomorrow is the day that their luck will change. I must admit that I am looking forward to the festivities. Not because of the emperor, but just for the change of pace.

Chaoxing steps forward and places a coin in Fiyanggu's hand so smoothly, I almost don't notice it.

"Is there anything else you can tell us about the emperor?" she asks, fishing for information.

Fiyanggu gives a small bow to her. "No, my lady." Chaoxing pouts since she just wasted a coin. I wonder if Fiyanggu truly has no more information to give or if the bribe simply wasn't large enough. Fiyanggu then dismisses himself to inform the ladies in the next palace of their honored invitation.

"This is so exciting!" Eumeh says. "We will finally see the emperor!"

"We must wear our best clothes!" Chaoxing says. "And the largest headdresses."

My neck starts to ache at the very thought.

"Our dresses should match the hairpins," Lian, the third roommate, says.

"That's a good idea," Chaoxing says, then she gasps. "I don't have a lavender qipao!"

"I have one," Eumeh says, and the three of them head to Eumeh's rooms to plan for tomorrow. I must admit, I do feel a little left out. I don't know why the other girls don't like me, but I haven't made an effort to be friendly either. I do at least have Wangli and Yanmei. I'm sure they will be here soon enough to discuss tomorrow's outing.

"This is a great opportunity," Suyin says when we are back in my room. "A chance for the emperor to see you. You must make a good impression."

"You think I will stand out among all the other shining jewels that will be there?" I ask, slumping into a chair. Tomorrow is going to be exhausting. I should probably go to bed now so I will have enough energy to get through the day.

"You always doubt your own beauty," Suyin says. "But, no, I do not think beauty will be enough to stand out."

"What would you suggest?" I ask and then immediately regret it. I don't want to stand out; I want to blend in!

"The feast is to honor Prince Honghui," she says. "But all the concubines will be focused on the emperor. I think the emperor would appreciate it if you honored the prince. You should give *him* a gift."

I consider this. It's a good plan. The other concubines will be so focused on the emperor that they will ignore the guest of honor. That is sure to displease the emperor, who clearly loves his brother. By honoring the prince myself, the emperor is sure to be pleased.

But I don't want to please the emperor. If I get too close to him, someone is bound to discover that I am not who I claim to be. The emperor could discover it simply by the way I speak or act. Or another concubine, in her jealousy, could try to discredit me and somehow stumble upon the truth. I don't want to make any enemies by attracting the attentions of the emperor.

"Perhaps it would be improper," I suggest, "if I were to give a gift to a man who is not my husband."

"Only if the gift was expensive or extravagant," Jinhai says. "But something small and thoughtful would be accepted as an innocent gift from a wife to her brother-in-law."

I squirm. I truly do not wish to stand out, but I can see that Suyin and Jinhai are set on the idea. And it is a good plan. If I refuse, that would surely be more suspicious. After all, it is supposed to be my great desire to become the bedmate of the emperor, the mother of his children.

"What would you suggest?" I ask.

~

The next day is a flurry of activity. The Summer Palace is several miles away, and we will apparently stay for a week, so almost all of our belongings must be packed into trunks to be carried on donkey carts to the palace.

The ride to the Summer Palace is hot and painful. The wooden carriage has a flat floor, so I must sit cross-legged. There are several layers of silks and furs, but it is still uncomfortable. Once the cart starts moving, I am tossed from side to side. Pillows keep me from bruising myself, but I am still jostled like a sack of potatoes. What's worse, the brocade curtains do not let any breeze pass through, so it is terribly hot, and it is already autumn. I am grateful we did not attempt this journey while it was still summer. Jinhai and Suyin are not allowed to ride in the cart with me, but must walk the entire distance! By the time we reach the Summer Palace, I nearly fall out of my carriage, little more than a pile of goo.

But I quickly decide that the Summer Palace was worth the trouble. It is more beautiful than it was described. The whole palace grounds is like a wonderous old-growth garden, with tall shade trees and thick flowering shrubs along every path. There is a wall, but it is must shorter than the wall around the Forbidden City, and I can immediately see that it would not be a difficult thing to climb over. The guards must be extra diligent to keep us safe here.

I am delighted to be taken to a palace all my own! Indeed, the Summer Palace is so large that there is no need for us to share. I can't help but wonder if I could ask the emperor if I could live here permanently.

No sooner have I arrived, though, than I must quickly

wash and change my clothes and prepare myself for dinner. I make sure the butterfly hairpin is given pride of place on my headdress, and I wear little else to detract from its beauty. In one of my sleeves I tuck the perfume pouch I have brought as a gift for the prince. I was actually making it for the emperor, something different than a handkerchief at least, but no one need know I have repurposed it for the prince.

It is dark when it is finally time for dinner. We are led along a path lighted with silk lanterns. At night, it is like walking through a mystical fairyland. I can see the gentle glow of fireflies among the trees and tall grasses and the air is clean and fresh.

The feast is held in a large, elevated palace with a wide open-air verandah that overlooks a lake that we cannot see very well, except for the reflection of the moon on the black waters.

The empress and the dowager are already seated when we arrive, and there are also dozens of men present, noble-men. There are then four long rows of tables and chairs to either side of the verandah, seating enough for the two-hundred concubines. As I take a seat somewhere near the middle, I can't help but laugh at the idea that anyone thinks she would be able to catch the eye of the emperor when we are all crammed together. It will be impossible for the emperor to single anyone out.

Suddenly everyone stands and bows, and I follow suit, assuming the emperor must have arrived, but I cannot see anything from my place.

"May the emperor live ten thousand years!" everyone says.

"Thank you!" he says. "You may rise. Thank you to all of

you for coming to celebrate the birthday of my dear brother, Prince Honghui!"

Everyone claps and I see the hand of the prince as he waves to everyone. I lean to one side to try and get a better look. When the prince's face comes into sight, I gasp.

It's the eunuch who saved my life.

16

I duck back behind the girls in front of me. No, it can't be him. He must look similar to the eunuch who saved my life. I peek around again to try and get a better look.

It's him!

The same eyes, the same chin, the same dimple.

But...how? How can the eunuch I met be the emperor's brother? Unless... I must have been mistaken in assuming he was a eunuch. But I thought real men were not allowed in the Forbidden City after dark. Or maybe that is just the inner court. I have seen the emperor in the inner court with men who are not eunuchs, his advisors or important noblemen, many of the same men here tonight, but that was always during the day. Perhaps the rules are different for men who are related to the emperor.

"What's wrong?" Yanmei whispers to me. "You look pale. Are you ill?"

I clear my throat, shake my head, and try to smile. "Not at all. It is just such a special night."

"Isn't it?" she asks. She reaches into her sleeve and pulls

out an embroidered pipe holder. "I was up all night making this. Do you think the emperor will love it?"

I nod. At least it isn't a handkerchief. "Of course he will."

"Please, sit," the emperor says after he and his honored guests—including the prince—have taken their seats. I sit quickly and slouch a bit, trying to hide my face behind the girls in front of me. Thankfully, it is not difficult to hide, we are so crushed together. I notice that Yanmei to my right and Wangli to my left are sitting as straight as chopsticks, their chins high as they try to keep the emperor within their sights. I wish I could melt into a puddle on the floor and wash away.

The prince. The prince! Of all the people in the Forbidden City who could have found me that night, why did it have to be the prince? What does this mean? Is that why he did not make any demands of me that night? What could I possibly have that a prince would want? Or is he simply biding his time? I stupidly gave him my name, so he can easily track me down. I have not met another Lihua among the concubines.

"We are all here for a special occasion," the emperor says. "My brother, Honghui, is twenty-four years old!" Everyone claps and cheers. "Still a very young man." The emperor chuckles. "In fact, I had despaired of ever having a brother. I was twelve years old when the gods finally blessed my father with another son. I was lonely for a very long time before that, but I was also old enough to know what it means to be a brother. To feel the bond that we share with no other person."

My eyes water a bit at the emperor's speech because it reminds me of my own dear sisters. My dear Junli. She must miss me so much.

"I have protected him, taught him to ride and shoot, and watched with pride as he grew into the man he is today."

Everyone claps and cheers again.

"Today, brother, I give you a mighty gift. Your own palace in Peking, the finest palace ever built outside the Forbidden City—Heshen Mansion. It is my greatest wish that you will soon fill it with wives and children of your very own."

I cannot see the prince's face in response to this, but I think he must be delighted.

"You have given me the greatest gift and honor, my brother. My emperor," the prince says, and I am now in no doubt that he is the same man who saved my life. It is the same voice, the same accent. What have I done? He is the emperor's brother! He will surely expose me. Why he hasn't already, I could not venture to guess.

Another man stands up and presents the prince with a tapestry sewn by his wife that depicts the emperor and prince as young boys together riding horses across the plains. Then another man give the prince a beautiful new bow and quiver of arrows.

I start to feel nauseous. I pray the emperor does not ask for gifts from among his ladies. I cannot expose myself. I look around for Suyin to tell her the plan is canceled. I will tell her that my simple, handmade present is not grand enough compared to all those being given by the great lords.

I look around and see her standing silently near the wall. I give her a small wave to get her attention and then beckon her toward me. She nods as if in understanding, but then she walks away!

"No!" I whisper, but she cannot hear me and I quickly lose sight of her.

"What's wrong?" Wangli asks.

"Nothing," I mutter, rubbing my forehead, but she doesn't look convinced. She reaches out and pats my leg.

"I'm sure we will all have our chance to present our gifts to the emperor soon enough."

"You brought something too?" I ask, and she nods, her smile tight. She must have been pressured by her servants to bring a gift too.

"Wangli..." I start to say, and she waits for my next words expectantly. I want to tell her not to present her gift to the emperor. That it might not have the intended effect. That she might even offend the emperor. But then I fear that she might take my words the wrong way. That I am trying to undermine her chance at being noticed.

I shake my head. "Nothing."

When I look back toward the emperor, I spy Suyin emerging from the crowd of servants and kneeling by the empress, who is seated at the emperor's right while the prince is seated at his left. The empress nods, and Suyin stands and whispers in her ear. I see the empress scan the crowd. I assume she is looking for me and duck out of sight. I stay hidden, but a few moments later, I see Suyin once again standing in her designated place nearby. She gives me a small smile and little nod. I try to smile back, but I feel like crying and quickly look away.

This can't happen. I have to get out of here. I can't let the prince see me. I look around, but I am in the middle of a middle row, I can't simply slip away unnoticed. I suppose I could slide out of my chair and crawl across the floor. The other ladies would see me, but I could feign illness perhaps.

"Ula Nara Lihua has a gift for the prince," I hear the empress say, and if I'd had a knife at that moment, I might have killed myself. I hear a murmur ripple through the crowd of ladies as all heads turn toward me. I can do nothing but stand. I keep my head downcast, hoping the prince will not realize who I am if he cannot see my face clearly.

"Does she?" the emperor says. "Then, please, Lihua, come forward."

Whispers break out among the concubines, and I see more than a few angry faces as I walk down the row of chairs to the end where Suyin is waiting to take my hand and escort me to the head table.

I can feel every single eye in the room on me, but one gaze feels stronger than all the others, and I know it is the prince. He does not need to see my face to know it is me, he knows my name. It cannot be every day—or even every life-time—that a prince saves the life of a reckless concubine who dared to sneak out of the Forbidden City. I know that he recognizes me without even looking up.

When I am standing in front of the table, Suyin releases my hand and steps back, lowering to my knees. "Your majesty," I say, my voice trembling, "if it is permissible, I wish to present his highness with a crude and simple gift made by my own hand."

"Proceed. I am quite curious to see what it is myself," the emperor says with a chuckle. I hear a chair scrape the floor as the prince stands. He then walks around the table to stand in front of me. I am frozen, unable to move, unable to look up. Oh, why can't I simply die!

"Well, what have you made for me?" the prince asks after an indeterminable amount of time.

I reach into my sleeve and pull out the silk pouch I embroidered with a scorpion, a snake, a centipede, a gecko, and a toad. It is believed that by wearing the pouch with the five most venomous animals, the wearer will be protected from evil. The pouch is filled with fragrant herbs that are supposed to bring the wearer good luck. When I hold the pouch up, I have no need to explain what it is.

"A xiangnang," the prince says. "What a unique and thoughtful gift."

"Certainly better than another handkerchief," the emperor says with a laugh. I hear a few of the girls let out little moans or groans and shift in their chairs.

The prince then holds his hand down for me. I hesitate, but I have no choice but to place my hand in his as he then gently pulls me to my feet. My fingers are freezing, but his hands are warm and soft. When I reach my full height, I come up to his chin. I'm much taller now in my pot-bottom shoes than I had been the night we first met. I can feel his gaze burning hotly upon my face, willing me to look up. I know I shouldn't, but I can't resist.

When I raise my eyes, I can see that he is smiling in a playful, mischievous way, and I realize that he has no plan to expose me right now. He lifts the xiangnang to his nose and breathes in deeply.

"Jasmine flowers," he says. "My favorite. The blooms are only at their most full, their most beautiful, under the light of the moon."

I am taken aback at his forward comment. I know that no one else in the room understands his reference, but if I had any doubts about whether he knew who I was, they are certainly gone now.

"I am glad his highness is pleased," I say, lowering my chin again.

The emperor chuckles and claps, and everyone joins him, though from the areas where the other concubines are seated, the clapping is not very enthusiastic.

"Lihua," the emperor says. "From the Ula Nara clan, did

you say?" he asks the empress, who nods. "I remember you. You were the last one chosen during the most recent consort selection, were you not?"

"Yes, your majesty," I say.

"It seems the gods knew you would be one of the most shining pearls in my harem," the emperor goes on. While I know he means to be kind to me, I am dreading the response from the other concubines at being singled out. I am grateful that I have my own palace. I will have to instruct Jinhai to lock the doors, or else I fear one of the other girls might smother me in my sleep.

"What is her rank?" the emperor asks the empress. One of her eunuchs steps forward and whispers in her ear.

"Sixth rank, your majesty," she says. "She is new and young and has not had a chance to prove herself yet."

"I think she has proven herself to be a thoughtful and industrious girl," the emperor says quickly. "Lihua, you are promoted to rank-four concubine."

I drop back to my knees, not out of respect, but because they cannot hold me. The other concubines do not even try to hide their displeasure as they gasp and mutter. I am not exactly well-versed in the ways of the court, but Jinhai has told me a few things. To be promoted is a great honor. To be promoted by skipping a rank is a *rare* honor, one the rest of the court is not likely to forget.

But what can I do but appear grateful? "Thank you, your majesty. I did not seek such praise. It only seemed proper that I should present a gift to the guest of honor at such an event."

"A practical girl as well," the emperor says. "You are a credit to your parents."

"Thank you."

"You may return to your seat, my dear," the emperor

says, but I cannot stand under my own power. Suyin rushes to my side and pulls me to my feet. We back away from the emperor, bowing the entire time. She releases my hand when we reach the row where I am seated, and I walk very slowly and deliberately toward my chair lest my legs give way again.

I do not see who it is, but someone places their foot under one of my shoes, knocking me off my balance and I tumble forward, banging my chin on the floor. Everyone gasps, but more than a few people laugh as well.

"My lady!" Suyin pushes her way down the aisle to be at my side. "Are you all right?"

I nod, but my resolve is broken and I cannot help but cry. I feel a stronger hand, that of a man, pulling me to my feet, and I expect to see Jinhai when I stand. But it is the prince.

"Are you injured?" he asks, and there is real concern on his face.

"No," I say, shaking my head, but I honestly don't know. One of my ankles is throbbing and my jaw aches terribly. The prince and Suyin lead me back down the aisle and outside where I see a sedan chair and two chair bearers waiting. Jinhai is there as well. He must have fetched it while the prince and Suyin were helping me. Jinhai holds the flap open as Suyin helps me inside.

"Are you sure you are all right?" the prince asks. "Shall I come with you? Or fetch a doctor?"

"Please, just go away," I whisper. I can't face him anymore tonight. He looks hurt at first, but then he nods in understanding. We certainly cannot speak freely in front of the servants.

"Send for me if she needs anything at all," he tells Suyin.

"Of course, your highness," she says. Jinhai closes the

flap, finally blocking the prince from my view. The chair bearers pick the sedan chair up, jostling me side to side in the process, but I finally breathe a sigh of relief.

That went as badly as it could have possibly gone. I knew the other concubines would be angry, jealous, but I never expected them to lash out at me in front of the emperor. And what of the prince? He seemed desperate to speak to me, but we cannot! The emperor would never allow it as it would call my virtue into question.

And what of the emperor? He promoted me by two ranks tonight! He will surely remember that. Will he summon me to his bed?

How could everything have gone so wrong so quickly? And what will happen to me now?

17

———

hat evening, a large trunk full of new clothes, hair jewels, pots of makeup, and embroidery and painting supplies arrives. I am also given a generous bag of cash.

"These are gifts from the emperor as befitting your new station," Fiyanggu explains. "You will also be given a new palace of your own when we return to the Forbidden City."

"The emperor is far too kind," I say, my voice tremulous. The more the emperor flatters me, the more frightened I become.

"He would also like your company tonight," Fiyanggu says, looking at me suggestively, and my face flushes hot. I look to Suyin for help.

"The mistress is not feeling well," Suyin says. "Her ankle is sorely damaged and she must rest."

"Of course," Fiyanggu says with a bow. "I will inform his majesty." He then takes his leave.

I put my hand to my mouth and let out a shuddering sigh. This is bad. This is so bad! What am I going to do? How could I be so stupid? I never should have let Suyin and

Jinhai talk me into giving the prince a gift. I can't blame them, though. They don't know the truth. Who I really am. Why I want to hide among the dozens of concubines. They want me to rise, want me to succeed. And I never thought a single small gift would have such results. I had hoped that it would be enough to show Suyin and Jinhai that I am trying but would not actually do anything to increase my reputation with the emperor.

Suyin is pulling the new clothes—qipaos, undergarments, fur wraps, pot-bottom shoes—out of the trunk one by one and examining them before putting them away.

"You are truly blessed, my lady," she says. "I knew the emperor would smile on you, but I never imagined he would increase your rank."

"Neither did I," I say. "The other ladies must be fuming with jealousy."

Suyin chuckles. "Of course they are. But don't worry about them. With the emperor's approval, they cannot touch you."

I have a feeling she's dead wrong about that. Jinhai enters the room carrying a large basin filled with water and fragrant herbs. He removes my shoes and places my injured ankle in the bowl. I can see it is swollen and dark blue on one side.

"Nothing is broken," Jinhai says. "But I can still send for a doctor if you are in much pain."

"No," I say, not wanting to draw even more attention to me. "I just need to let it rest." Jinhai nods and then helps Suyin finish unpacking the crate. When they are done, I hand Jinhai the bag of cash I was given.

"Divide it between the two of you evenly," I tell him, and his eyes go wide. Suyin's mouth drops.

"My lady," he says, "that is far too generous. You will

soon have many more household expenses. And it never hurts to save money for a later date."

I shake my head. "My allowance will be increased to cover the expenses, will it not?"

"Yes, my lady."

"It is because of the two of you I was elevated today. You earned that money, not me."

Jinhai and Suyin look at each other for a moment, then they fall to their knees in front of me and knock their foreheads to the floor.

"You are the kindest mistress of all!" Suyin exclaims.

"I am not worthy of your service!" Jinhai says.

"Please, stop," I say, and they sit up on their heels and look at me. I want to tell them how unworthy I am. How much I don't want to be here. How much I wish everyone would stop praising me. But I cannot. If I continue to protest, they will surely begin to wonder if I really am a high-ranking lady.

"I...I am indebted to you for my situation," I tell them, and then I force myself to say, "thank you."

They both return to their feet. "It is now we who are indebted to you," Jinhai says. "We will always support you and remain by your side."

I nod, unable to think of what else to say that won't continue this round and round conversation.

~

The Summer Palace is indeed a magical place. It is deep autumn, and the trees are every shade of red and gold. The yellow ginkgo leaves break free and flutter across the ground. Rabbits skitter across the grass and squirrels jump from tree to tree. There are countless birds, each singing a sweet song. In an expansive pond there are pleasure boats, and the ladies take turns out on the water. There is an opera troupe performing almost constantly, so the ladies come and go from the performances at all hours. Many of the ladies sit outside under the trees painting and embroidering, taking advantage of the fresh air and cool breeze.

I partake in none of these activities, but stay sequestered in my palace. I do not want to draw attention to myself, nor do I want the emperor to think my ankle is sufficiently recovered that I may visit his bed. I can only hope that he will forget about me soon.

One day, a fine mist descends over the Summer Palace, and there is a gentle rain. The temperature drops considerably, and I no longer hear the laughter or conversation of the palace ladies drifting through my window. I open the front door and look outside; I see no one. I breathe in the clean air. Everyone seems to be hiding from the damp, but I find it refreshing and inviting. I would like to explore the Summer Palace, but did not want to court unwanted attention. This seems like a good time to finally venture out of doors.

"I would like to take a walk," I say.

Suyin gasps. "It is cold and wet, my lady! You could catch a chill."

I smirk and think to myself about all the nights I spent in my little hutong house where the air was so cold, we would wake with frost on our eyelashes. Those were not the worst of days. We would snuggle together to stay warm and sleep late, waiting for the sun to rise. I blink away tears that are threatening to form.

"The cold doesn't bother me," I say. "But bring me some leather slippers. My ankle is still sore and I don't want to risk falling or slipping." My ankle is fine, but I am anxious for an excuse to walk normally and not balance precariously on tiny platforms.

Neither Suyin or Jinhai seem happy about venturing out, but they cannot deny their lady her wishes. I am in a simple qipao, and my hair is tied up around a bian fang, but I do not have any headdress attached. I am sure I look more like a high-ranking maid than an emperor's concubine, but I doubt many people will see me.

As we leave the palace, Jinhai tries to walk by my side, holding an umbrella over me, but I feel crowded.

"I can hold my own umbrella," I tell him. He hesitates, but then relents, handing me the umbrella. "I just need some space and fresh air." He nods and seems to understand my meaning as he and Suyin both stay several paces behind me as I walk.

I feel as though I am in a fairyland. The mist is so thick, I can only see a few feet around me. But every step also reveals stunning new sights. There are, of course, gardens and pagodas, but so much more. Stone steps rise up and disappear into the mist far above me along a path to a Buddhist temple. A bronze dragon guards the Hall of Benevolence and Longevity. Smoke from smoldering embers inside an incense burner four times my height disappears into the fog. As the rain comes down a little harder, we walk along a covered corridor that stretches from one end of the Summer Palace to the other, and I hand Jinhai my umbrella to carry. We pass a pond that is full of green lotus leaves and I stop to take in the sight.

For a brief moment I forget who I am, what I am, and the great danger I am in. It all washes away as I lean against the railing and I lose myself in the lotus leaves. I sigh and allow myself, just for this one moment, to feel happy. It is so quiet, so peaceful here, and I can see nothing beyond the fog. I am at peace and wish I could remain in this place, this frame of mind. The Summer Palace is truly the most beautiful place in the world, and I am so fortunate to see it. A girl like me, a Han Chinese from the poorest part of Peking, could never even imagine being in such a magical place. Yet, here I am. Despite everything, I know that I am truly blessed. Whatever happens, I have this moment, and I know my family is safe and cared for. Could I ever ask for more?

"My lady."

The prince has appeared at my side so silently, I did not realize he had approached me until he spoke. I fall to my knee, water seeping through my gown and dampening my leg, and drop my head.

"Your highness!" I say. "Forgive me. I did not see you approach."

"Please stand," he says, and I obey, but I keep my eyes downcast. "Please don't do that. You may look at me like a normal person." I raise my eyes to his face and feel a flutter in my stomach. "Thank you. I hate that you are required to speak to the ground and not to my face."

"Those are the rules," I say, turning away and looking back over the lotus pond.

The prince laughs. "Since when are you one to follow the rules? Did you forget how we met?"

I quickly look around to make sure Suyin and Jinhai are not lingering nearby where they could hear us. I see that they are still keeping a respectful distance away from me, but they can clearly see what is going on. I am grateful for that; it would be quite improper for me to be alone with the prince.

"No," I finally say. "I have not forgotten."

"Then why do you treat me like a stranger?" he asks, sitting on the railing so we can face each other as we talk.

"Because I value my life," I say. I think the prince must have expected me to say something funny or witty, but the slight smile he had been wearing transforms into one of seriousness.

"I understand," he says with a nod. "But I have longed to see you again. I've never met a woman like you before."

"What are you even doing here?" I ask. "I thought men were barred from the inner court if not accompanied by the emperor."

"The rules don't exactly apply the same way here," he says. "There is no inner or outer court."

He is right about that. In the Forbidden City, the inner court is physically closed off from the rest of the palace by a wall. Here, there are no large, imposing walls to contain us. We ladies are free to wander where we will. And it seems the emperor's male guests enjoy the same privilege. My heart races at this realization, but I am not sure if it is from fear...or something else.

"I should go," I say, but as I turn to leave, I feel him gently tug on the sleeve of my robe.

"Stay," he says. Not only my face, but my entire body flushes hot. If he had been speaking to me—to Daiyu—I would not need to be convinced to stay. But I am not. I am Lihua, and I am married to the emperor.

"I am your brother's wife," I whisper. "I cannot be seen in the company of another man."

"Then tonight," he says, "can I come to you?"

"No!" I whisper harshly. "The servants!"

"But you can sneak out," he says. "You've done it before. I'll wait for you outside your palace when the gong is struck for the hour of the ox."

Of course I want to say yes. He is so handsome, and so insistent. I have a fleeting vision of running away with him, away from this place. Away from these people. Away from the fear and loneliness. But I shake my head and pull my sleeve from his grip.

"No," I say and turn away to go back to my palace.

"I'll wait for you," he says. I pause, but I do not look back. I neither shake nor nod my head, but continue walking toward my servants. Who is this dangerous, reckless man? How could he ask such a thing of me, putting both of us at risk? And what is wrong with me that I want to say yes?

18

—————

I shouldn't go, I tell myself as I lay on my bed in the darkness. It's dangerous. Stupid. Bumping into the prince while I was walking and having a conversation within the watchful eyes of my servants is one thing. It was perfectly innocent. But if I sneak out of my room in the middle of the night and am caught, there would be no acceptable explanation.

How would I be punished? What a stupid question. I would surely be put to death. Probably not by beheading or publicly, but I would certainly be given a white scarf and be expected to kill myself for the dishonor I have brought to the emperor and my family.

My family. What would they think? Would they hear the story of the concubine who betrayed the emperor with his own brother and was put to death? Would they know it was me? Mingxia would most certainly hear of it, and the real Lihua. They would probably be glad to know that I was no longer alive. I would no longer carry the secret truth with me that Lihua defied the emperor and sent another—a Han—in her place.

As I roll away from the wall and look into the darkened room, I think about how unfair it is that Lihua retained her life—or at least a free life—outside the palace walls. She still has a future. Can still marry and have a family of her own. Still has her mother by her side while I am completely alone.

I hear a gong struck to mark the hour of the ox. Suyin is sleeping peacefully at the foot of my bed while Jinhai snores softly on the floor.

I shouldn't go, I tell myself as I slip out from under the covers. *I shouldn't go*, I think as I pick up my satin slippers and silk cloak and tiptoe across the room. *I shouldn't go*, I whisper silently as I pull the front door of the palace open just enough for me to squeeze through and into the chill night.

I shouldn't go. But if I don't, I know I will regret it for the rest of my life. Not for the prince, I hardly know him. I am thankful he saved my life, but it is no more than that. It might be nice to one day count him among my friends, but that is all.

No, I do this for me. For one grasp at freedom. Once act of...dare I say defiance? Defiance of the emperor. Defiance of the stupid rules that brought me here. Defiance of the rigid constraints that doom me to be alone for the rest of my life.

I wrap my cloak around my shoulders as I look for any sign of the prince. He only said to meet him outside my palace, he didn't say where.

"*Psst.*"

From the left, I hear the noise, so I walk in that direction. I am nearly at the end of another building when I feel a hand reach out and touch mine. I jump even though I expected him to be there. I guess I did not expect him to touch me.

"*Shh*," he says almost silently with a finger to his lips. Then he smiles and leads me away. The prince seems to know the layout of the Summer Palace by heart as we walk quickly along paths, around buildings, and down stairs. It is a wonder we aren't seen by a guard, but we somehow manage to avoid all of them. Finally, we end up along the river where a great stone boat juts out from the walkway that lines the waterfront. He leads me down to the boat and to the very front where we are surrounded by water on three sides. The moon is bright and reflects off the water, giving just enough light to see ripples skipping across the black mirror.

"It's beautiful," I say, my breath fogging in the cool night air.

The prince smiles. "I thought you might like it."

I give a rueful laugh. "You don't know the first thing about me."

Honghui chuckles. "I know you are defiant and brave. But also reckless." The smile leaves my face as I look at the water and not him. "I know you don't treasure your life here, and perhaps have no care for your life at all. You risked death to slip out and see your family when you could have just written them a letter. I suppose you must have some great secret that you couldn't put in writing. But why you came back... Hmm, now that is a puzzle."

My heart races as I realize just how much danger I am in. I don't know how the prince could know so much about me from our very brief meetings. Perhaps it is because he is so well-educated while I am an ignorant fool. I take a step away from him.

"I should go," I say. "I shouldn't have come." I start to walk away, but I feel his hand grip mine.

"Stay."

I let him pull me back to the bow of the great stone boat and stand much closer to him than I probably should. I like being near him. He is warm and smells like winter pine trees.

I always knew that my marriage—if I married—would be arranged. But I had hoped that once we were man and wife, my husband would be kind and romantic. He would perhaps kiss my forehead in the morning and bring me fresh mulberries in the autumn. We would eat dinner together and maybe play throwing dice. If he were a working man, I would help him. When I had children— even girls—he would praise me and thank me. Eventually, I would love him.

But my marriage to the emperor has been nothing like that. Before the birthday celebration, I had not seen him since I had been selected except for fleeting glances. He had not sent for me or inquired about my health. He had forgotten I existed until I gave his brother a present. I do not feel married. He owns me, yes, and I must live in his home. But I am not a wife.

"Tell me about it," I say.

"What?" Honghui asks.

"The boat," I say. "Why is there a boat made of stone here? It cannot float. It cannot sail. What is its purpose?"

"Must there always be a purpose to something?" he asks. "The Qianlong Emperor built it because he could."

"Hmm," I say, thinking. I recall an old saying. "Water can support a ship, but water can also overturn it."

"Water is beautiful and deadly in equal measure,"

Honghui says. "Much like this boat itself. It is a place of beauty and joy, but it could also collapse, bringing fear and death."

"Like you," I say, looking him full in the face to gauge his reaction. "You are pleasant company. But if we were to be caught, I would be put to death."

My words do not seem to surprise or hurt him. Instead, he smiles. "And yet here you are. Why?"

I give a small laugh. I had been so preoccupied thinking about his motives, I had not considered my own. I knew it was dangerous, and yet I could not resist. What did that say about me?

"I'm lonely," I finally say, and he nods in understanding. There is much more I could say, of course. About being trapped. About not loving the emperor. About missing my family. But it all comes down to how alone I feel.

"You do not have any companions among the other ladies?" he asks. "Or your maids?"

"I do," I say. "But I cannot truly be myself around them. I feel as though I must constantly put on a performance. Act the part of the perfect lady when I am far from it."

"You are the daughter of a celebrated general," he says, speaking of Lihua's father. "Are you not a lady?"

I look at him but say nothing, which I realize too late is the wrong thing to do. My silence says volumes.

"You aren't his daughter, are you?" he asks.

"He died," I say, remembering what Mingxia told me about her husband. "I never knew him." At least that much is not a lie.

The prince nods. "My father died when I was quite young as well. People say that because I am the son of the emperor, I must be a great man. But in truth, I don't know how that could be possible. I was raised by my mother, by eunuch servants, by tutors. Everyone except my father. I often wonder just what it means to be the son of an emperor if he was not here to teach me."

"You have your brother," I say. "He must be of help to you."

"True," he says. "You don't know him, but he is a decent man who loves his country."

I let out a small snort and immediately wish I hadn't when I see Honghui's face drop.

"I'm sorry," I say. "I didn't mean that."

"But you did," he says. "And now I am curious. What makes you doubt him?" I say nothing for fear of walking into a trap. "Please," he prods. "Tell me."

I chew my lower lip, considering my words. Is it possible for me to tell him how hard life is for people just beyond the red walls without giving myself away?

"He lives in such opulence," I say. "A huge city of his own filled with palaces. An army of servants. A harem of wives, each one with more food and clothes and money than they could ever need all while people just beyond the walls of the Forbidden City starve to death."

The prince nods, and now that I've started, I can't seem to stop myself.

"The money the emperor gave me last night after he elevated my rank could have fed a poor family for the rest of their lives, and I threw it away. I gave the whole bag of it to my two servants to do with as they wish like it was cast-off rubbish. And that was only last night. I'll get just as much money next month. Can you imagine? Every month one woman is given enough money to support a family for decades. There is so much good that could be done with that money. If the emperor did not have so many wives, the money could be given to the people instead."

He sighs and leans against the bow, giving a small nod as he considers my words.

"I'll not ask how you know so much about the city's poor," he says, and my cheeks burn. "You must know that it is more complicated than that. There are millions of people in this country."

Millions? I mouth. I don't know how many that is, I'm still learning to count to a hundred. But the way he says it, I know it must be a lot. More people than I can imagine.

"However, your point is well-taken," he says. "You think our lives are extravagant to the detriment of the people." I nod. He runs his hand over his chin. "There is some truth to what you say, and I will give it much consideration and speak to my brother about it."

"You mustn't tell him what I said!" I say, grabbing his arm.

"No," he says. "Of course not." He reaches up and runs his thumb along my cheek. "I would never want any harm to come to you."

I lean into his touch. It has been so long since I have had any physical comfort. Just a hug for reassurance or a pat on the head in praise. I miss my family so much and would give just about anything to have them near me right now.

A gong is struck indicating the hour of the tiger. I've been gone for two hours. I step away and wipe the tears from the edges of my eyes. "I really must get back before I am missed."

He nods. "I know." But we both hesitate. I don't know what it is, but *something* is drawing us together. I dread to think that it might be something more than friendship after all. Something I dare not name for fear that it could undo me. What good would it do to...feel something for a man I can't possibly be with?

Finally he takes my hand and leads me from the boat back to the winding paths through the Summer Palace back to my rooms. When my palace is in sight I start to walk toward it, but Honghui does not release my hand. I look back and he pulls me to him, pressing his lips against mine. I am shocked at first and pull away from the kiss but not out of his arms which are now wrapped around me holding me close. A shock ripples through my body. Not a painful shock, but a pleasurable one. I reach up and pull his face back to mine, this time welcoming the kiss and taking it greedily. And yet I want more. It is as though I cannot hold him close enough, pressing my full body against him. His kisses move from my lips to my jaw to my neck and I pant with the desire for yet more. I feel one of his hands on my backside, squeezing it, and I know we must stop. If we don't, I won't be able to stop what happens next.

"No, no, no," I whisper, unwrapping his arms from around me and stepping back. "Please don't. I can't. The emperor..."

He shakes his head and steps back to catch his breath. "I know. I'm sorry. I just... You are... But...I do love my brother and would not want to hurt him."

The question neither of us wants to ask—*then why are you seducing his wife?*—hangs heavy in the air like a precariously placed boulder threatening to crush us.

I can't speak as I back away, afraid of what dangerous words might fall from my lips. I slip back inside my palace and close the door. I lean my forehead against it as I catch my breath. I smooth my hand through my hair and take off my robe and slippers, placing them to one side as I quietly enter my room and tiptoe across the floor.

I get back into bed and neither Suyin nor Jinhai stirs. Once again, I have managed to sneak around without being caught. I should be relieved, proud even.

But I only want to cry.

19

The next day is spent packing all of our items and returning to Peking. Everyone seems a little down, a little slow as they go about their assignments. I think I am not the only person who is sad to be leaving the Summer Palace. It is truly a beautiful, magical place. The sky is a little bluer here, the greens a bit more vibrant. There is a freedom here I have not experienced since I first entered the Forbidden City. And I don't mean just my freedom to sneak out and see the prince. Life is slower here, more calm and easy. I feel at peace, and I am sad to be leaving that behind.

The ride back to Peking is uneventful and I am more than ready to get out of the carriage and stretch my legs when it finally stops shaking me back and forth, rattling my very bones. But when we step out, I see we are not in front of my palace.

"Why have we stopped here?" I ask.

"This is your new home, my lady," Suyin says. "A palace all your own, as befitting your new rank."

I am taken aback by this. I suppose a part of me had

hoped that the emperor—and everyone else—would forget about the rank thing and let me go back to living my life of obscurity. But, apparently, that is not meant to be.

I step through the door and see that the palace is not much larger than the last one, but it is all open—all for me. Far more space than I could possibly need. A reception area, a sitting room, a bedroom, a separate dressing room! I think about the years my family spent huddled together in one small room and shake my head. I can only hope they have found larger, more comfortable lodgings. I wish there was some way of knowing.

Three maids and two eunuchs enter the front door and kneel down in front of me.

"We are honored to serve Lady Lihua," one of the maids, the eldest of the three, says. She appears to be in her late thirties or early forties. This surprises me since most maids are quite young, too young to yet marry. I suppose this woman never had an offer of marriage.

"What do you mean?" I ask, looking at Suyin.

"You now need more servants, befitting—"

"Befitting my rank," I say with an annoyed sigh. What am I supposed to do with seven servants? I'm still only one person. I look to Jinhai, who is apparently reading my mind as he gives me a small nod. I must now pay for seven servants from my allowance. I suppose Jinhai and Suyin are also deserving of a raise, considering I would never have been elevated without them.

"So, what are we all to do now?" I ask. I really have no idea what they are supposed to do all day.

"You must be tired from your journey, my lady," the older woman says. "I'll draw you a bath."

"We will unpack your things," the younger maids offer.

This all seems reasonable to me, but I have no idea what the eunuchs are supposed to do. I look to Jinhai.

"You are in charge of them," I tell Jinhai. "Do what you will."

He gives me a nod. "Yes, my lady."

I am about to go to my new bedroom to undress when it is announced that Fiyanggu has arrived at my door. When he steps in, all the servants bow to him, and in his turn he bows to me.

"How are you settling in, my lady?" he asks. "Is everything to your satisfaction?"

Of course everything is *not* to my satisfaction. It is too much! Far more than I could ever need. But to say such would undoubtedly hurt his feelings and make me appear ungrateful. I give a smile and nod.

"Yes, of course. Thank you."

"You are truly blessed, my lady," he says. "The emperor has requested your company tonight."

"What?" I feel sick. Frightened. Why is this happening?

The maids all jump up and begin squealing. I suppose I should be excited as well. Believe myself fortunate. But all I want to do is cry. Hide. I try to force a small smile, but have to fight back tears.

"Are you sure he has asked for me?" I ask, hoping there has been a mistake. "There must be dozens of ladies of higher rank than I who are more deserving."

"The emperor made his wishes quite clear," Fiyanggu says. "He did not even draw your name, but asked for you specifically."

There is no getting out of it then. He knows my name. Knows who I am. My plan to hide in obscurity has failed. So what do I do now?

"I will return at the hour of the pig to convey you to his

majesty's bed-chamber. Your maids should know how to prepare you accordingly."

Suyin gives a small bow and tells him that she knows what to do. She then walks him to the door as they talk about the details, but I can't hear them. Nor do I care. I know there is no way out, so I will just have to suffer through it.

"No need to be frightened, my dear," the older maid says as she tasks my hand. I hadn't noticed I was shaking until now. "One of the reasons I was selected to serve you was to prepare you for tonight."

"Prepare me?" I ask, growing nervous about what that is going to entail.

"Come," she says as she leads me to the bathing room. She moves to help me undress, but I pull back. I should be used to servants dressing and undressing me by now, seeing me naked. But this woman is a complete stranger to me.

"What is your name?" I ask her, hoping that a little more familiarity might help.

"Nuwa, my lady," she says.

I nod. After a few calming breaths, I look away as I let her undress me and help me crawl into the bath. As another maid scrubs my body and hair, Nuwa sits at the other end. "Do you know what will happen tonight? What it means to be the emperor's bedmate?"

"Yes," I say. I had four younger sisters. I know where they came from. Nuwa seems surprised at this for a moment, but then nods. "Good. That will make things easier. At the appointed hour, we will wrap you in a blanket and his majesty's eunuchs will carry you to his bed."

"Wrapped in a blanket?" I ask.

"*Only* a blanket," she says. I'm stunned for a moment. I'm to be carried naked wrapped in a blanket to spend the night with the emperor. How ridiculous! I then have a sudden memory of seeing eunuchs carrying such wrapped parcels across palace grounds and burst out laughing. I thought they were just taking bedding or rugs to be cleaned! I had no idea a woman was wrapped inside.

"Why do you laugh?" she asks, and I see that she is genuinely surprised by my reaction.

"Does it not sound very silly to you?" I ask. "Why can I not just go to him in my nightdress in a palanquin or something? It would certainly be more dignified."

"It is for the emperor's protection," she says, and I know I look confused. "If you were wearing clothes, you could conceal a weapon and do the emperor harm."

I am now even more confused. "Why would I carry a weapon?"

"I am sure you would never do such a thing," she says. "But such things have happened before."

It takes me a minute to understand what she is saying. "You mean an assassination!"

"Shh!" she says, motioning for me to lower my voice. "It is treason to speak of the death of the emperor."

I am somewhat annoyed. I am only asking a question, not wishing him harm. "But why would anyone—especially a concubine—want to hurt the emperor?"

"Many reasons. Anger, jealousy. She could be bribed by his enemies to act for them. You must understand, my dear. The emperor's bed is when he is at his most vulnerable." I'm not sure what she means by that, so she goes on.

"The emperor will be dressed when you arrive, but eventually he will be naked too. He would have no way to defend himself from an attack. And when a man is finished, he is often very tired. Almost in a drunk-like state."

I nod, not needing her to say more. I still think it is

excessive, and a terribly embarrassing way to be conveyed around the palace. But what can I say? These are the rules.

"When you are in bed with the emperor," she goes on, "he prefers women who are...enthusiastic."

I wrinkle my nose.

"Some girls will simply lie there, like a dead fish, allowing the emperor to do what he will, but they don't respond to him. They show no signs of pleasure or enjoyment. He doesn't like that."

I give a slow nod. "But...I won't know what to do."

"I understand," she says. "But try not to worry overmuch. It is a very natural experience. And the emperor is a very kind lover, so I have been told. If you let yourself enjoy it, your body will know what to do."

My face flushes hot and I think about the kiss I shared with the prince. I wanted to grab him, hold him close. As he ran his hands over my body... Oh, I nearly shudder at the thought. I wanted more, so much more. What that more was exactly, I can't quite say. But I am sure that if I had been willing, my body would have known precisely what to do.

Nuwa chuckles. "There is no need to be embarrassed. You will do well, I am certain of it." I nod and let the maids wash my hair, pouring buckets of warm water over my head.

～

Even though I have had several hours to prepare for my night with the emperor, I am terribly nervous when the eunuchs arrive. Nuwa and Suyin wrap me in a blanket and two eunuchs lift me up on their shoulders and carry me away. Even though I know what will happen— Nuwa explained a bit more about the physical act, how it might hurt a bit—I suppose I can't help but be nervous about lying with a man for the first time.

Especially a man I did not choose.

The prince continually comes unbidden to my mind. I try to shake the vision of his face from my memory, but it always comes back. And when I think about having to lie with the emperor, I remember how much I wanted to be with the prince. It feels...dishonest somehow to be going to the bed of another man when I only have feelings for the prince.

But I have no choice. The eunuchs finally set me down on a bed and I hear them shuffle away. A hand reaches up and unfolds the blanket from my face and I start.

"Did I frighten you?" the emperor asks.

"I didn't expect you to already be beside me," I say, and he smiles, opening the blanket a bit more.

"How do you like your new palace?" he asks. "Does it suit you?"

"Yes. Your majesty is very generous." I don't know where I find the words to speak, but it feels strangely like talking to any man, not an all-powerful emperor.

He shifts on the bed and loosens the tie of his robe. My heart races and my mouth goes dry. I hope it does not take too long. He reaches up and strokes my cheek, much in the same way the prince did when we were standing by the lotus pond. My body pulses at the thought of him, but I force myself to look at the emperor. For the first time, I notice the similarities between the two men. The emperor is much older than Honghui, but they have the same eyes and nose.

As the emperor shifts closer to me, cupping my cheek and kissing me, I suddenly realize why some women might lie like a dead fish and try to pretend it isn't happening. I don't want this man touching me. I don't want to give myself to him. I don't know him! I only want Prince Honghui.

But I can't have him. He isn't my husband, my owner. The emperor is, and I must do my duty. I remind myself that the emperor paid a great price for me. A price that I pray helped save my family from poverty and starvation. I must do this.

When the emperor kisses me again, I kiss him back. I know how, after all. The kisses come faster and grow more passionate, which surprises me. I hear him let out a low growl as he opens the blanket around me even more, exposing most of me.

I let my body take control. It knows what to do.

20

─────────

The emperor must find me pleasing because he sends for me several more times in the coming weeks. And the following day, he always sends gifts—including cash. According to Jinhai, we have not needed to use any of my regular allowance to pay my expenses thanks to the extra gifts from the emperor.

It's not a bad way to earn a living. Hadn't I at one time considered selling myself to a brothel? Not that I consider what I am doing now prostitution. I am the emperor's wife, after all. He is simply a far more generous husband than most.

Occasionally, the prince still comes to my mind. But I know I have to push him away. There is no room for three in the emperor's bed.

"Join me today," the emperor says one morning as I rise to leave his bed-chamber.

"What do you mean?"

"Wear the gown I sent you yesterday," he says. "The blue one with the cranes. I have to meet with a lot of important people today—*boring* important people. It will bring a little joy to my day to have you beside me."

I am surprised by this, and not a little delighted. My daily life is so monotonous, it will be a welcome change. I can't suppress the smile that crosses my face, nor would I want to. The emperor walks over and taps my nose.

"Besides, I would like to show you off. It never hurts to make those below me a bit jealous."

"Why would they be jealous that you have me? I'm nothing special."

The emperor chuckles. "Go on. Get dressed. I'll send a sedan chair for you after you greet the empress."

I bow and back out of the room. I wrap my robe around myself and slide my feet into my slippers. I might arrive naked, but when I leave I am allowed to wear some clothes and am carried back to my palace in a sedan chair. It's far more dignified and I feel much less self-conscious when I leave the emperor's palace than when I arrive.

After being bathed and dressed in my own palace, I walk to the empress's audience hall. Along the way, I spy Wangli and Yanmei and wave at them. They give me small waves back but make no attempt to approach me, so I go to them. When I get close, they each bend their knees and bow their heads. Now that I am ranked above them, they are supposed to show me extra respect, but it makes me terribly uncomfortable.

"Good morning, Lady Lihua," they say.

"Please, you don't have to do that," I tell them. "We are old friends, aren't we?"

"I'm afraid we must," Wangli says as she and Yanmei stand up. "If anyone thought we were being disrespectful, we could be punished."

Sadly, I know she is right. From the corner of my eye, I

can see other concubines and consorts watching us closely, whispering behind their hands. I step closer to my friends so I can speak in a lower voice.

"Will you please visit me soon? I miss you both so much."

They look at each other and then their faces soften at me.

"We have been rather unkindly lately," Yanmei says. "And jealousy is a most unbecoming feature in a woman. Why don't we have lunch together, then I can show you the paintings I've been working on."

I'm so excited I nearly accept right away, but then I remember that the emperor wanted me by his side today and my face falls.

"I'm sorry, I can't today," I say.

"Why not?" Wangli asks. "Are you very busy during the day as well?"

"The emperor wants me by his side during audiences today...to keep him from being too bored."

Wangli's eyes narrow and Yanmei looks near to tears.

"I'm sorry, I shouldn't have said anything," I try, but Wangli is not having any of it. She grabs Yanmei's arm and tugs her away toward the empress's audience hall. I try not to notice the other women staring and laughing.

"Ignore them," Suyin says. "She is only punishing herself by eating vinegar."

I know Suyin is right. There is no reason for anyone to be jealous of me. I am the favorite today, but tomorrow it could be someone else. Even now, the emperor does not see me exclusively. I know that on nights he does not send for me he has sent for another woman. And I didn't ask for this. Wangli knows that. Does she forget how we met? When she was weeping in my garden, just as sad as I was at being chosen. I wonder what has changed to make her so jealous.

I am so lost in my thoughts, I don't realize that I almost step in front of Lady An, but Suyin pulls me back—but not before Lady An notices.

"How dare you try to walk in front of me?" Lady An snaps. I drop down to one knee.

"I am so sorry, Lady An. I did not see you. I would never knowingly disrespect you."

"You should be punished for your insolence!" she says, stomping her foot, and my heart races. It is within her right to punish me, and the punishments meted out within the harem can be severe, from the loss of servants or a palace or even a physical beating. I am not sure why Lady An is so angry with me, but I dare not ask.

"I humble myself before you, my lady," I say. "I'm sure you are right."

"What is going on?" I look up and see that the empress has stepped out of the audience hall and walked to us.

"This concubine insulted me!" Lady An says. "She needs to be punished."

"It was an accident," I try to explain to the empress. "I did not see her. But that does not excuse my disrespect, and I am truly sorry."

"See!" Lady An says. "The concubine admits it!"

"She is not a concubine," the empress says, her voice even. "She's a consort."

"A rank four," Lady An says, and I can hear her voice wavering. "She owes me her respect."

"Yes," the empress says. "I will take care of her."

I feel faint. The empress could even have me put to death if my transgression was serious enough. What I did was not bad enough for that, I am sure, but still, she could make my life very difficult.

"Inside, everyone," the empress announces. "I shall deal with her later," she tells Lady An. Lady An stammers and stomps her foot again, but she then does as the empress orders and takes her place within the audience hall. Suyin pulls me to my feet.

"What was that about?" she mutters. I shake my head.

"I have no idea," I say. "Could she possibly be jealous too? But she is a rank three. The mother of the emperor's daughter."

Suyin shakes her head. "But he has not called her to his bed for years," she whispers.

"Years?" I ask, bewildered. Suyin nods and leads me to my seat, which has been moved closer to the empress—as befitting my station. I can see Lady An from here, and the way her lips are pressed together tightly.

Years? I don't understand it. If she fell pregnant once, she could do so again. She is also a rank three. It is his duty to give her precedence. Why would the emperor neglect her so?

We all greet the empress, the dowager, and then Lady An. I do my best to avoid her gaze. After the empress dismisses us, she orders me to stay behind. When everyone else is gone, I kneel before her.

"I await your decision, your majesty," I say.

"Do not worry," the empress says. "I have no plan to punish you. Your offense was an accident, I know."

"Thank you, your majesty," I say, tears escaping my eyes. The empress stands up.

"Walk with me," she commands. I get to my feet and follow behind her out of the audience hall. We go past the sedan chair that I know the emperor sent for me, but I cannot disobey the empress any more than I can disobey him. The empress motions for the servants to stay back so we may converse privately.

"The emperor tells me that you have served him well," the empress says, and I blush. Do they really speak of such private matters?

"I have done my best, your majesty," I say.

"You must realize that this is only a temporary situation, do you not?"

"Of course," I say. "I am grateful for the favor he has shown to me, but I am only one consort of many. I have no expectations of him."

"Good," she says. We stop next to a lotus pond and she lays a hand on her stomach. "Because things are sure to change dramatically around here."

It takes me a moment to realize how round her stomach is under her thick autumn robe.

"Majesty..." I say. "Are you with child again?"

"I am," she says. I drop to my knees.

"You are truly the most blessed among women. I pray for the health of yourself and the emperor's son." One must always assume a child is a boy in order to persuade the gods to make it so.

The empress motions for me to stand. "During my pregnancy and confinement, the emperor may not touch me," she says, and I nod. "It is important to me that he is well taken care of by someone I can trust until my return. Are you that person?"

I am not exactly sure what she is asking of me, but I have no choice but to agree.

"Good," she says. "I also will need competent women by my side during this time. The emperor has insisted you be among those chosen."

"The emperor has spoken too highly of me," I say. "I am just a stupid, common girl."

"Perhaps," she says. "But it never hurts to have those whom the emperor holds dear close to myself as well."

"I shall serve you both to the best of my abilities," I say.

"Good," the empress says. She nods and I see that the sedan chair bearers have followed us at a distance. "The emperor is waiting for you."

"Thank you, your majesty," I say as I back away. Suyin helps me into the sedan chair and the windows are closed.

It would seem my plan to stay hidden and anonymous has utterly failed. I have not only caught the attention of the emperor, but the empress as well. I will have to be extra careful not to give myself away. I really do hope the empress has a son. Perhaps then the emperor will return to paying her attention and forget about me. After all, if she can give birth to one son, she can have another.

My own stomach feels a bit queasy as I consider the possibility that I could fall pregnant as well, especially if the emperor spends more time with me while the empress is in her confinement. What would I do then? It would be truly terrible. Everyone would know my name. My "family" would be honored. But the child wouldn't even be Manchu.

This is the secret knowledge that worries me the most. As much as I despise the Manchu, I cannot deny that the emperor is the chosen emissary of the gods. The Son of Heaven. Surely the gods would not want Han blood defiling the royal family.

And yet I am here. I share the emperor's bed. Is that not offensive enough? If anyone ever found out who I truly was, they would be horrified. Disgusted.

For a moment, I think I forgot that I was not Manchu. I have had to wear their clothes and practice their customs for months now. I have been so convincing, I even fooled myself for a while. But I cannot forget who I am, where I came from. I don't belong here. I am not one of them. The sooner the emperor forgets about me, the better.

By the time the sedan chair stops and the flap is opened, any excitement I might have felt about accompanying the emperor today has fled and has instead filled my stomach with bile.

But the hand I hold to climb out of the chair is not Jinhai's or Suyin's. It is larger and warmer.

"Lihua," Prince Honghui says, giving me that arrogant, self-assured smile.

Could this day have gotten any more precarious?

jerk my hand back. "What are you doing here?"

"I'm to escort you inside," he says. "The emperor is already holding audiences."

I grumble to myself as I place my hand in his and he helps me from the sedan chair. He then continues holding my hand as he leads me inside the audience hall—to keep me steady on my shoes, of course.

"It is quite an honor," Honghui says, "that the emperor would have you stand behind him today. You have certainly grown in his estimation."

"I am only his favorite for today," I say. "I've done nothing special."

"You do realize that the more you act like you don't need my brother, the more he will want you," he says.

I wrinkle my nose. "What do you mean?"

He chuckles. "To be a concubine or consort is the highest position in the land for a woman. Almost any woman would die to be in your position. The ones who are fortunate enough to be chosen continue to work toward his favor in hopes of having the emperor's son. He has never had to work to gain the affections of a woman—except the empress, I suppose. But you, you act as though none of this matters to you. The emperor's favor means nothing to you. You have given him a challenge for once. He is having to actually seduce you."

I wonder if the prince is speaking earnestly or teasing me. Why would the emperor—the most powerful man in the country—care a bit about my feelings for him?

"Are you teasing me?" I ask. "Certainly the emperor doesn't care about my feelings. What am I?"

The prince chuckles again. "Believe me, I know men. And my brother is still just a man in many ways."

"So...what should I do?" I ask.

His steps slow and he looks at me as if I had just asked him an impossible riddle. "You...really don't want his favor? You aren't just playing some game with his affections?"

"No," I say plainly. "I never wanted it."

He stops and looks at me, rubbing his jaw as he regards me. "Because of me?"

I almost bark a laugh but catch myself as his eyes bore into mine. I feel a weakness in my knees, a desire that I never feel when I am with the emperor. I have to wonder if sharing a bed with the prince would be far more pleasurable.

"You aren't making things easy," I manage to say, but it is nearly a whisper.

We look at each other for a moment more before the prince finally looks away. I can't help but see a pain on his face. Regret, I think.

He clears his throat. "There is nothing you can do," he says. "You...you are the emperor's woman and must do as he wills."

"I know," I say, wondering why he is stating a cold fact

that I have known since I first stepped into the Forbidden City.

The prince takes my arm again and gives me that carefree smile he usually carries on his face. "Come."

It is only when I finally look away from him that I notice the grandeur of the audience hall I am in. It is a palace unto itself, with long wide corridors leading off into an infinite number of rooms. The ceilings are high, supported by tall, red pillars. I have never been in this building before. Since it is outside of the inner court, women are forbidden from entering this area without permission from the emperor.

We come to two large doors, and eunuchs on either side open them as we approach. I have to stifle a gasp when I see the actual audience hall. The floor is polished marble that shines so brightly, I think it must be like walking on ice. There is a raised dais on which a large golden throne sits. There are stairs up the front and both sides of the dais. Behind the emperor is a thin silk screen. Behind the screen and set lower than the emperor's throne are two smaller thrones. The empress dowager sits on one, the other is empty. I suppose it must be where the empress sits when she is invited.

There are dozens of men present, more men than I've seen since entering the Forbidden City. Each is dressed in a fine robe with crests embroidered on the front. They all have long queues and wear tasseled hats. I see several of them look my way. I don't like the feeling of being the center of attention and look away.

As I approach the dais, my eyes are drawn upward to an enormous golden dragon with a pearl in its mouth. I have to hesitate as I look at it. It seems to me that the pearl could easily slip out of the dragon's fangs and crush the emperor. But then I think how silly that must be. Surely the emperor would not sit below something dangerous. When the emperor sees me, he gives a small smile and nod, and I cannot help but blush at his attention. Seeing him here, among such splendor, set above all other men, he truly seems to be the Son of Heaven.

The prince leads me up the side stairs to the empty throne behind the screen next to the empress dowager. The dowager looks at me, but she does not smile or nod. She looks away, sitting up a little straighter.

"You must stand here," the prince whispers to me. I nod, understanding that it would be inappropriate for a mere concubine to take the empress's throne, even in her absence. The prince then walks away, and I see Suyin and Jinhai take their places behind the dais. *Now what?* I wonder to myself.

I hear a name announced and a man approaches the throne. He kowtows to the emperor. Once the emperor acknowledges him, he sits up and begins speaking to the emperor about some trade issues with a place called Chosan. The man and the emperor talk for a bit, then the emperor says he will write to the king of Chosan personally. I think we must be done when another man is called forward, and the same procedure is followed. This happens again, and again, and again.

Every time a new person is called forward, I feel like I am going to topple over. My feet, legs, back, and neck are killing me. I have to pee. I glance to the dowager, who simply sits primly in her chair, paying me no mind, saying nothing. This cannot be what the emperor intended for me, is it? I am so bored and uncomfortable. I see several men inch their way around the dais to where they can see me, nodding appreciatively, making my skin crawl. I hate everything about this. Did the emperor think he was paying me an honor by inviting me here?

Finally, an announcement is made, calling an end to the audiences for the day. Several men at the back of the room groan in frustration. I guess they came all this way for nothing and will have to return another day.

The emperor stands and stretches. He walks around the screen and speaks to his mother for a moment, but I cannot hear what they say. The emperor then comes to me, a wide grin on his face.

"What did you think?" he asks, and I'm not sure what to say. "Terribly boring, isn't it?" I'm so surprised I can't help but laugh.

"Yes," I say. "I don't know what I expected, but it wasn't that."

He chuckles and offers me his arm. "Come. There is something I wish to discuss with you."

I smile and nod, though I can't imagine what he might wish to talk with me about. We leave the audience hall and walk back to the inner court together, side by side, our servants following behind.

"My brother tells me that poverty has become an issue within Peking," he says, and my heart thumps in my chest. Surely the prince was not stupid enough to tell the emperor that we had conversed privately. "He thinks that some of that could be alleviated by the ladies of the inner court. What do you think?"

I am stunned into silence for a moment, then I slowly nod. "I cannot speak for all of the ladies, but I would be happy to give part of my allowance to help the poor. Your majesty is generous and gives me far more than I need."

"I think many of the ladies would object," he goes on. "They enjoy their servants and silks."

"I would not want to force anyone to donate their allowance," I say. "I know many of the girls use their money to support their families."

The emperor nods and is thoughtful for a moment. He then rubs his chin in a way that reminds me of his brother. "I think this is a good idea. It is proper for such privileged people to help the less fortunate."

"Thank you, your majesty," I say.

"I will put you in charge of this," he says. "Lady An handles many of the financial aspects of the harem. I will inform her that I want this plan implemented. You can be in charge of collecting the donations from the other ladies."

This causes a lump to form in the pit of my stomach. Such a task would draw much attention to me, and there will certainly be ladies who object to the idea. It will, of course, be voluntary, but I am sure many ladies will feel pressured to contribute funds. I certainly do not need to be making any more enemies among the ladies.

"I...I...I am not sure I will have time for such a task," I say. "The empress has asked me to attend her during her pregnancy."

The emperor nods. "She has informed the inner court, then," he says.

"She has not announced it to everyone," I explain. "She told me after our morning greetings. I wouldn't have known her condition if she hadn't told me. It is not apparent."

"I see," he says. "Lady An can assist you in finding helpers," he says. "And your own maids can help as well. Perhaps they can solicit the donations while you are attending the empress."

"I...suppose that could work," I say slowly, wracking my brain to come up with some excuse to distance myself from this task, but I can think of none. And as much as I don't want the attention, I am excited at the prospect of helping the people of the hutongs. My family might be gone, but there are thousands more just like them facing starvation and nakedness every day. My foot itches as I recall how, not very long ago, I was walking barefoot just beyond the palace walls. That seems a lifetime ago even though it was mere months.

"I will see it done," he says, then he turns to me. He lowers his face to mine and kisses me tenderly on the lips. "I will send for you tonight."

I nod sheepishly and I feel a blush on my cheeks. For the first time, I feel a real tenderness toward him. I realize that he sees me as more than a bedmate, more than a woman he is trying to impregnate. He asked my opinion. Asked for my assistance. And he doesn't know it, but he took my suggestion and acted upon it. For the first time, I feel like a real wife.

The emperor chucks me under the chin and then walks away, back toward the audience hall. I am sure his duties have no end during the day. I watch him go and see him pass his brother. He waves for Honghui to follow him, but instead, the prince looks back at me, giving me a knowing smile.

I feel terrible guilt wash over me. The emperor has been so good to me, shown me nothing but kindness. He provides for me and has now given me a task to fill my empty days. He is a good man—a good husband.

And I have already betrayed him.

I have kissed another man. His own brother. I have felt lust and desire for Honghui. Let him touch me in intimate ways.

I turn away from the prince, disgusted with myself, and rush back toward my own palace. I cannot deny my attraction to the prince. I am eternally grateful that he saved my life. But I cannot let those feelings overwhelm my common sense. I must stay away from the prince as much as possible lest I betray the emperor further and risk deadly consequences.

22

"Massage my feet," Empress Caihong says to me, and I do my best not to wrinkle my nose at the idea of the task.

Though, to be fair, massaging the empress's feet is a far less gross task than unbinding, washing, and rebinding my mother's feet every night back home. Mama had the tiniest, most lovely feet. Perfect little lotus flowers. Honestly, with feet like that, I'm surprised she married so low. But in order to maintain the shape that had been created when she was a child, the feet had to remain bound with strips of silk for the rest of her life. The wrappings would make the feet sweaty and sometimes break out in pus or blood if she tried walking too much. We could not afford to buy her new silk wrappings very often, so we had to wash and reuse the same bindings every night for as long as possible. I used a tiny pair of sewing scissors to keep her toenails short so they would not grow into the ball of her foot, which could cause more pain and leave the foot open to infection.

Still, as arduous as the task was, it was one of my

favorite parts of the day. The repetition of it was soothing, and it was the time of day when I had Mama all to myself. With four sisters, time alone with my mother was rare indeed.

It is this memory that I hold in my mind as I remove the empress's silk slippers—it is too dangerous for her to walk on pot-bottom shoes while pregnant—and press my thumbs into her soles and squeeze her ankles, which seem to be a bit swollen.

"Refresh my tea," she tells a maid.

"Can you adjust my pillows," she says to another consort she has tasked with attending her.

The empress is not unkind in her demands, there are simply a lot of them. Her every whim must be seen to, no matter how small. She cannot do anything for herself lest she tax her body too much and lose the baby. I know how important the baby is—especially if it is a boy—but I am not sure complete bed rest is healthy. My mother carried five successful pregnancies while working as much as possible. In fact, where I grew up, no woman was privileged enough to lie in bed for months on end to grow a baby. They had to work, doing embroidery if nothing else, and still care for their husbands and other children. As I look at the empress's fat ankles and cheeks that are a bit more round than before, I worry about the weight she might be gaining. Though, I am sure the royal physician knows best, and he pampers her as much as anyone.

We all get to our feet and then kneel as Lady An, the third-rank consort, arrives with her and the empress's daughters in tow. The little princesses are so darling with wide eyes and their long black hair allowed to hang down around their shoulders. They are each dressed in the finest silk outfits and wear silver bracelets. Lady An's daughter seems to be around six years old, while Caihong's daughter is around four. They kneel before the empress.

"Good morning, Mother. We wish you and our little brother good health."

"My darlings!" Caihong says, holding her hand out to them. "Come, sit with me. Maybe you will feel your brother move."

The girls both climb up onto the bed and put their hands on the empress's stomach. It reminds me of how I would touch my mother's stomach and feel each of my sisters moving around inside.

"Such strength this one has," Baba would say when he felt the kicks. "It is surely the son we have been praying for." Of course, it never was a son. Still, my eyes mist a bit at the memories as I watch the empress with her daughters. The scene seems to affect everyone, as we look at each other with smiles and tears.

But Lady An seems to be the most affected. The woman has always been thin, her cheeks sunken. But now, she looks to be little more than a skeleton. She clenches her teeth, setting her jaw tight, as she watches. She turns away and walks toward one of the latticed windows and looks out. She takes a few deep, shuddering breaths before turning back to the empress.

I am never sure what to make of Lady An. I know she would be a beauty if she took better care of her health. She is the third-highest-ranking woman in the harem after the empress and the dowager. She has a huge palace with lots of servants and a large allowance. She has a child of her own. Yet, she seems to be the most miserable among women.

I follow Lady An's gaze toward the empress and wonder if the fact that Empress Caihong is considered Lady An's daughter's mother has something to do with it. There is nothing unique in this, and Chinese families follow the same custom. A man can only ever have one wife while the other women he takes into his home are concubines, the sole purpose of which is to help the family have as many children as possible. The concubines are little more than property, so the children belong to the husband and wife. Usually, the concubine and wife raise the children together. After all, in a large family with many children, the wife needs as much help as possible. And, of course, the concubine will nurse her child for several years. The wife has the final say in how the children should be educated and in arranging their marriages, however, as is her right as mother. As a concubine myself, if I were to fall pregnant, I know I would have to submit to the empress when it came to how the child would be raised. That is the way of things.

I have, of course, heard of cruel wives who take the children from the concubine and forbid her from even seeing her child. But I think this is quite rare.

The empress has not done this to Lady An. In fact, from my observations, it is Lady An who takes charge of the children more than the empress since she is so busy with managing the harem. So why does she now look at the empress with such...anger? Malice? Hurt? I can't quite make out her expression other than know it is not love or adoration the way the other women look at her.

But perhaps she is not looking at the children at all, but the empress's pregnant belly. Is she jealous that the empress is pregnant again? I can understand that. I personally am not jealous since I don't want even more attention on me.

But for most other women here, their only dream in life is to have a son. To see the empress, the woman with the most honors, who spends the most nights with the emperor already, blessed with a second child when all the others except Lady An have none, it must cut them to the core. It is quite strange that the emperor should have more wives than any other man in the country but so few children. I can't understand it. But Caihong *is* the empress. I think that if any woman was able to give the emperor a son it should be her by right. She is the Daughter of Heaven, after all.

I am about to go to Lady An to... I don't know. Pat her on the shoulder? Offer her some cold comfort? I have no idea, only that she seems too distressed to ignore. But I stop when I hear a eunuch announce that the dowager has arrived. We all fall to our knees again, even the little princesses, except for the empress, who sits up proudly in her bed.

"Good day, Mother," Caihong says. "What brings you here today?"

The dowager wears a thunderous expression on her face, as if the empress has greatly offended her. "What are you doing?" she demands.

The empress looks confused. "What is wrong?"

"Why haven't you cut your hair?" the dowager asks. "You are selfish to steal vitality from the emperor's baby."

I have no idea what the dowager is talking about and wonder if it is a Manchu custom. But the empress—and the other ladies—seem just as bewildered as I am.

"That is...such an outdated belief," Caihong says. "If the physician thought it necessary, he would have told me so."

"The doctor is a man," the dowager spits. "What does he know of childbirth? Are you stupid?"

The empress gapes like a fish, opening and closing her

mouth as she grasps for a response. I have seen the way the dowager looks down her nose at the empress at almost all times, but this is the first time I have heard her use such cutting language. I thought the dowager would be happy that the empress is pregnant again and coddle her the way the rest of us do. But that seems not to be the case.

"I...I will cut it at once, Mother," the empress finally says, and I hear some of the other ladies gasp. I don't know any woman who has ever cut her hair other than as an absolute necessity...and I can't remember any specific instances of that ever being the case. Nuns shave their heads, but that is a completely different situation as only widows are allowed to be nuns.

"See that you do," the dowager says, then she turns to Lady An. "Bring the girls. It is time for their lessons."

"Yes, your highness," Lady An says with a bow. "Come along, girls." The princesses sulk away, looking back at the empress longingly, who I can see is doing her best not to cry. As soon as they are gone, we all rise to our feet and silently wait for orders from the empress. It takes the empress a long moment to collect herself enough to speak.

"Lihua," she finally says, her voice quiet. "There are scissors in my embroidery basket. Get them and take them to the kitchen to be sharpened."

I hesitate. I can't believe she is actually going to do it. All of us, maids and ladies, exchange glances, unsure of what to do.

"Was I unclear?" the empress snaps, and I go to the basket to look for the scissors.

"My lady," I hear her closest maid say in a low voice, "you cannot go through this with this. The dowager is being unreasonable. If you send for the emperor—"

"Ask the *emperor* to intercede in a harem issue?" the empress asks, aghast. "Are you insane?"

"But...my lady—" the maid tries again, but the empress refuses to listen.

"Do as I say!" she yells. I find the scissors, which already seem exceptionally sharp to me. But, not wanting to upset her further, which seems more of a danger to the child than long hair to me, I bow my way out of the room and outside. Suyin follows after me, since I cannot go anywhere alone.

"Where...where is the kitchen?" I ask, realizing I have no idea where it is. Why would I?

"This way," Suyin says, taking a narrow path in the opposite direction I was heading.

"But why hasn't the emperor sent for me?" I hear a voice say. I stop and peek around a bush and see Lady An and the dowager conversing while the princesses feed fish in a pond. I know I shouldn't be listening, but I can't help myself when I hear my own name mentioned.

"I am doing my best," the dowager says. "But he is obsessed with that Lihua girl."

I look to Suyin, who I think will tell me that we need to walk away, but instead, she holds a finger to her lips, telling me to be quiet.

"So is the empress," Lady An says. "Why? What am I doing wrong?"

"Nothing, my dear," the dowager replies using a voice kinder than I've heard her use before. "Caihong is simply jealous of you. She always has been. Ever since you fell pregnant first and were elevated."

"She's ruined my life," Lady An says through sniffles. "The emperor has never called me back to his bed since my daughter's birth. It must be her fault."

"Of course it is," the dowager says. "She has much sway

over who the emperor favors with his attentions. The fault lies with her, it always has."

I find this strange since it is not what Jinhai has told me about who is selected as the emperor's bedmate. I will have to ask him about it.

"What am I to do?" Lady An asks.

"Don't worry," the dowager says. "Her days are numbered. If the child is a girl, he will surely put the empress aside in favor of someone else. In favor of you, as the next highest-ranking woman in the harem."

"But what if the child is a boy?" Lady An asks.

"Then we will be glad of it," the empress says.

They are both quiet for a moment, and I wish I could see their faces. It sounds as if neither of them wants the baby to be a boy. But why? I can't understand it.

"Come," the empress says. "I am going to see my son now. Bring the girls. He will be happy to see you, I'm sure."

I hear them walk away, but I remain hidden for another few moments to make sure none of their attendants see me.

"How strange!" I say to Suyin as we continue our walk to the kitchen. "Does the dowager favor Lady An over the empress?"

"I am not sure," Suyin says. "We will have to ask Jinhai about it."

We continue our walk to the kitchen and back in silence. I am uneasy carrying such sharp blades while wearing pot-bottom shoes. It would be far too easy to trip and impale myself, so Suyin carries them back for me.

Back at the empress's palace, I hand the scissors to the empress. She holds them in her hands warily, like an animal she is not sure will bite or not.

"Go," she says after a long moment.

"My lady?" her maid asks.

"All of you, go! Except for Delun."

Delun is her chief eunuch and hairdresser. The rest of us bow our way out of the palace and then stand around awkwardly, wondering if she is going to call us back or if we should return to our own homes. But no one leaves. So, we will wait here, no matter how long it may be.

23

"It's beautiful," I say as I admire a pale-green vase the emperor has given me. "Is it made from jade?"

The emperor laughs. "No, silly girl. If it were carved from jade it would be much heavier than that. It's ceramic, but it is made with a special glaze called qingci to give it that beautiful green color. A little old-fashioned, I know, but I think jade is one of the most perfect colors in the world. Wouldn't you agree?"

I nod as I turn the vase in my hands, admiring the tiny cracks in the glaze that give the vase its character. Jade is beautiful, and highly prized. Instead of naming me Biyu, green jade, like many other girls, my father named me Daiyu, black jade. When I asked him why he named me after such an ugly rock, he said it was because black jade was far more rare, and thus more precious. I learned to love my name after that, and I sorely miss it now. Even after all these months, a part of me still twitches whenever someone calls me Lihua.

"It gives me great joy to see you happy," the emperor

says. "Is there anything you need? More money? New jewels for your hair?"

I shake my head, but then something comes to mind. "I...I just have a question, if you don't mind."

"Of course," he says. "Anything."

It still takes me a moment to gather my courage. "It's about Lady An," I finally say. The emperor frowns and turns away from me. "I'm sorry. I shouldn't have said anything."

"What about her?" he asks. "Is she bothering you?"

"No," I say. "Nothing like that. But I see how sad she is, how thin she has gotten. Perhaps it would do her heart good if you were to invite her to your bed."

The emperor shakes his head. "I never liked that girl. So quiet, so timid. When she is in my bed, I might as well be making love to a pillow for all the response she gives me."

I'm a bit shocked by the emperor's words, but then I remember what my maid, Nuwa, told me the first night I was summoned to the emperor's bed. The emperor preferred girls who were... What was the word she used? Enthusiastic, not a cold fish. I wonder if she was thinking about Lady An when she told me that.

"I will never understand how she came to be with child," the emperor goes on. "I only slept with her once."

This takes me back. It can happen after only one time? I've lost track of how many times I've been in the emperor's bed. I don't think I'm pregnant. I don't feel any different. But I suppose it could happen at any time.

"I'm sure she was just intimidated by your presence," I say. "Perhaps if you gave her another chance—" He waves me off. "I only mean that, since she fell pregnant once, she could again. And perhaps give you a son."

"Is that what you are worried about?" he asks. "Are you afraid you aren't going to give me a son?"

"Not...afraid..." I say, trying to explain myself. "But... Well, I haven't yet. I'm sorry." I'm not sorry, I'm just not sure what else to say.

"Do I make you unhappy?" the emperor asks, narrowing his eyes at me.

"No!" I say, wondering what gave him that impression.

"Do you not want me to call you to my bed anymore?"

"Of course I want to be here," I say, growing afraid. I mean, if he did stop summoning me, I wouldn't mind. But I certainly don't want him to be angry with me.

"Then, what is it?" he asks. "Why would you push another woman, one I despise, at me so forcefully?"

I don't think that asking a simple question, making such a small suggestion, was me being forceful at all. But I guess I have overstepped my bounds.

"I'm sorry," I say, tearing up. "I... The other ladies..." I'm just not sure what to say!

"Oh," the emperor says, nodding his head. "I see."

"You...you do?"

"The other women in the harem, Lady An especially I suppose, are jealous of you," he says. "Is that it?"

I nod slowly. I don't want to get any of the other ladies in the harem in trouble. But it is true that Lady An is jealous of me.

The emperor is thoughtful for a moment. "It is good of you to want to keep peace in the harem. Caihong usually makes sure of that, but I know she cannot keep an eye on everything as she usually does. She told me that she thought Lady An would do a good job managing the harem in her place, but I suppose that is not the case."

I open my mouth to protest but then close it again. I've already said far too much.

"I will speak to my mother about it," he says. "Other

than Lady An, I'm not sure who else has the experience necessary to manage things. I will ask her opinion."

The dowager! She favors Lady An for some reason. If the emperor tells her that I accused Lady An of being jealous, she might turn on me even more.

"Please don't mention my name," I blurt out. "I mean, if she thinks that I accused Lady An of...of being unkind to me, she might think I was the one trying to cause discord among the ladies."

"Don't worry," the emperor says, kissing me on the forehead. "I know how to handle my mother."

I nod but doubt his words. I don't think the emperor really knows what it is like living the harem. And why would he? Whenever he visits, we are all smiles and kindness. No one would want the emperor to think any of us were unhappy. I have no doubt that the dowager will suspect I was the one behind the emperor's doubts of Lady An. I was stupid to say anything.

"How is the collection of funds for the poor coming along?" the emperor asks.

"Very well," I say with a nod. I don't tell him that the vast majority of money I have saved has been my own. I dismissed all of my servants except for Suyin, Jinhai, and Nuwa. I still don't think I need two maidservants, but Nuwa has been in the palace a long time and has been very helpful to me. I think it is wise to keep her with me.

The money I saved from not having to pay their salaries, I have set aside to be donated. I have also requested less food and sold some embroidery. Suyin has mentioned my fundraising efforts only to the maids she knows well, and they have told her which ladies would be agreeable to donate as well. But that has not been very many. I think only three other ladies have donated, and it has been a pittance. I know I need to try harder, but I don't have the courage.

"Good," the emperor says. "Come, speak to Honghui about it. He will know better than I what to do next since it was all his idea."

"What?" I ask, trotting along behind him as quickly as I can. I've gotten far more nimble on my pot-bottom shoes than I ever thought possible.

We leave the emperor's bed-chamber and he leads me to a large sitting room where his brother, Honghui, is already waiting. I give the prince a bow, but he bows even lower to me. The emperor's consort apparently outranks the emperor's brother, even if I am one of dozens. The two men embrace, and then the emperor beckons me to them.

"Brother," the emperor says. "Lihua has been raising the funds for the poor among the ladies. You two can discuss how best to proceed. How to make sure the money reaches the people and doesn't end up in some bureaucrat's pocket."

"Of course," Honghui says with a bow. "It will be my honor."

The emperor then kisses me on the cheek. "I am sure you have a busy day ahead, my dear. I will send for someone else tonight—but *not* Lady An." He shakes a finger at me but gives me a smile as if he is making a joke. I chuckle even though I don't find his words amusing.

"Of course," I say with a bow.

The emperor goes to attend his morning audiences, leaving me alone with Honghui—and his charming, mischievous smile.

"Did you arrange this?" I ask, my arms crossed as though I am in a huff. The prince glances around and sees that we are alone for once. Suyin and Jinhai would be standing near my waiting sedan chair at this time. They are probably wondering why I am so delayed this morning.

"That's depends," he says, stepping closer to me. "Does it make you glad that I have found a way to spend more time with you?"

I sigh and turn to walk back down the hall to the emperor's bed-chamber. "I enjoy your company. But you know we shouldn't be doing this."

"Doing what?" he asks. "Making donations to the poor? It was your idea."

I reach over and pinch his arm. "You know what I mean."

He squirms as if I actually hurt him. "I know. I know. But I can't help it. I'm just so intrigued by you."

"Why?" I ask. "I'm just a girl. You can have any woman you want. Shouldn't you be married already? You must be an old maid by now."

He chuckles. "You are starting to sound like my brother. My mother died when I was young, and Father died before he could arrange a marriage for me, so...it just hasn't happened yet. But..." He cuts in front of me and squeezes my chin. "It's you I want to talk about. Are you ever going to tell me the real reason you snuck out of the palace that night?"

I turn my head away so that he has to release my chin. "No."

We've reached the emperor's bed-chamber, but I hesitate to go inside. I don't want to be in a room alone with Honghui. If he tried to kiss me, I might not be able to stop myself.

"I think you will," he says, standing next to me. "I just have to be patient."

We are quiet for a moment. In truth, I wish I could tell

him. Tell anyone. It's such a weight in my chest. I'm so terri-fied that the truth of my identity is going to come out somehow and ruin everything. If I could tell someone the truth first, someone in power, the prince, the empress, the emperor even, then perhaps they could protect me. But I can't do that. Not yet. There is no one, not even the prince, I trust that much.

"So," he finally says, "since giving away your money to the poor was your idea, how do you think it would be best to do so? Use it to buy grain? Give them all new shoes?"

I remember how I had to sell my shoes just to buy food and shake that idea away. "Every family is different. They all have different needs. Some need shoes. Some need food. Some need a place to live. I think we should put the money directly into the hands of the poor."

The prince scoffs. "Don't you think they would just spend it all getting drunk at a public house?"

"Some might," I say. "But even drunkards have children who need to eat. Give the money to the people. They will know what to do with it."

"Then what?" he asks. "When that money runs out, what then? They will be hungry once again. Should we just give them more money?"

"Yes," I say, looking at him defiantly. I wish I could tell him why. Tell him how even a small amount of cash can change a family's life. Can buy them enough food to have strength for work. Can help them move to a neighborhood with better prospects. Can provide a dowry for a young girl that can get her into a better family and out of poverty alto-gether. At this last thought, I think of my sister Mingming. She will be of a marriageable age soon. I'm sure my family will use the money Mingxia paid for me to provide her with a dowry. Just how high will she be able to climb, I wonder.

I wish I could tell him all this and more. But I can't. He would want to know how I know these things. He would perhaps figure it out on his own.

Honghui looks at me expectantly, waiting for me to explain, but he finally realizes I am not going to do that. He lets out a sigh as he looks back down the corridor. "You're a good person, Lihua. I suppose you want to assume the best in others as well."

I'm frustrated that he thinks my ideas are born from being naïve and not from experience. But I say nothing. I can't tell him the truth, not yet.

"I will do as you ask," he says. "When you have collected enough money, I will just go out into the streets and hand the money out myself."

"Thank you," I say. I wish I could go with him, but I know that wouldn't be proper. I look down at my hands as I feel his fingers touch mine.

"Will you meet me tonight?" he whispers. "At the hour of the ox?"

"We shouldn't," I say, but it is only because I have to. The prince walks away, confident that I will meet him at the appointed time.

24

———

*S*ince I dismissed all the other servants, sneaking out should be as easy as it was before. Suyin and Jinhai are still deep sleepers, and Nuwa sleeps in another room. Still, I'm careful and quiet, walking barefoot until I am out of the palace. As soon as I am in the garden, I feel Honghui's hand in mine. I don't start, I've grown so used to his presence. He kisses me as soon as we meet, not waiting until we've moved into a more secluded area, and I cup his jaw as I kiss him back. I feel his kiss turn into a naughty grin as he pulls away and leads me through the garden.

I feel a tingling in my belly, an anticipation. I can't wait for him to hold me, caress me. All my worries melt away when we are together. I know I should let my guilt, my fear, control my actions, make me stop, but I can't. I only want him. Those feelings are for later when I am once again alone.

He leads me to a building that is often occupied during the day—a hall with good lighting where ladies sit to work on their painting or embroidery—but now, it is completely empty. And completely dark. The lattice shutters are closed, blocking the moonlight. When the prince closes the door behind us, I can see nothing, but I can feel his presence near me. A presence that burns as hotly as my own.

We say nothing as he grabs me to him, his kisses hungry, as if he will steal the very breath from my lungs. His hands slip up my sleeping gown, caressing my bare legs, and my knees go weak. I wrap my arms around his neck to keep from falling, holding him that much closer against me, and yet it is still not close enough.

I suddenly understand what true passion is. True desire. It is something I have never felt with Emperor Guozhi, and I know I never will. That is duty, a mere job I must perform. But this... Oh! This is pure pleasure.

I lean my head back and Honghui kisses down my chest, between my breasts, tugging at my gown, pulling it from my shoulders. I slowly sink to the ground, pulling Honghui down with me.

"Are you sure?" he asks me, breathless, and I answer with more kisses, opening his robe, revealing his smooth, muscular chest. He lets out a breathy chuckle and removes his belt, letting his robe fly open. I untie my own belt, and in a moment, our warm bodies are as close as two humans can be.

I am no innocent maid. I know exactly what I am doing. I know it is stupid. Dangerous. I know what will happen if we are caught. But I don't care. I have given up everything to be here—my family, my home, my name. I know I will never have a real husband of my own, children of my own. I never thought I would know love, know passion. But now that I have it, I will not let go. This is for me.

The emperor has taken my virginity. He will never know that I laid with another man. And if I fall pregnant? Well, the emperor will be delighted. He would never suspect the child was not his own.

I have to bite my lower lip to keep from crying out as ecstasy washes over me, taking me to the highest peaks and then dropping me into a freezing cold river. The prince follows right behind me, and then we are lying in each other's arms as we wait for our senses to return.

"That...that was not my intention in seeing you tonight," he whispers, and I cover my mouth as I giggle.

"I would never have known that," I reply, and he laughs as he nuzzles my neck.

"I didn't believe you would ever want to," he says. "It is dangerous, and I did not think you would take such a risk."

I chew my lower lip as I consider my response. My whole life is one huge risk. This seems like nothing compared to the secrets I already hold in my heart every day.

"I thought you knew me better than that," I say. I feel his lips smile as he kisses me again.

"I think you should work to remain the emperor's favorite," he says. "As long as he takes you to his bed, we don't have to worry about...consequences of our own meetings."

I let out a sigh and he holds me tight. As much as I would like the emperor to forget about me, Honghui is right. If the emperor did not take me to his bed and I fell pregnant, there would be no explaining it away. And I would have no way to hide it. My maids, since they wash my laundry, would know as soon as I missed my courses.

"This is all a dream," I say. "We can never freely or openly be together. We could never marry or even run away together. You are a prince and are sure to be discovered no matter where we might go."

The prince says nothing because he cannot disagree with me.

"And you must marry," I finally say. He humphs. "I mean it." I turn his face to mine so that I know he is listening even if we cannot see each other in the dark. "If the emperor has no sons, or should his future sons die, your son would be the next heir to the Dragon Throne. You must do your duty by your brother, as I must."

"How did one so young become so wise?" he asks me, teasingly.

I sigh and snuggle close to him. "I only know how precarious life can be."

He holds me for another minute before we both have to admit that we have lingered too long. I crawl around on the floor, groping for the belt to my sleeping gown and my slippers. Finding them, I then attempt to dress myself in the dark. Hopefully I will not look as disheveled as I feel in the morning when Suyin wakes me. If I do, I'll just have to tell her I had a nightmare.

When he is ready, Honghui takes me by the hand and leads me to the door. He opens it carefully and I have to blink as my eyes adjust to the moonlight. It's still the middle of the night, but anything seems brighter compared to the pitch black we just came out of. The prince leads me by the hand back toward my palace. When we are about halfway there, we hear a noise.

We both freeze and glance around. I don't see any lantern light, so it can't be a guard. Still, it could be anyone. And if we are caught together... I don't hear anything else for a long time, and we start to relax, but then we hear it again, the unmistakable sound of slippers on stone. Someone else is here.

"Go," I whisper so quietly, it is little more than my mouth moving.

"Not without—" he starts to say, but I put my fingers to his lips.

"Go." He looks at me for a moment, panic in his eyes. I can tell he is frantically searching for an alternative, but there is none. If we are caught together in the middle of the night, no explanation will save us. And if the prince is caught in the inner court at night, even alone... Well, no one would believe he was there for innocent purpose. At least I can say I couldn't sleep and went for a walk or something. He finally nods and then darts off in the other direction, away from the noise. To then mask any sounds he might make, I continue walking toward my palace, my head held high, as if I have nothing to hide.

I reach the end of a garden walk and look left and right, my eyes scanning the darkness for any movement. I am about to turn right, toward my palace, when out of the corner of my eye I see a shadow move. I put my hand to my mouth to keep from crying out and crouch down. It takes a moment for my heart to stop racing enough for me to realize it wasn't a ghost or spirit, but a person. A person dressed all in black. It is this realization that both calms me and sets my mind spinning.

Who would be out at night dressed all in black?

I peek to the left again and can now clearly see the dark shape slinking quickly down the path. It looks to be a man, probably a eunuch. For a moment, I consider returning home. Whatever is happening, it is surely not my business. I think back to the night I snuck out of the Forbidden City dressed all in black to try and find my family. If anyone but the prince had seen me, my life would have been over. Perhaps I should let this person go, pretend I saw nothing.

But there is a sinking feeling in my stomach. Why would a eunuch be sneaking around at night? Eunuchs have much more freedom than us ladies. They can leave the Forbidden City on errands or even to visit their own families. They are allowed to walk around the palace grounds, both the inner and outer courts, unescorted. I can't help but think that if this man is sneaking around the palace at night, it cannot be for good reasons.

When I see the shadow turn down another path, I follow. I suppose I could scream, call him out. The guards could come and put to an end whatever he is doing. But then I think of the prince and me sneaking around. Perhaps this eunuch means no harm, but is meeting a lover? No, of course not! He cannot have a lover. He could be delivering a love note to one of the ladies on behalf of a lover on the outside. A love left behind when she was chosen. If that is the case, I will say nothing. Pretend I saw nothing. But until I know for certain, I think I should continue to follow. Just in case...

Several times I lose sight of the shadow moving about in the dark, but I always manage to find him again. Finally he stops and crouches along the wall of a palace and waits for a long while. I realize with growing dread that he is outside the empress's palace. This cannot be right. The empress would have no lover. She wouldn't dare... No. Something is very, very wrong. But what should I do? Call for the guards? Scare him away myself?

I'm debating what to do when I see him stand up and open a lattice shutter. The same lattice shutter belonging to the window I saw Lady An standing near a few days ago. The lattice shutter that covers a window to the empress's bed-chamber! With surprising ease, the eunuch grabs the edge of the window and climbs through.

I have to do something. Have to stop him! I almost run to the front door. But if he hears me make a commotion, he could slip back out the window and into the dark night, escaping. Instead, I run to the window. Standing on my tiptoes, I look in. With horror, I see him standing over the empress, his hand raised as if to strike!

A scream rents the air, and it takes a moment for me to realize that I am the person screaming.

"Stop!" I yell. The man turns to run toward the window, as I thought he would, but he stops when he sees m.

"Help the empress!" I scream, and I finally hear the voices of her many servants as they are ripped from sleep. The man turns to run toward the door of the room, but the empress's own eunuchs are already entering the bed-chamber. I finally feel that the empress is safe enough for me to call for the guards. I run back to the main walkway in front of the empress's palace.

"Help! Guards! The empress!" In only a moment, over a dozen guards with lanterns and swords drawn are running toward me. I turn to lead them into the palace just as a maid throws the doors open.

"We caught him!" she says excitedly. "Please, hurry!" She is surprised as I rush into the palace, the guards right behind me, but she says nothing. I stop when I reach the bed chamber and see that several of the empress's eunuchs have the man in black pinned to the ground beneath them. Someone has lit the lanterns of the empress's room, and she is sitting up in bed, her face confused, her arms wrapped around one of her maids.

"The scissors!" someone says, and all the ladies scream. There on the floor, next to the skirmish, is a small pair of scissors. Not a pair large enough to cut hair, but one that might be in a lady's sewing kit. Small, yes, but very sharp.

One of the guards picks it up and waves it in the man's face.

"What is this? Were you going to kill the empress?"

"No...no!" the man cries. It is then that I realize he is familiar, but I cannot place him.

"Peizhi!" a maid finally says. "He is one of Lady An's eunuchs." There is a round of gasps, including my own. She's right. I have often seen him following behind Lady An with his head bowed, which is why I did not recognize him right away.

"The emperor approaches!" a eunuch announces, and all of us drop to our knees, even the eunuchs holding Peizhi.

"What is happening?" he yells.

"He tried to kill the empress!" someone explains.

"What?" the emperor roars, and for the first time, I see him truly angry. "Who?"

The eunuchs move aside, all of them pointing to Peizhi. "Him!"

The emperor storms forward, grabbing Peizhi by the collar, pulling him up and backhanding him across the face, his nose instantly spewing blood.

"Who are you? Why did you do this?"

Peizhi can form no coherent words, only sputters and cries. The emperor, disgusted, drops Peizhi to the ground.

"Arrest him," the emperor orders. "Torture him. Find out exactly why he did this and who sent him."

"Yes, your majesty!" the guards say as they get to their feet and go toward Peizhi. But before they can reach him, Peizhi lunges toward one of the empress's eunuchs. He manages to grab the little scissors, and before anyone can stop him, he stabs himself in the neck, blood spurting into the faces of a nearby eunuch and a maid. This leads to another round of screaming, and even I feel sick.

The emperor grabs Peizhi, not caring about the blood getting on his hands or yellow robe. He grabs the assassin's collar and slams him to the ground. "You bastard! Tell me who sent you!"

Peizhi's mouth opens and closes, but only blood bubbles forth. I think it takes less than a minute for his body to stop moving. The emperor lets out a yell in his frustration and starts barking orders at the guards. He doesn't see that the empress has gripped her maid in pains of her own.

I run across the room, trying to avoid looking at the dead body on the floor, and kneel by her side. "My lady!"

"It...hurts..." she says, clutching her stomach. It cannot yet be her time! That is at least three months away.

"Call the physician!" I yell. I fear she is losing the baby.

25

———

When I was seven years old, my mother had a miscarriage. I was so young at the time, I didn't know what was happening at first. We lived a little better then, since the only children were myself and Mingming, who was only two years old. Mingming and I slept on one bed while Mama and Baba slept on another. A moaning sound woke me. I tried to roll over and go back to sleep, but then I heard Mama cry out in pain.

"Daiyu!" Baba yelled. "Light a lamp!"

It was the middle of the night, so it took a while for me to find the lantern and then light it in the dark. But when I did, I wished I hadn't. There was so much blood. My hands shook and I could only stare at the nightmare before me. Mama looked at me, her eyes wide with terror.

"I'm losing the baby."

Now, I had heard this phrase before. Every so often there would be a rumor that such-and-such had lost a baby. I thought it must be so terrible, to lay your baby down and not be able to find it again. I had supposed the babies were snatched away by some wicked person hoping to sell them.

Or that the woman had simply put the baby somewhere, perhaps while she worked, and then forgot where she put it! *That would never happen to me*, I thought, believing my parents to be better than most.

As I stared at the blood and Mama's words echoed in my ears, it was only then that I realized that it meant the baby was dying.

"What should I do?" I asked her.

"Fetch the midwife!" she cried through gritted teeth. I didn't even put on my shoes as I fled out the door into the night. I ran down the hutong and around the corner to the home of the midwife. I banged on the door for what seemed like hours before someone finally answered. I don't remember what I said. In my memory, even I don't understand my words through my crying. But the midwife probably knew that there was only ever one reason why someone knocked frantically on her door in the middle of the night.

Back at the house, I felt completely helpless as I sat on the bed, holding Mingming, who wouldn't stop crying. I watched as the midwife tended to Mama, massaging her belly, giving her bitter tea.

Mama lived, thanks to the skill of the midwife. We paid her what little money we could and she carried away the little bloody bundle that was supposed to have been a little brother or sister. But she warned Mama and Baba not to risk any more children, at least not for a while.

I was so terrified of Mama dying that anytime I woke in the night to hear her and Baba...umm... "doing what married people do," as we were told when we were too little to understand, I would jump out of my own bed and into theirs between them. They didn't scold me. I'm sure they knew it was for the best if Mama didn't fall pregnant again.

It was six years before Mama became pregnant with Junli. By that time, I was a little older and wiser and knew that miscarriages were actually rather common, and that most of the time the mother didn't die. It was just a part of child-bearing. Still, I laid awake every night, always the last to drift off to sleep, as I waited for the cries of pain that would tell me that she was losing the baby...

The empress did not lose her baby. While we waited for the physician, I held the empress's hand, massaged her belly, and asked for bitter tea. I helped her breathe slowly and evenly. By the time the physician arrived, she had calmed considerably, and so had her pains. The doctor gave her more herbal remedies to calm both her and the baby and said it was simply the fear and shock of the night that caused her nerves to shake. If she remained calm and relaxed, she—and the baby—would recover.

Weeks later, I'm lying in the empress's bed, between her and the wall, holding her hand in mine.

The dawn sun is just starting to peek through the windows, turning the room from black to gray. The birds tweet. I hear servants shuffling about outside, delivering food, laundry, fresh flowers, and other items to the various ladies' palaces. You would think it was just any other day.

But it is not any other day.

Today is the day that Lady An has been ordered to kill herself. Even though the assassin never said it was Lady An who sent him, since he was her eunuch, that was the only conclusion. Lady An protested her innocence, of course. Said she loved the emperor and would never harm the empress or her son. But the emperor was so thunderously angry, he refused to believe her. She was banished to the Cold Palace—palace that is nothing more than a room with a single chair—and given a long white scarf. A consort of the emperor could never be executed like a common criminal, no matter how heinous her crime. Women such as Lady An, ladies of rank and dignity, are expected to do the honorable thing and take their own lives.

I swallow as I lean back against the headboard and peer over the empress to the spot on the floor where the eunuch died. The empress is too weak, too delicate, to be moved to another palace. Even though the rugs on the floor that had been stained red were thrown out and replaced with new ones, I think I can see a spot on the floor that is a little darker than the rest.

Even though there is no evidence that the eunuch was acting under order from Lady An, I did not speak up for her. I did not plead for mercy. No one did. The emperor was so angry, I think he would have killed anyone who questioned his judgment.

I think about how very close to death I could have been had all the focus not fallen on Lady An. It was eventually discovered that I had been the one to scream and alert everyone to the intruder. When asked why I had been outside the empress's palace that night, I only said that I could not sleep and heard a noise, which I then followed. I think everyone was so relieved that the eunuch had been caught, no one thought to question my story.

But they still could.

When all is said and done, when Lady An is dead, when the prince is born, even then, no one will forget that night. No one will forget the assassin in the empress's bed-chamber. No one will forget the concubine who was so jealous she sent her own eunuch to kill the empress and the unborn prince. People will talk about that night for years to come, I am sure of it. And my name—the name of Lihua— will be remembered too. In all the times the story and told and retold, will someone eventually question *why* I was truly there that night?

I had thought that my position as the emperor's favorite made me invincible. No one would suspect that I was having an affair with the prince. No one would question the identity of any child I might conceive.

But I had been a fool. Stupid. Reckless. There is no proof that Lady An was the person behind the plot on the empress's life. She has never wavered in protesting her innocence. Yet everyone believes she is guilty. The emperor believes it. And she will die because of that belief, whether she is guilty or not.

The same thing could happen to me. If the emperor ever suspected, ever doubted my loyalty, he could put me to death without question. And just like Lady An, no one would speak up for me.

The empress starts and wakes with a gasp.

"My lady?" I ask, lightly touching her arm and then her forehead to check for a fever.

"Lihua," she says as she tries to adjust her position.

"Don't strain yourself," I tell her as I move the pillows to make her comfortable. "What's wrong? Do you need some water?"

"No. No..." she says as her eyes adjust to the light. She pushes her hair, now only chin-length, behind her ears. "I had a dream. A terrible dream."

"I'm sure it was nothing," I say to reassure her. But as she wakes more, I can see the worry on her face.

"I dreamed I was standing on the edge of a cliff," she says, "overlooking a beautiful valley. There were endless green trees and a winding river down below. The wind was gently blowing around me. And in my arms, I held my newborn son."

"That sounds like a good omen," I say. I know some people put great importance on the meanings of dreams. I do not know if dreams carry messages from the ancestors or not. I can only say that I have never had one to make me believe it is so.

"No," she says, shaking her head as her eyes water. "For we were dressed in white, me and my son. And I could not see his face."

I do not know what to say to this, and I can see why she is scared to have dreamed of herself in the color of mourning.

"When I looked out over the valley, there on the breeze, a white scarf danced by." As she wipes tears from her cheeks, a heavy stone lodges itself in my stomach.

"Lihua," Caihong says, gripping my arm, "has there been a terrible mistake? Is Lady An innocent? Are the gods going to demand my death and the death of my son as payment?"

"No!" I say with as much conviction as I can muster. "You have had nothing to do with her. The assassin killed himself. The emperor sentenced Lady An to death. You are completely innocent in all of this. It was only a dream, nothing more."

"Do you really think so?" the empress asks.

I do my best to give her a reassuring smile, but I am not sure if I am successful. "I'm sure of it."

The door to the empress's bed-chamber slides open and a maid steps in with a tray of tea things. I help the empress sit up in her bed. Before, I think the empress only feigned helplessness because she enjoyed being doted on. But now, now I do believe that fear and stress have made her weak. All of us ladies wait on her every moment and help her at all hours without complaint. Any energy she has must be conserved to birth the prince.

After the maid prepares the tea and hands it to the empress, she then leaves the room to attend other duties. The empress has only taken a sip when she turns to me.

"Lihua, I need you to do something for me."

"Of course, my lady."

"I need you to go to Lady An in the Cold Palace." My heart drops and I am so frightened I nearly run away. My fear must be clear on my face because the empress grips my arm and continues. "Please, do this for me."

"I cannot," I whisper. The last thing I want is for the emperor to hear that I spoke with Lady An. What if he thinks I was part of her scheme?

"You must," she says, her eyes wild. "I must know the truth! Go to her, beg her to tell you what really happened. She is going to die today no matter what. What is the point in maintaining her lie? Surely it would be better for her to die with a clear conscience."

"But...to what end?" I ask. "Is it not enough that she will die for her crimes against you?"

"I cannot send an innocent woman to her death!" she says, dropping the teacup to the ground and grabbing both of my arms. She looks me in the eyes so intently, I fear she can read my very mind. "If she is innocent, I know I shall die too! The gods of justice will demand it! Please, please go to her. Get her confession. Set my spirit at ease."

I don't want to do it. I would almost rather throw myself into a well and drown than speak to Lady An. But I know I must. I cannot defy my empress. And, in truth, a part of me is curious as well. If Lady An is guilty and admits is, I know I would rest easier.

"Fine," I say. "I will do as you ask."

She breathes a sigh of relief. "Thank you. Go, now, while it is still early. Before it is too late."

I bend down and pick up the broken shards of the teacup and then bow my way out of the room. I put the pieces of porcelain into a rubbish basket and then dust off my hands. I return first to my own palace to wash my face and change my clothes. Suyin brushes my hair and pins it up in a simple style merely to keep it off my neck and out of my face. She does not even bother with a bianfang. When I tell her, Jinhai, and Nuwa what the empress has ordered me to do, they are horrified and try to convince me not to go. But I must. I order all of them to stay behind. Should the emperor fault me for my actions, I do not want them to be punished as well.

With a heavy heart and my shoes feeling as though they are made of boulders, I make my way to the Cold Palace alone.

The Cold Palace is located in a shady, isolated part of the Forbidden City. I had thought the palace was named such simply because it is where ladies are sent to be punished, but I now see that the meaning is much more literal. The palace, even from the outside, appears cold and drafty, with the lattice shutters falling from their hinges and the door showing a splintered crack. The building has not been maintained for some time.

On either side of the door, two guards stand sentinel, and they eye me suspiciously as I approach.

"The empress has sent me to speak to the prisoner," I say. One of the guards holds his hand up to stop me.

"No one is to speak to her," he says. "She should already be dead."

"Is she already dead?" I ask, eyeing the door. I see movement through the crack and realize that she is not.

"She has refused to carry out the emperor's orders so far," the guard says. "But she will either hang herself, or she will starve. Her choice."

I hear a whimpering and realize that Lady An can hear us. The pitiful sounds of her cries tug at my heart. I raise my head and speak with more conviction than I feel.

"Would you dare defy the empress?" I ask. "The empress is the head of the inner court, *not* his majesty. She has ordered me to exact a final confession from Lady An and I will not leave until I have carried out my task."

The guard looks to his companion, who shrugs. He hestiates, but finally he steps aside.

"Be quick about it," he orders. I nod as I walk past and go to the door. I try to open it, but it is locked fast. I look to the guards, but their backs are to me. I decide not to press my luck by asking them to open the door. I kneel down to where the door is cracked.

"Lady An?" I say.

"Who...who is there?" she asks. "Fenfang? Is that you?"

"No," I say. "It is not the dowager. It's only me, Lihua."

She is quiet for a moment, and I think she is refusing to speak to me, but then I hear her voice.

"Why have you come?"

"The empress sent me," I say. I hear a shuffling noise and can see part of her face on the other side of the door.

"Has she spoken for me? Has she begged mercy of the emperor?"

The hope in her voice nearly tears me apart. "No," I finally say. "She wants you to confess."

"Confess?" she asks as though confused. "Confess to what?"

"To sending your man to kill her."

"But I didn't!" she says emphatically. "I would never do such a terrible thing! Why should I?"

"Because you are jealous she is pregnant," I say.

"Of course I am," she says. "And so are you! And so is every other woman here. But that does not mean we kill one another. We are sisters!"

I hate to admit it, but I believe her. Her voice does not waver. There is no malice in her words. I do not believe she did this terrible thing.

"If it was not you, then who was it?" I ask. "Why did your own eunuch try to kill her?"

"I don't know," she says, her voice choking. "I can only think someone bribed him to do it. They must have paid him a very great amount. He had to have known that he would be caught and put to death. Even if he had succeeded in killing Caihong, he never would have gotten out of her place alive."

I consider this for a moment. She's right. The scissors were small. They were sharp enough for the eunuch to kill the empress, but surely she would have woken up and screamed before she died. There were also maids in her room. They hadn't heard him sneak in, but they would have heard the scuffle.

"Do you think he wanted to get caught?" I ask. "Could that have been his plan? Maybe he never intended to be successful?"

"Why?" Lady An asks. "It doesn't make sense. Why bribe a eunuch to commit a crime he is sure to be caught doing?"

A sudden terrible thought fills my head and I am a little less sturdy, crouched on my pot-bottom shoes. "Because he was *your* eunuch."

"What?"

"He was your eunuch," I say. "What if Caihong was

never the intended victim? Whoever it was, what if they always intended the blame to fall on you?"

Lady An goes quiet for a long time. "No," she says. "That can't be true. Who would want to hurt me?"

"That is the question," I say. "Can you think of anyone who hates you enough to want you dead?"

"No," she says. "I'm no one! The emperor hates me. Why should anyone hurt me?"

"I don't know," I say. "Maybe I'm wrong. I don't know. Maybe he was supposed to kill Caihong and I'm just being stupid."

"But you believe me, don't you?" Lady An asks. "You know I would never hurt the empress, right?"

I nod. "Of course I do."

"Then, can you tell Caihong? Tell the emperor? He loves you. He will listen. Ask him to spare my life."

I wish I could. I wish I could give her comfort. I wish I could even save her life. But I can't. No one can. I am wracking my mind to come up with a reply, but no words come to me.

"I understand," Lady An finally says. "No one wants to risk their life for a nobody like me."

A sob escapes my throat. It's all so terribly unfair. She's innocent! I'm guilty! But she will die, and I will live. Yet I am too much of a coward to speak up.

Lady An slips her fingers through the crack. I reach up and hold them as best I can.

"Protect my daughter," she says.

The princess! The emperor's eldest daughter. I hadn't even thought of her in all this. What will happen to her now? Will the emperor send her away? Disown her? Will the stigma of her mother's reputation as a murderer follow her for the rest of her life?

"I will," I promise. I don't know how, but I cannot let that innocent little girl suffer. I will do whatever I must to keep her in the emperor's good graces.

She pulls her hand back and moves away from the door. I know she will say no more. What else is there to say? I sit for a long moment before finally pushing myself to my feet and walking away. I have only just passed the guards when I hear a bang and a yelp from inside the Cold Palace. The guards hear it too and they rush over and fling the doors open.

I look and see Lady An's thin body hanging from the rafter by a white silk scarf, her black hair hanging long around her shoulders. It is an image that will haunt me for the rest of my life.

I don't remember the long walk back to the empress's palace. I don't even realize where I am until I hear the empress's voice, see her face anxiously looking at me.

"Well?" she asks.

"Huh?" I say.

"Did she admit it? Did she send the eunuch to kill me?"

I want to tell her the truth. That Lady An was innocent. That she was possibly only a victim as much as the empress was. But the words catch in my throat. What good would it do? The empress is terrified that she is going to die in exchange for the life of an innocent woman.

Lady An is dead. I cannot save her. I cannot comfort her. But I can comfort my empress.

"Yes," I say simply.

The empress lets out a great, heaving sigh of relief and tears stream down her face. She collects herself and grips my hand.

"Thank you," she says. "Thank you. I owe you so much. You have saved my life twice."

I try to smile, but I cannot. I turn and leave her palace. I need to be alone.

I walk aimlessly, losing myself along the endless, twisting paths among flowers, trees, and trickling brooks. I feel so tired, as if a great weight is pushing me to the ground. I come to an open grassy area surrounded by tall flowers. Perhaps I can hide here for a while. I lie down on the grass and look up at the sky, so blue, with only white wisps of clouds. I cry silent tears, letting them slip down the sides of my face and into my ears.

I cry for Lady An. I cry for the princess. I cry for the empress. But mostly, I cry for myself. I cry for my mother, my father, each of my sisters. I cry for the life I lost and the life I gained. I cry for the red walls that keep me trapped like a caged animal. I cry for the life I can never have with Prince Honghui. I cry for all the lies upon lies I have told, lies so thick I no longer know who I am anymore.

I cry because, like Lady An, I know I will die here. I cry because I am already dead. I am not Lihua. I am not Daiyu. I am a mere figment of the imagination. A ghost. A shade of a person who never existed.

I close my eyes and drift away, praying that oblivion claims me.

———

26

Oblivion does not take me. I wake several hours later, my skin pink and tender from lying in the sun for so long. When I make it back to my palace, my servants are frantic in their search for me. They were afraid that I had been so traumatized after seeing Lady An's body that I had thrown myself into a well. I tell them that I was not traumatized, merely sad over the whole situation but would recover in time.

I fear that if I tell them the truth, that I *had* been severely affected by what happened, they will coddle me endlessly and never let me out of their sight again. So I stuff my emotions deep down inside my heart. I dare not tell anyone what was said that day. How I truly felt when I saw Lady An's body swinging from the rafter.

Days later, sitting in the empress's bed-chamber working on my embroidery, the other ladies and I keep the empress company, tending to her every need. There is smiling and laughter. Lady An seems all but forgotten. No one else notices the large dark spot on the floor where the eunuch died. The days pass much as they did before, in anxious anticipation of the birth of the emperor's son.

When the emperor's chief eunuch visits us, everyone except the empress rises to greet him, expecting him to have brought kind words for the empress on the emperor's behalf.

"The emperor has requested that Lady Lihua be escorted to his audience hall," he says.

"Me?" I ask as everyone looks at me. "Why?"

"You saved the empress's life," he says, as if I should have known. "The emperor wishes to reward you for your brave actions."

My mouth gapes and I look around the room. I see that many of the smiles on the ladies' faces have faltered. The empress, however, looks away from me sheepishly, and I know she knew this was coming.

I put my embroidery circle in my chair and step around the other ladies as I follow the eunuch out of the palace. There is no sense in fighting whatever is about to happen. The emperor is waiting for me.

I am carried to the audience hall in a sedan chair, but I am not taken to the side door I entered through before, but the front door.

"Are you sure?" I ask him as Suyin, who trotted along beside the chair, takes my hand. Jinhai accompanied us as well and moves to stand by the door to the audience hall and await any orders.

"Quite sure, my lady," he says with a bow. I am, of course, even more nervous now than I was before and am wishing that I had taken better care with my appearance. Nothing I can do about that now. I take a breath as I follow the eunuch through the door.

The room is filled with important men who all part to let me pass when my name is announced. I walk carefully toward the emperor, who is sitting on his dragon throne on the raised dais, so I do not trip and make a fool of myself. When I reach the dais, Suyin backs away, and I kneel, bowing my head.

"May the emperor live ten thousand years!" I say. I try to speak clearly and loudly enough for all to hear, but my voice cracks and I hear some of the men chuckle, even the emperor.

"Rise, Lihua," he says, and I do but keep my eyes downcast. "Ula Nara Lihua, you have proven to be the bravest woman in my harem. You saved the lives of my son and the empress, and for that, you will always have my deepest thanks."

The men in the room clap and I blush.

"Even before that, you showed yourself to be thoughtful and wise. And you have brought nothing but joy to my life night after night."

The men laugh again, but now with an undercutting tone that makes me nauseous as they imagine me in the emperor's bed. I try not to shrink into myself, but it is difficult.

"Ula Nara Lihua," the emperor continues, "it is because of these selfless qualities that I appoint you as my rank-two consort."

I hear Suyin cry out in excitement just before all the men erupt in cheers and clapping. But I cannot have heard him right. Rank two? That's impossible.

"Do my words not please you, my lady?" the emperor asks.

"No," I say, "it's not that. Of course I am glad. Only surprised. I thought...I thought the rank-two position was reserved for the concubine who gave you a son. I...I am not even with child...I don't think. Much less a son."

"How humble she is," the emperor says, and the men chuckle again. "That is normally the case. However, extraordinary bravery deserves extraordinary honors. Never before has a concubine saved the life of an empress before. I can think of no better way to show my gratitude."

I can't believe it. Rank two! The only women in the palace who would rank higher than me would be empress and the dowager. How...how did this happen to me? Me! The barefoot Chinese girl from the streets is now the third most powerful woman in the kingdom. I... I...

"She is speechless," a voice says, and I recognize it as Honghui's. I close my eyes, not daring to look at him.

I lose my balance, falling off my shoes and onto my knees. Suyin rushes forward, but I bend forward, putting my forehead to the ground in a full kowtow as if that was my intent.

"His majesty honors his worthless slave!" I say. "I am not worthy."

"You are worthy," he says, "because I deem it to be so."

The men clap and cheer again, and Suyin tugs my arm so that I sit up. I let my eyes drift up to the emperor and he is smiling wider than I ever saw before. I feel a fluttering in my belly. Is this really happening to me? Do I dare believe it? Do I dare let it make me happy? The emperor has no suspicions of me, that much is clear. I am safe.

The emperor claps his hands and several eunuchs rush forth carrying large trunks. They place them around me, opening each one. They are full of silks, jewels, furs, porcelain cups, bowls, and vases, and so much more. The last one opened, the one placed right in front of me, is filled to the top with gold ingots, and my eyes swim. I never imagined in my life that I would see such wealth—or that it would be given to me!

"His majesty is too...too generous," I say as I begin to cry. Suyin wraps an arm around me and blots a handkerchief to my cheeks as the men make sounds as if appreciating an adorable child.

"No, not too generous," the emperor says. "Rightly generous. You will be moved to the Palace of Earthly Honor and given dozens more servants. Every morning, the ladies of the harem will greet you and pay you honor. And while the empress is in her confinement, the management of the harem will be your realm."

This stops my tears and reawakens my concerns. The other ladies are surely not going to be happy about this.

"I feel I am unequal to the task," I say. "I cannot read. I can barely do numbers. How can I possibly perform such a role?"

"Worry not," the emperor says with a wave of his hand. "You will learn all you need to know. I will hire you the best tutors. Empress Caihong will tell you everything you need to know. And my gracious mother, the dowager empress, will guide you while the empress is indisposed."

For the first time, I realize that the dowager has been standing behind and to the side of the emperor the whole time. She is perhaps the only person in the room who is not smiling. She does not look angry, merely unimpressed, I suppose. As she should be. She cannot think that I am worthy of the position the emperor has granted to me, and I agree! I will have to do my best to let her know that I did not want this. It was never my intention to rise so high. But now that I have, I certainly cannot refuse. The emperor would only take it as a grave insult. So once again, I bend over in a kowtow.

"May my gracious mother live ten thousand years!" I say.

The emperor laughs. "Wonderful! Rise, Lihua. I pray that the rest of your days see nothing but joy and contentment."

Suyin helps me to my feet and I give the emperor another bow. "Thank you, your majesty." Suyin guides me as I bow my way out of the audience hall. As soon as I am outside, I pull away from her and vomit into a nearby planter.

"My lady! Are you ill?" she asks. I shake my head.

"No. Only terrified."

"Of what?" she asks. "The emperor loves you. You are the most honored among women! The Palace of Earthly Honor is a beautiful home. You are sure to love it."

I see the eunuchs who carried the trunks into the audience hall now carrying them out, and I have to assume they are being taken to my new palace.

"Suyin," I say close to her ear. "The other concubines, they will be furious. I cannot imagine they will willingly accept me as their superior."

"But they must," she says plainly. "The emperor has appointed you as rank-two consort. They must all bow to you or face the consequences."

At the mention of consequences, my stomach clenches. "Please don't seek to get anyone in trouble on my behalf. I don't want to make enemies."

A terrible thought troubles my mind. I truly believe that Lady An was innocent and did not pay her eunuch to kill the empress. In that case, the true murderer is still out there. Is he—or she—among the members of the harem? What if the killer comes for me next? Lady An had been the only rank-three consort, and now I am the only rank-two. Am I in danger?

"Jinhai," I say, and he is instantly by my side. "How many eunuch servants will I be entitled to now?"

"At least twelve," he says. "Possibly more. It has been a long time since there was a rank-two consort. I will confer with the department of household affairs."

"And how many of them will be guards?"

"Guards, my lady?"

"Yes. How many will be there solely for my protection?"

"Umm..." He shares a glance with Suyin, and I am sure they think I am being paranoid. And maybe I am. But I don't care. I can't risk being unprotected while a killer lurks the inner court.

"There will always be someone patrolling the palace, day and night for your safety."

"The empress has patrols," I say. "The whole Forbidden City has patrols. Yet that eunuch was still able to slip into the empress's bed-chamber unmolested." Jinhai blushes at this. I know that many of the guards and patrols have been punished for various offenses since that night.

"I want guards," I go on. "Real guards, with weapons. At least for a while. I'll pay extra if I must."

"Yes, my lady," he says. "I will see it done."

"Immediately," I say. "I'll not be able to sleep a wink until I know the palace is secure."

"Yes, my lady," he says, and he bows away from me before running off.

"You will be safe, my lady," Suyin says. "No one would dare harm someone so loved by the emperor."

I start to argue, but then I remember that Lady An was *not* loved by the emperor. She did not have the benefit of his protection as I do. Perhaps I am being silly and the guards are completely unnecessary. Maybe in time, I will truly believe that. But for now, I will take no chances.

The doors to the audience hall open and the men begin filing out. Suyin helps me climb into the sedan chair and closes the flap behind me. As the chair bearers lift me up, though, the flap flies open for a moment and I catch sight of Prince Honghui. Our eyes meet and for once, he does not have the confident smile he usually wears.

I close the flap and the chair is carried away quickly. The prince is the very last person I should be thinking of right now. I cannot risk what I have only just gained.

27

I haven't slept since the emperor "honored" me with the promotion to second-rank consort. I was not taken back to attend the empress, but to my new palace so I could get settled in. The palace is nearly as large as the empress's in size and grandeur. There are at least ten rooms, not including storerooms. There is a large bed-chamber with a huge kang-style bed nearly as large as the emperor's. There is also another, smaller bedroom with half a dozen individual beds for the servants. They don't have beds of their own, but sleep in shifts so that there is always someone to attend me. There is a separate room to store my clothes and jewels, and another room to dress in and have my hair styled. A washroom has a copper tub set up at all times. There is also a private kitchen where all my food will now be prepared. The palace reminds me a lot of Mingxia's house in its design. The wide main doors open up into a private courtyard garden and pond, and the rooms are all arranged around the courtyard. It's beautiful, peaceful, and I have to admit that if I were Manchu, if I had wanted to become the emperor's favorite, I should feel joyful indeed.

But I don't. Instead, I am afraid. Afraid for my safety. Afraid of being caught. Afraid of failing in my new duties that I don't even understand. I am constantly watched now. There are guards posted outside my palace doors and two more who patrol around it at all hours. I have at least a dozen eunuch servants and a dozen maids. I haven't seen all of them at one time to count them properly. I've hardly learned any of their names. But I've been told that someone will always be awake and alert to attend me, even while I sleep.

But even now, in the middle of the night, I'm not sleeping. In the morning, I am to host my first audience as head of the harem in the empress's absence. And I am dreading it. What will everyone think? What will they say? Will they even bow to me? Surely none of them will believe that I am worthy of such respect. Even *I* don't think I'm worthy of such respect. I *know* I'm not worthy of it. I'm not Manchu! I'm not the daughter of a great general and a fine lady. Everything about me is fake and a lie. I shouldn't even be here!

I climb out of bed and a maid is immediately by my side with a candle.

"Are you all right, my lady? Do you need to pass water? Shall I prepare your bowl?"

"No," I say, holding up my hand to shield my eyes from the light. "I can't sleep. I thought I might walk in the courtyard."

"Yes, my lady," she says, dropping to her knees and putting my slippers on my feet. She offers me her hand to help me stand, then another maid rushes over with a fur-lined cape. I hadn't even seen her before. The constant attention is unnerving and makes me feel helpless, but there is nothing I can do about it.

Eunuchs open the door to my bedroom for me, and then the doors that lead to the courtyard. I step out into the cool, crisp air. It's late autumn now, so the nights are cold and I can see my breath in front of me. It doesn't bother me, but I see the maid beside me shiver.

"You don't need to come with me," I tell her.

"But I do, my lady," she says, and I give a small nod. Of course she does.

"Then, hang back at the very least," I say. "I'd like to be alone."

She bows, chewing her lower lip. I know she won't be more than a few paces back, but as long as I can't see her I can at least pretend she isn't there. It isn't completely dark out. There is the moon, of course, but the Forbidden City simply isn't *dark* the way my old hutong was. There are lanterns outside every palace, and guards patrol with lanterns. Even here in the courtyard, there are lanterns layered with thick silk so that there is at least a soft glow in every corner.

I walk around the pond and see ripples in the black water where the koi dart about. I pass by a window cut into the concrete wall that surrounds my palace and stop. The little hairs on the back of my neck and arms ripple down my skin. I look through the window, but see nothing. And yet...I know someone is there. I step closer and peer through, squinting in the dark. Across a wide walkway, there is a garden. I can see a few small green bushes, but not much else. But...there, next to one of the bushes is a shadow that... doesn't quite fit. I focus my vision, trying to see...

I yelp when a guard walks by, scaring me half to death. The maid is instantly by my side.

"Are you all right?" she asks.

"Yes, of course," I say, my hand on my chest to soothe my

racing heart. I glance back through the window, but I don't see anything out of the ordinary. I let the maid lead me back to my bed-chamber, even though I am no more likely to sleep now than before. But no point in making her wait out in the cold for me.

Back in my bedroom, the eunuchs close the doors behind me. The maid moves to the bed to tuck me in, and I reluctantly climb in. I lay with my eyes open, staring out into the room, and my thoughts drift to Prince Honghui. Could he have been the shadow I saw outside? Was he hoping I would meet him? That would be impossible now, considering how closely I am watched. I'll probably never be able to speak to him privately again. And certainly never touch. Never kiss. Never...

I have to wipe a tear from my cheek. I had already lost so much when I came to the Forbidden City. Everything. The one thing I had claimed for myself, my relationship with the prince, has now been taken from me as well.

I am surrounded by people in my new palace. But I am completely alone.

~

I am shaking so badly as I am carried in a sedan chair to audiences the next day, you would think I had caught a deadly chill. But I am nervous. Terrified! Since my appointment, the dowager has never paid me a visit as I expected her to. I thought she would want to begin my training right away. Instruct me in exactly how I am supposed to manage a harem of dozens of ladies—all of whom must hate me.

When the chair stops, I nearly vomit as my stomach clenches. Thankfully, the sensation passes by the time

Suyin offers her hand to help me from the chair. I look at the ground so that I can't see if anyone is watching me. But when I enter the audience hall, what sounded like a swarm of bees instantly quiets. I can feel hundreds of eyes on me as Suyin leads me to my... I want to say chair, but it is not a chair. It is a throne. I can't believe I am about to sit on a throne.

My throat is completely parched, and when I open my mouth, no sound comes out. Which ends up being for the best because it is then that the dowager enters the room and stands next to me in front of her throne, which is set just as high as mine on the dais. I had thought it was lower and slightly behind the empress's throne before, but perhaps I had been mistaken.

The dowager sits without a word, and I follow suit. Everyone is silent, waiting for me to address them. I try to remember what it was that the empress said to us every morning, but my mind goes blank. I look to Suyin, and she mouths something to me, but I can't understand her. I look out over the crowd of ladies and hear whispers from somewhere, and then giggling.

"Good morning, ladies," the dowager finally says, and all the ladies drop to their knees.

"Good morning, Empress Mother," they all say at once, and then they wave their handkerchiefs over their shoulders. Then they look to me.

"Good morning, Consort Lihua," they say, but it is not in unison, and not nearly as loud as their greeting for the dowager. Then, only some of them wave their handkerchiefs at me. I'm completely mortified and wish I would die.

"How dare you snakes show such impertinence!" the dowager snaps, and gasps ripple through the gathered ladies. "Is this how you show respect to your superiors? I should have each one of you whipped!"

All of the ladies cry out and bend over with their heads to the floor in full kowtows, muttering their apologies.

"Do it again," the dowager orders.

"Yes, Mother," they all say as they sit back up. They turn to me and, this time loudly and in unison, they greet me.

"Good morning, Consort Lihua." All of their handkerchiefs are waved at me three times.

"Good morning, ladies," I manage to say. "Please, sit." When they are all in their chairs and quiet again, I am once again at a loss for what to say. I look at the dowager from the corner of my eye.

"Since Lady An's betrayal, there are going to be a lot of changes around here," the dowager says. "Empress Caihong has been too lax, allowing all of you to show disrespect, slack in your duties, and spend money frivolously. All of that will change."

"Yes, Mother," everyone says, including me. Fenfang shoots me a glance, and I realize I should not have spoken.

"All positions within the harem will be reassigned," the dowager continues. "And a new set of rules will be issued shortly. I expect all of you to comply with whatever Consort Lihua tells you to do." I stiffen. Are the assignments and rules supposed to come from me? "Remember, it is the first and foremost duty of the harem to bring honor to the emperor and dignity to his house. Do you understand?"

"Yes, Mother," everyone says, except me this time.

The dowager stands, and I follow suit. The girls all fall to their knees again.

"You are dismissed," she says.

"Thank you, Mother. Thank you, Consort Lihua," they say. Then, row by row starting in the back, the ladies leave the audience room. Soon, only the dowager and I and our maids remain. I turn to the dowager and give a respectful bow. "Thank you for the assistance, Mother," I say. "I am completely at a loss as to what to do."

"That much is apparent," she says, somehow looking down her nose at me even though we are nearly the same height. "Your actions earned you your place, but it is clear that this is a task you are not equipped to handle."

"I agree," I say. "I never asked for this."

The dowager stares at me for a long moment. I am sure I misspoke. What Manchu girl wouldn't wish to be where I am now? But I can't take back what I said now. I will have to be more careful about what I say in the future, even more careful than I have been.

Finally, a slow grin spreads across the dowager's lips. It is a small grin, barely perceptible, but a grin nonetheless.

"Do not worry, child," she says. "I will take care of everything."

I nearly cry with relief. "Thank you! Thank you so much!"

"I will call on you later today and make sure you have everything you need."

"Of course," I say, bowing again. "Thank you again."

The dowager leaves the room and I let out a long breath I was holding. "I thought for sure she would hate me as she does Caihong," I say to Suyin.

"She doesn't hate you," Suyin says. "You are not a threat to her position."

"What?" I ask, confused.

"You know she's not supposed to be here at all," she says. "She's not the head of the harem—you are."

"But...but you know I can't do this," I say. "If the dowager wants to take the lead, why should I not let her?"

"You *can* do this," Suyin says, holding both of my hands in hers. "Caihong was fifteen when she became empress. You are three years older than that now, and you've been living here for months. If she could lead the harem, then so can you."

"But she was a princess," I say. "She was raised to be an empress."

"Fenfeng wasn't," Nuwa says. "She was selected among Manchu ladies just as you were. She was thirteen when she became a concubine. A rank six, just like you were. But she gave birth to the emperor's son, the current emperor. That's the only reason she is dowager now. She wasn't trained for it. She didn't earn it by saving an empress's life. She wasn't elevated because the emperor loved her. She lucked into it by falling pregnant."

The other maids all nod and murmur in agreement. *But I'm not Manchu*, I want to say, but I can't. If I had been born Manchu, I would have at least known that life in the palace was a possibility for me. I shake my head.

"You just don't understand," is all I can say.

Suyin gives me a smile and pats my hand. "Everything will be all right. You'll see."

All I can do is smile back, even though in my heart I know she's wrong.

28

"This one says, 'a new era of happiness is sure to never end'," Jingfei, Empress Caihong's daughter, says as she points to a square on the quilt we are sewing together.

"Does it?" I ask. "You are quite clever."

"I can't believe you can't read," the little girl says, and I just shake my head and smile.

"I never imagined I would become an imperial concubine," I say. "I should have prepared better."

"I'm going to marry a prince, you know," she says. "Maybe in Mongolia. Then I can ride horses!"

She then prattles on about horses while I continue to work, Suyin and Nuwa along with me, and also Dongmei, Lady An's daughter. The girls are only a year and a half apart in age, but they could not be more different in disposition.

Jingfei is loud and outgoing. She runs everywhere and laughs with ease. She has round cheeks and a short nose like her father, but her eyes and skin coloring she gets from her mother.

Dongmei is quiet and reserved. She's willowy with long arms and legs and an equally long face and nose. While Jingfei is pretty, I'd say Dongmei has a more classic beauty, like a girl from a painting.

I've been inviting the girls to work with me every day for an hour or two in the afternoons on a "One Hundred Blessings Quilt," a gift for Caihong's son made up of one hundred squares embroidered with good wishes from loved ones. The squares were donated by the wives of important officials of the emperor's court, the dowager empress, and a few ladies of the inner court. It's a lot of work, but it will be beautiful in the end. I only hope we complete it before the baby comes...and that the baby is a boy.

Everyone is confident that this child will be the much-needed heir...but I have my doubts. I don't give voice to them because it might seem as though I am cursing the child to be a girl. And I don't need anyone looking at me more critically than they already are. But there is no way to know if a child will be a boy before it is born, and no way to force such an outcome. Oh, there are old sayings and superstitions, of course, about how to conceive a son, but I don't think they really work. Otherwise every family would have a son. In my mind, there is just as much a chance that the child will be a girl as a boy. But I hold my tongue.

I rarely leave my palace except for the morning greetings, but when I do, I am mostly ignored by the other ladies. They see me, but they will walk the other way and talk about me behind their fans. They don't try to hide it. Suyin and Jinhai have offered to find out what is being said, but I would rather not know. It can be nothing kind, I'm sure.

I have tried to befriend the other ladies, sending gifts of painting supplies or hair ornaments when I can. I have not asked any of them to donate to poor relief like I had wanted. I have even invited Yanmei and Wangli to visit me, but they have politely declined every time. So, I have contented myself with spending time with the little princesses. They are so very clever for their ages, and I suppose that comes with the fine education they must be receiving. They remind me of my sisters. And while my heart is still pained that we cannot be together, having the princesses around me soothes the pain a bit.

A kitchen maid appears with a tray of sweet treats and tea. Jingfei doesn't bother asking for permission before jumping up and running over for a snack, nearly toppling her sewing basket in the process, but Suyin catches it. Dongmei watches her sister, but then continues her work.

"You may have some," I tell her.

"No, thank you," she says, keeping her head down, but I think I see her fingers shaking. I nod to Suyin and Nuwa that they may take a break, so they leave me alone with the little girl.

"Is something the matter?" I ask her quietly.

"No," she says, but it is nearly a whisper, and then I see little tears slip down her cheeks. I put my hand on the square she is working on to stop her, then I put an arm around her shoulder.

"You can tell me the truth," I tell her.

She is quiet for a long minute, staring at my hand, her needle poised. "My mother is dead."

My mouth gapes as I struggle for words. It has been weeks since Lady An killed herself. Did Dongmei not know until now?

"Who told you?" I ask.

"I heard the maids talking," she says, wiping the tears from her eyes after dropping her needle into her basket.

"They said she tried to kill the empress and was put to death. Is it true?"

"When did you hear this?" I ask.

"A few days ago," she replies. "They...they had told me Mama was sick, and that was why she hadn't come to see me for so long. I didn't...didn't know she was...was..."

I wrap my arms around her and hold her close as she bursts into tears I am sure she's been holding onto for days. The poor darling must have been in shock at the news.

I have not used my authority in the harem even once. I don't conduct morning greetings, I don't manage spats or arguments, and I have not issued any punishments, not even for the smallest infraction.

But I think I must now. Dongmei's servants should not have been gossiping about Lady An, and certainly not within earshot of the princess.

"Is it true?" Dongmei whispers as she sniffles.

"Your Mama has died," I say. "But she did not try to kill the empress, I am sure of it."

"Then why is she dead?" Dongmei asks, looking up at me.

I run my hand over her hair, smoothing where it has come out of its pins. "It's very complicated, darling. Some people think she wanted the empress dead, but I don't believe it. I think—I *know*—she was innocent."

She shakes her head, laying it on my shoulder. "I don't understand."

"I know," I say, rocking her. "When you are older, I will tell you everything. But don't believe anything the maids say. They are only spreading hateful gossip. I will make sure they stop."

"Okay," she says, still sniffling. "Where is Baba? He hasn't come to see me in a long time either. Is he dead too?"

"No! No, he's fine. He's just been very busy, I'm sure. He will see you soon, I promise."

Dongmei looks at me, her eyes glassy, and I can tell she doesn't believe me, but she nods and leans against me again. We sit together for a long time and my heart aches for Lady An, that she will never be able to hold her daughter again. I miss my mother so much, but I was already at marrying age when I left. I can't imagine how hurt and lonely Dongmei must feel. I hardly feel up to the task, but I know I must do my best to be the mother she so desperately needs.

"The empress dowager approaches!" a eunuch announces just before the dowager enters my courtyard. We all rush over to her, the servants getting on their knees while the princesses and I just bow.

"Welcome, Mother," I say.

"Ah, the girls are here," she says.

"Yes," I say, standing upright. "They have been helping me sew a blanket for their little brother. It is coming along nicely."

"Hmm," she says, and then looks to her own maids. "Escort the girls to their palaces." The maids bob and then try to take hold of the girls' arms and lead them away.

"I don't want to go!" Jingfei protests, digging her heels in, and I see tears rush to Dongmei's eyes.

"Wait!" I say. "Why should they leave?"

"Are you standing in the way of their education?" Fenfang asks me.

"No!" I say. "Of course not. But I was under the impression that their lessons were in the mornings, so I saw no harm in having them spend their afternoons with me."

The dowager cocks her head and the maids pull the little girls away more forcefully. "That is when they have their academic lessons. But their entire life is an education. An education preparing them to become fine ladies. Do you think you are up to such a task? Can you truly teach the girls how the daughters of an emperor should comport themselves?"

Of course I'm not, but I don't want to admit that. But neither can I say yes. I know nothing of raising imperial children.

"With Lady An...gone and the empress confined, the girls need a mother, or an elder sister at least," I say. "They are lonely."

"Lonely?" Fenfang barks a laugh. "They are surrounded by maids and tutors. How can they possibly be lonely?"

"You think a maid is an acceptable replacement for a mother?" I ask. "You would have the children raised by *servants* instead of wives of the emperor?"

The courtyard had been quiet before—no one would dare speak without permission in the dowager's presence—but now, it is so silent not even the crickets make a sound. The dowager's jaw is set tight, but I stand firm. Normally I would cower before her, but seeing the girls dragged away stirs anger in me. I made a promise to Lady An to protect her daughter, and I will hold to that.

The dowager's face softens and she smiles, but I think it is the way a fox would smile at a chicken when it knows the chicken cannot escape.

"You are so very new to life here," she says. "I will forgive you for speaking out of turn this time. But in the future, I would encourage you to remember your place."

I don't know how to respond, which gives her time to turn and leave, the girls dragged away behind her.

"Lihua!" Dongmei calls out, and I feel a sharp pain in my chest.

"I'll see you tomorrow, darling!" I call out to her, trying to pretend that nothing is the matter. But as soon as the girls are out of sight, tears of my own sting my eyes. Suyin comes to my side and tries to comfort me.

"What did I do wrong?" I ask her. "Why did the dowager take them away?"

Nuwa answers. "You've given complete control of the harem to the dowager, and that includes the princesses. I think that she doesn't like the idea of you influencing them, even if you meant no harm."

"What can I do?" I ask.

"You have to take your rightful place as senior lady of the harem," Nuwa says. "You need to lead the morning greetings. You must mediate disputes. You need to visit the other ladies in their palaces and insist that they come here when you summon them. It is unacceptable that they ignore your calls."

My bladder clenches at the thought and I suddenly have to pee. "I don't know. I wouldn't know how to begin! I don't have any idea what I'm doing."

"We will help you," Suyin says, then she looks to Nuwa. "But she needs allies, don't you think? If Lihua simply starts making demands, the other ladies will ignore her and follow the instructions of the dowager. They know where the real power lies."

Nuwa sighs. "Perhaps. What should we do?"

Suyin looks at me. "You should speak to the emperor. Tell him that you are ready for more responsibility. Ask that he speak to his mother about being *your* assistant."

"Are you sure I should speak to him about harem matters?" I ask. "Will he not think it is beneath him?"

"Perhaps," Nuwa says. "But he will defer to *you*. He will tell *you* to do as you wish, and that should be enough. He tries to get involved in harem matters as little as possible, but he understands the hierarchy. He knows you are second only to the empress and should be making all the major decisions. He will support you, I am sure of it."

I nod. "I will speak to him the next time I am summoned." I feel a bit more hopeful at this. In truth, I don't want to take all authority from the dowager. I don't *want* to be the head of the harem. I only want to watch over the princesses. If she gave me that much, I would be content.

"I do have an idea," I say, and I wave Jinhai over to me. "Dongmei said that she heard some maids gossiping about her mother. It was how she found out her mother had died. I want the maids found and demoted."

"You should have them dismissed," Nuwa says.

"No," I say. "I know that many of the maids support their families, so I don't want them dismissed completely. But I don't want them serving the princesses, either of them. Tell the ministry of household affairs they are to be given the lowest positions. The scullery or chamber pots."

"I will see it done, my lady," Jinhai says. "It might take a few days...and a few bribes to find out which maids it was. The princesses have more servants than you do."

"You manage my income so do what you must."

Jinhai bows and then rushes off to do his work. I've made him my chief eunuch, and as far as I know he has managed the position well.

"That is a good start, my lady," Nuwa says. "But may I make another suggestion?" I nod. "Hire tutors of your own, not merely eunuchs, but proper teachers."

"You don't think Jinhai is doing a good job?" I ask, concerned.

"For a rank-six concubine, he was more than adequate.

For a rank-two consort..." She shakes her head. "You must be able to read and do basic math in your position. You cannot learn those things studying only occasionally when both you and Jinhai have time."

"He has been so very busy lately," Suyin says, and I nod in agreement.

"You should prioritize your education as much as possible," Nuwa says. "Hire a tutor and have lessons every day."

"I think this is a good idea. Please find me someone as soon as possible. I wouldn't have any idea how to find a tutor."

"Of course, my lady," she says.

My heart feels a bit lighter. I am nervous about having to stand up to the dowager, but I think I might be on the path to making things right.

29

"How are things in the harem?" the emperor asks me that evening as we lie in bed together. His arm is around my shoulders and my head is on his chest. I fuss with the edge of his robe as I consider my answer. He doesn't really want to know how things are. He only wants to hear that everything is well.

"Things are well, your majesty," I say.

"Are you becoming accustomed to the way things are done?"

"Slowly," I say.

"That is good. Mother has been pleased with you."

"Has she?" I ask, wondering just what the dowager has been telling the emperor about me.

"She says you are a kind and tolerant mistress, as I knew you would be."

I press my lips to keep from responding. Of course she would say that. I have tolerated allowing her to run the harem however she wishes. I'm no threat to her power the way Empress Caihong was—and will be again once she is free of her birthing bed.

I hadn't considered what will happen once Caihong is no longer confined. She will surely want to put Fenfang back in her place. But will she be able to? Once authority is given, is it easily taken away?

"The empress is mere weeks away from giving birth to my son," the emperor says with a contented sigh. "Then all will be as it should be."

"We are all eagerly awaiting news of the prince's birth," I say. I open my mouth to mention the princesses, but stop myself. I'm not sure how to broach the subject. I do not wish to imply that he is neglecting his children...but that is exactly what he is doing.

"Something seems to be on your mind," he says, and I realize I am doing a poor job of pretending everything is perfect. I sit up in bed so that I can see his face, better gauge his reaction.

"I have been spending more time with the princesses," I say, "Jingfei and Dongmei. They are the smartest, sweetest girls I have ever known."

The emperor is not smiling. He rolls away, getting out of the bed on the other side. Already, I feel the anger coming off of him and I say no more. I'm not sure why he should be so angry at the mere mention of his daughters.

"And this...disturbs you?" he prods.

"No, of course not," I say.

"Then why did you bring it up?" he asks. "Did you think I would be proud of you? Pleased? The girls fall under your preview as head of the harem while Caihong is indisposed."

I feel as though I am walking into a trap. I remain sitting, my hands folded in my lap. I tug the edges of my robe closer together, feeling exposed. Vulnerable.

"Speak!" the emperor orders.

"They miss you," I mumble.

"What? Speak clearly!"

"They miss you," I say, looking right at him. "Your daughters love you, but they are very alone right now. Caihong cannot see them for more than a few minutes each day. And Lady An is—"

"Don't mention that woman to me again!" he yells.

"I am sorry for offending you," I say. "I don't mean to mention her. But Dongmei is greatly distraught. She has heard the servants gossiping—"

"Then punish them," he says.

"I have, your majesty," I say. "Or, I will, as soon as I learn which ones it was."

"These are harem issues," he says, turning from me and pouring himself a cup of wine. I take the opportunity to stand. Having him tower over me in such a way has made me uncomfortable. "Why bring them up to me?"

"As I said, the girls miss you," I say. "They know you are busy, but Dongmei is especially—"

"Her mother was a whore and a traitor!" The emperor turns back toward me and throws his cup against the wall, wine splashing on the floor. I suppose the outburst has it's desired effect as I say no more. But this seems to enrage him more. It is as if he *wants* to fight with me.

"Dongmei is fortunate be allowed to stay in the palace at all," the emperor goes on. "I should disown her. Send her away. She is sure to bring bad luck upon this house."

I'm so disgusted by his words, I cannot stay silent. "She is an innocent child. Your daughter."

"Is she?" he asks, his face dark. "That woman betrayed me, was a murderer. She was cunning, that one. How do I know that Dongmei is really my daughter? I only slept with the woman once. She could have had a lover, had another man do the deed to ensure her place."

"You don't really believe that," I say. "Dongmei looks like you. She has your eyes."

The emperor waves me off. "That proves nothing."

I want to protest, but then I remember the night I spent with Honghui, his own brother, and my cheeks go hot. I did not fall pregnant, for that was months ago, but still, the guilt gnaws at me. Lady An was not unfaithful, but I was.

"You spoke to her," he says, interrupting my thoughts. "You spoke to her only minutes before she killed herself, didn't you?" I stand stone still, not even nodding my head. "Caihong told me what you said, what the woman told you. She told you she was guilty, did she not?"

My eyes water as I remember Lady An at that moment. She knew that she could not be saved. Her only thoughts were for her daughter, dear Dongmei. *Protect my daughter*, she said, and I promised. I rush to the emperor and drop to my knees, knocking my forehead to the floor.

"Please do not punish Dongmei for her mother's sins," I say. "She is a child. A child! Please, please, my lord, do not forsake her. She loves you."

"Get up!" he growls. "Groveling does not become a woman of your station." I sit up on my heels, keeping my eyes low.

"The care of Jingfei falls to you," he says, "until her mother is out of confinement. But as for Dongmei..." He shakes his head. "I cannot bear to look at her. And I don't want her poisoning Jingfei's thoughts about me."

"She would never—"

"Dongmei must be sent away," he says.

"No—" I start, but the emperor interrupts me.

"She must! Her mother was like poison in a well, infecting every person it touches. Dongmei carries her mother's hate, her malice. She cannot stay here."

"No. Your majesty, please!" My heart races frantically. "Please don't separate the sisters from one another."

"I cannot use her in a marriage alliance now," he says. "No family would accept a girl with such a notorious mother. I'll send her to Kaifu Temple to be raised."

"She cannot be a nun," I say. "She's a child. A maid. Only widows become nuns."

"Then perhaps I will banish her altogether!" the emperor yells, stomping toward me. I fall backward and he stands over me, panting with anger, his eyes full of hate...or is that hurt? I can't tell the difference. "Throw her out into the street and let her find her own way."

I don't know where this is coming from. How any man—but especially an emperor—can speak so cruelly of his own child. He cannot mean it. He must know what would happen to her if she were abandoned. But...he cannot mean it. I want to fight back. Yell and scream for Dongmei. Force him to see just how terrible he is being. But something holds me back. I would like to think it is common sense, but it could also be cowardice. Either way, I know I cannot continue the way I am. If I continue to fight him, he will only become more determined to send her away.

"I am sorry for mentioning the troubles of the harem to you," I say, getting back to my knees. "It won't happen again. Dongmei's fate should be left to the empress, as befitting her station."

The emperor is silent. I cannot see his face, but the tension between us lessens.

"I am a stupid girl, one who cannot comprehend the complexities of an imperial family. You have blessed me with responsibility far beyond my understanding. I...I await your punishment." I did not want to add that last part. I don't want to be punished! But it is something I have heard the servants say many times to irate mistresses. It is meant to show the ultimate humility, and something I need to demonstrate now.

The emperor is quiet for so long, my knees start to ache, but I dare not move. Finally, he speaks.

"Leave me," he says. My eyes shoot up to him. He's never dismissed me in such a way before. The first few times I was brought to him, I was carried in naked, and when he was finished, I was taken away in a sedan chair. But the last time that happened was months ago. Now, on nights I go to him, I stay the whole night. To be ordered away so callously is a great insult. But not only that, he has not given his decision regarding Dongmei. I can't let him send her away, but I do not know what else I can do.

"Go," he says again. "I am tired. You have no idea the weights upon my mind. What it means to rule an empire and then have to deal with the petty squabbles of home life."

I do not think that Dongmei's future is a petty issue, but I cannot say so. I rise to my feet and bow, but I do not leave, not just yet. I have to hold out hope that he will give me some reassurance that Dongmei will not be sent away.

"I think that you are not ready to deal with such weighty issues within the harem," he says. "Perhaps I did promote you too quickly. From now on, any major issues should be put on hold until Caihong is out of her confinement. If there is an emergency, it should go to the dowager. Do you understand?"

"Yes, your majesty," I say. At least, I hope I do. I think he is saying that a decision about Dongmei's future shall be put before the empress later. For now, Dongmei is safe. I think that this is for the best. I know that Caihong loves Dongmei as her own child and would never send her away.

After all, all children of the harem are *her* children. To treat them as anything less would be dishonorable on her part.

I stand still, waiting to see if he changes his mind about dismissing me. I hope I have not damaged our relationship. I don't love him, but I need him. I need his goodwill, his protection.

"Go," he says, and my eyes water as I back away from him.

"Yes, your majesty," I whisper. He was not unkind. In fact, he only sounded tired. Still, his dismissal stings. And the way he yelled at me, threw his cup, towered over me...I have never felt so afraid of him.

When I am finally out of the room, the sedan chair is waiting for me. Suyin rushes over, rubbing her eyes as she helps me inside. She had probably fallen asleep in another room, thinking that I would spend the night with the emperor as I usually do.

"My lady?" she asks, realizing that something is wrong. But I say nothing as I climb into the chair. She is going to be disappointed when she finds out that I did not gain the emperor's support to run the harem. Quite the opposite happened. All decisions are to be postponed or put before the dowager. I am now even more powerless than I was before.

It could have gone much worse. He could have demoted me. Could have punished me. Could have done any number of things, but he did not. For that, I suppose I should be grateful. I have to hope that his anger toward me will quickly cool. I try to reflect on what I said, what could have made him so angry. I suppose it was the mere mention of Dongmei, for I can think of nothing else. He grew irritated at the very mention of his children. Why? I cannot fathom it.

These thoughts are still swirling around in my head as we reach my palace and Suyin helps me out of the chair.

"My lady! Lady Lihua!" I look and see a maid from Empress Caihong's palace running toward me.

"Yes?" I ask. I look up and see that the moon is high in the sky. It is very late.

"You must come at once! The empress's labor pains have started!"

30

———

"It's too early!" Suyin says, but I can hardly hear her as the blood thumps in my ears.

"Call the physician!" I say as I run toward the empress's palace.

"My lady!" Suyin calls, but I do not stop. I can run far faster than any chair can carry me, and the empress needs me, now!

When I reach her palace, it is lit up bright as day, surrounded by bright lanterns. A dozen servants are sitting outside on their knees, their hands folded together as they pray. I step around them and enter the palace, the place in a flurry of activity. Maids rush about carrying bowls of water and clean linens. Eunuchs carry buckets of coal to the various braziers to keep the palace warm and well-lit. My heart seizes as I hear the empress cry out in pain.

I push my way into the room. The empress, lying on her bed, turns her head to me as tears fall down her cheeks. I rush to her side, pushing the maid who was mopping her brow out of my way as I take the empress's hand.

"You...you told me..." the empress starts to say, but she cries out with another birth pang.

"Don't try to speak," I tell her. I toss her quilt aside and a maid screams. There's so much blood. I remember the night my mother nearly died and shake myself from my stupor. If my mother lived, so can the empress.

"My...my baby!" the empress cries. "My boy!"

"Shh," I say as I take over with the rag, dabbing cold water on her forehead. "You'll be fine. The baby will be fine."

"You...said that...that she confessed," the empress says with wide, terrified eyes, gripping my wrist. I open my mouth to confirm what I had said, but it's too late. I know the truth is showing on my face. The empress looks away from me and cries out as another pain grips her, her short hair sticking to her cheeks.

"Where's the physician?" I yell.

"He's been sent for, my lady," someone answers.

"The midwife?" I ask. Before anyone can answer, the doors to the room swing wide open and everyone drops to their knees.

"What are you—" I am about to ask how they can just abandon their empress, but then I see that the dowager has entered the room. I don't care. I look back to the empress, trying to keep her calm.

"It's all right," I tell Caihong.

In a moment, the dowager is at my side, standing over the empress. "What have you done?" she demands.

"Nothing!" the empress cries. "I did nothing!"

"You worthless—" She raises a hand to strike the empress, but I jump to my feet, grabbing the dowager's arm. Her eyes go wide in shock. "You dare—"

"Get out!" I tell her, releasing her arm. "The empress needs to focus on giving birth. Get out!"

The dowager seems to have forgotten all about Caihong as her gaze narrows at me. "You will regret this," she says through gritted teeth.

I know I will, but I do not stand down. The empress can't handle any more stress if she is to have any hope of surviving. The dowager and I continue to stare at one another, but then I turn away from her and sit back at the empress's side. I think the dowager originally thought to cower me with her glare, but the fact that I simply ignore her instead of appearing frightened does not have the intended effect. Instead of her appearing superior to me, I insulted her. The fact that I don't seem to care only adds salt to the wound. Still, I ignore her. Ignore the scared faces of the maids. Ignore the whispers that dance around the room.

Finally, the dowager turns away, her robes swishing by me, and she stomps from the room. I've now managed to anger the emperor and the dowager both in one night. I am sure I will pay for it later. The empress squeezes my hand and I look down at her.

"Thank you," she says, and I nod. If the empress lives, she will surely protect me from the dowager's wrath. But should she die...

The midwife arrives then, and I make way for her. It is custom for a royal birth to be attended by a doctor and a midwife. As women, we know a doctor is unnecessary, but the emperor insists.

The midwife feels the empress's belly, but her face gives nothing away. She then moves to the empress's feet, lifting her nightgown and looking between her legs. She is not at all bothered by having to sit on the blood-soaked bedding.

"My lady," the midwife says to the empress, "the child

has decided to be born. This is not something that can be stopped."

"It's too early..." the empress cries. "It's too early..."

"Not necessarily," the midwife says. "Babies born this early can survive. But we must hurry."

At this, the doors open again and the doctor rushes forward. Behind him is the emperor. This time, even I drop to my knees. The doctor begins giving the empress the same exam as the midwife did, and the two whisper together. The emperor crosses the room, and I move out of the way as he sits on the bed next to his wife.

"I'm sorry," she says.

The emperor shakes his head and gives her a smile, but it quavers. He touches her cheek and then kisses her forehead.

"You can do this," he whispers. "Do it for me."

The empress kisses the palm of the emperor's hand. As he pulls away, he glances at me and gives me a nod. I bow and then take his place by her side. He cannot stay, so he entrusts her care to me. As soon as he is gone, the room is once again busy, and the doctor and midwife work together to save the empress and her son.

~

A day and a half later, the baby still has not come. The empress is so weak, she can barely keep her eyes open. She no longer screams, her body having become numb from the pain. The midwife and doctor check between the empress's legs one more time and shake their heads.

"Your majesty," the doctor whispers so only she and I

can hear, "we can delay no longer. The baby will not come on its own. We must cut him out. I'm sorry."

The empress puts her hand to her face as she nods. Tears run down my cheeks, but I do not contradict her. It is a death sentence for her, but it is the only chance the baby has of survival. As the doctor moves away to prepare for the surgery, the empress pulls me to her.

"He will need you now," she says, and I know she means the emperor. I nod as I hold her tight.

"My lady," the doctor says, tugging gently on my shoulder. I look around and see that there are very few people in the room, only two senior maids and the helpers for the doctor and midwife. I know he thinks I should leave. That I should not have to see what happens next. Watch my empress die. But I can't leave her. I shrug him off.

"I'm staying."

The doctor only gives me a small bow as he prepares his instruments and lays a clean cloth over the empress's stomach.

"She...she was innocent, wasn't she?" the empress asks me. "She never would have hurt me."

I cannot lie to her. Not now. Not when she knows the truth already. Not when she has only moments left on this earth. I nod, too choked up to say anything.

The empress grunts, and I see that the doctor has made the first incision. I look away, back to the empress's face. I can't watch.

Tears stream down her face and she grunts again, gritting her teeth. She gasps and looks at me. "You are in grave danger," she spits out with surprising force. "If it wasn't Lady An... I don't know... I don't know..." She screams and I see the doctor pull the baby from the empress's body, the thing tiny and red.

"I did it," she says with a sigh, and I feel her grip loosen. "I did...my duty..."

Her eyes flutter closed as the blood from her body pours out, seeping into the bedclothes, my gown, and dripping to the floor. The midwife and doctor have not bothered to stop the bleeding or clean her up. All their focus is on the child, who they are tending across the room next to a brazier. The assistants are there as well. One maid has fainted, while the other has fled the room to tell the others what has happened.

Pain seizes my chest and I lean forward, wrapping my arms around the empress, crying out in a pain of my own. How could everyone just abandon her? This beautiful, brave woman who sacrificed her very life for the empire. She cannot simply be discarded, tossed aside like a useless husk. I hold her tight, my cheek to hers.

"I'll remember you," I whisper. "I'll tell your son about you."

I don't know how long I sit there, waiting for my tears to stop. Waiting for the pain to release me. But eventually, I realize that I have not heard the baby cry. I look over and see the doctor and midwife still working.

"No," I whisper as I stand. My gown is heavy with blood and I slip on the slick floor. But I must see. I must know. The empress cannot have died in vain. The prince must live!

When I reach the light of the brazier, I look between the midwife and the doctor at the tiny wrapped bundle between them. The midwife is crying, and the doctor is shaking his head.

"What...what is wrong?" I ask. I know the answer, but I must hear it.

They both look at me, and I see both sadness and fear on their faces.

"The prince," the midwife says, "he is dead."

My head swims and think I might swoon. The doctor grabs my arm to hold me steady.

"There was nothing we could do," the doctor says. "The...the cord wrapped itself around his throat. The prince was already dead from the start of the empress's pains."

I don't know how they can know this, nor how they could not have known it before now. If they had known, then perhaps the empress could have been saved. She didn't need to die.

I look back at the empress's body, the large cut across her abdomen, and feel sick. How could this happen? She was so young. Healthy. She'd given birth before. It shouldn't have happened... It shouldn't have happened...

The doors to the room open and the emperor staggers in, swaying, and I think he must have spent the last day and a half drinking. He looks at the empress, then he leans against the wall and vomits. The smell of it about makes me sick as well. I put my sleeve to my hand, which is not much better as it smells of blood and the empress's perfume.

"My son," the emperor says, walking toward us. We all drop to our knees, the midwife holding tight to the bundle. "Where is my son?"

"Your majesty..." the doctor says, shaking, and I suddenly realize why I saw fear on his and the midwife's faces. "The child...c-c-could not survive."

"Where is my son!" the emperor roars, pushing the doctor out of the way. The midwife staggers to her feet, offering him the wrapped bundle. I am afraid he will drop it, but the emperor takes the baby with surprising gentleness. He nudges the wrapping away from the face, then he brings it to his lips and gives it a delicate kiss.

"It was a boy, wasn't it?" he asks, looking to the midwife for confirmation. The midwife nods.

"Yes, your majesty."

I am not sure if this is a comfort to him or only makes the deaths more painful, but either way, the news seems to undo him. He backs into a wall and sinks to the ground. There, holding the body of his only son, he cries.

I am not sure what to do. My own heart aches so much, I wish I could just lose consciousness. Sleep for a thousand years. Long enough for the pain to dull. But I cannot. Still on my knees, I crawl to the emperor's side and wrap my arm around his shoulder. He turns into me, crying into my chest. I hold him tight, his son between us, and together we mourn the loss of our empress and our hope for the future.

31

———

e mourn the empress and the prince for ten days. We dress in white robes and kneel in the courtyard behind the emperor's main audience hall from dawn until dusk. We do not eat, do not pass water, don't stand up until the sun sets. On the other side of the emperor's audience hall, in the main grand courtyard, all of the emperor's advisors, officials, princes, and elevated lords and ladies perform the same ritual.

I do not see the emperor in all this time. After we cried together, he left the empress's palace, carrying the tiny body of his son, and retreated to his own palace. Jinhai carried me back to my palace, where my ladies washed me and combed my hair, folding it into a simple plait. We cannot wear makeup or style our hair in any elaborate fashion while in mourning. I do not know anything about Manchu death rites, but no one seems to notice. I think everyone chalks it up to my own grief muddling my mind.

But why have I grieved so? I was not particularly close to the empress. She had not been exceptionally kind to me. I suppose it is just the tragedy of it all.

When I lived on the dusty streets of Peking, I thought that the Manchu lords and ladies, the emperor and empress, on the other side of the great red wall lived such easy lives. They never knew hunger, or cold, or went without shoes. And while that is all true, that does not mean that they did not still suffer. Suffer loss, suffer pain, suffer loneliness. The empress should have been the happiest, safest, most privileged woman in the world. But the last time I saw her, she looked like nothing more than a slaughtered animal. The memory makes me sick, and I think it always will.

This morning, eleven days after the deaths of the empress and the prince, the emperor's chief eunuch appears at my door. Even though no one told me what is going to happen—I know.

I am going to be crowned empress.

"Please prepare yourself and follow me," is all the eunuch says. I nod and return to my washroom, where Nuwa bathes me, scrubbing me from head to toe until my skin burns pink, and then rinsing me with cow milk scented with rose petals. I did not think it was possible for my skin to appear so light in color. I am then massaged with oils and my hair brushed one thousand times.

Suyin uses the best quality makeup, making my face even more pale, painting my eyes with black and gold and a strip of red painted down the center of my lips. Nuwa styles my hair with a headdress befitting an empress. Then, I am dressed in a yellow robe embroidered with a nine-tailed phoenix. The emperor and the empress are the only people in the whole country allowed to wear imperial yellow. I am given a long string of jade beads, and gold enameled nail protectors are placed on three of my fingers on each hand. I am then helped into pot-bottom shoes taller than any I have worn before. I am carried in a sedan chair to the main audience hall and led through a side door into a small room, where I now wait alone.

I wish I could pace, but I cannot walk on my own accord without falling. The shoes are too elevated, the headdress too heavy, and the long train of my robe tugs me down. My maids are instructed to wait outside until I am summoned. I wish I could cry, but I do not want to spoil my makeup or look a fool when I am called for. I do not want this, but it is impossible for me to refuse. The least I can do is act with as much dignity as I can muster.

I hear a door behind me open and close and I hold my breath, expecting it to be the eunuch, telling me it is time. But it is not the eunuch's voice I hear.

"Lihua."

Prince Honghui's eyes are rimmed red, the same as mine have been these last two weeks. He is no longer in his mourning clothes, but in a robe of another shade of yellow embroidered with a three-toed dragon. Only the emperor may wear garments depicting a four-toed dragon.

"What are you doing here?" I ask him.

He takes my hand, and I know I should pull it back, but I don't. He steps close to me, too close, and puts his forehead to mine.

"I had to see you," he says, his breath shaking. "Had to see you one last time before…"

Before I am crowned empress, is what he cannot say. After today, we will not be able to see each other again, at least not privately. I can never risk sneaking out of my palace, not that I would have the opportunity. I have not had a moment alone since I became rank-two consort, and it will be even worse when I am empress.

Any independent identity I thought I had been forming

since my arrival here is now gone. I am no longer a mere Manchu lady. Nor a concubine. Not even a consort. In only a few minutes, I will be the empress of China. When I was younger, I thought that such a title was the pinnacle of power. But now I know that it is the opposite of that, complete servitude. I will no longer live for myself, but for my country, my emperor. Pregnancy will not be an unhappy consequence of my position, but my sworn duty. A duty that killed my predecessor.

"No matter what happens, I will be here for you," he says, and my heart hurts. It is a beautiful sentiment, to think that I am not alone. But I am alone. So very alone. Whatever happens, I will not be able to turn to him for help. For support. For kindness or friendship. And do not mention love.

But I nod, unable to stop a single tear from slipping down my cheek. "I'm so afraid," I whisper, at first surprised that I said the words out loud. Then I realize that this is my last chance to speak freely, to express what's truly in my heart.

"I know," he says. "You never asked for this, never wanted it. You strange, wonderful, beautiful girl." I can't help but laugh. "You never told me what secret burden you carry, and now I suppose you never will."

I am not Lihua! I want to tell him. Tell anyone! It isn't only that I don't want to be here. I *shouldn't* be here. I'm not Manchu. I'm not a lady. I should never have even been admitted to the Forbidden City, and now I am about to sit on the empress's throne. How did this happen?

"You should go," I finally say, pulling my forehead from him and looking into his eyes. "You can't be caught here."

He nods, but then he places his lips on mine...one last time. Tingles rush from my lips, down my spine, and into my stomach. It is a gentle kiss, one where our lips barely meet for fear of disturbing my face paint, but there is so much contained in that small touch. So much love and loss, joy and fear, passion and pain.

The prince finally pulls back, wiping his mouth of any paint, and he bows his way away from me—as befitting my new station as his empress. I turn away from him, for I cannot watch him leave me.

The doors in front of me open, and the light is blinding. I hold my arm up to my eyes as they adjust. Nuwa and Suyin enter the room, each taking one of my hands. They tug me forward, but my feet feel stuck to the floor.

"I cannot do this," I tell Suyin.

Suyin moves to stand in front of me, taking both of my hands and looking deep into my eyes. "Do you remember what I told you when we first met?" I shake my head. That feels like a lifetime ago! "I said that you were sure to be chosen, and I was right. You were chosen for a purpose, my lady. Everything has led to this."

Could there be some truth to what she says? Am I *supposed* to be here? Would Heaven allow a Chinese girl to sit on the throne if they did not will it?

Suyin squeezes my hands one last time and then stands beside me once again. This time, as she and Nuwa tug me forward, I place one foot in front of the other and enter the great audience hall.

The room is full of important men, even more than last time. When I enter, they all drop to their knees and then bend over, knocking their foreheads to the ground in honor of me. I gulp as I remind myself to put one foot in front of the other, and then to breathe. As I follow the red carpet, I see the emperor up ahead, at the top of the stairs of the raised dais, waiting for me.

When I reach the bottom of the stairs, my knees are shaking so badly, I cannot raise my foot. I dare to raise my eyes and look at the emperor. The last time I saw him, we cried together. But the last time we spoke, it was in anger and he sent me away. What if he is still angry with me? What if he is only doing this because he has to? Will he set me aside at the first opportunity?

But when I look up, the emperor meets my gaze. He is not smiling, but neither is he angry. The pain is still clearly etched on his face, as I'm sure it is on mine as well. He nods, and I know he means it as a comfort. The past is forgiven, perhaps even forgotten.

I lift my foot to the first step, and then the next, and the next, Suyin and Nuwa still by my side. As I reach the top of the dais, the emperor takes my hand in his, and my maids step away. The emperor leads me to a throne that has been brought forward and set next to his, a throne of gold carved with a phoenix. The emperor helps me turn around and face the gathered people, who are all still kneeling, but now they have sat up, a thousand eyes watching me. Somehow, out of the sea of people, there, to the left toward the very back of the room, I see Prince Honghui. He gives me a small smile and nod, and I give a smile back—only for a moment.

I sit down and perch on the edge of the throne, and the emperor takes his seat next to me, in the dragon throne, and takes my hand. My eyes lift to the massive golden dragon above him with the pearl in its mouth and for a moment, I think I see it quiver, as if the dragon can no longer hold the weight of the pearl and is about to drop it, crushing the emperor. I hold my breath, but nothing happens.

As I face forward once again, the empress dowager appears and places a gold phoenix crown on my head in front of my headdress. I had expected it to be heavy, but it is so light, I hardly notice it is there. She then bows as she backs away. Through all of this, I do not look at her face. I cannot bear her scrutiny right now. A eunuch steps forward and reads from a scroll.

"Presenting Her Imperial Majesty, Ula Nara Lihua, consort of His Great Imperial Majesty, Emperor Guozhi, Empress of the Great Qing Empire, Empress of the State of Manchuria, Khatun of Mongolia. May the empress live ten thousand years!"

Everyone in the room kowtows to me, repeating, "May the empress live ten thousand years!"

As I scan the crowd, a large smile crosses my face and a laugh chokes my throat. It is inappropriate, I know, but I cannot stop it. Every person of wealth and dignity in China is kneeling before me—*me!* The daughter of a laborer without even a pair of shoes is now the empress of China. *I am the empress of China.*

I only hope my parents hear of me, and that I make them proud.

THANK YOU FOR READING!

Daiyu's adventure continues in Empress in Hiding, available for pre-order now at your favorite bookstore!
https://books2read.com/u/b5ZNKl

Be sure to sign up for our mailing lists so you never miss a new release!
http://zoeygong.com/subscribe/
http://amandarobertswrites.com/empress-in-disguise/

EMPRESS IN HIDING

EMPRESS IN DISGUISE BOOK 2

https://books2read.com/u/b5ZNKl

She thought that the favor of the emperor would keep her safe. She was wrong.

At the center of power and privilege, Daiyu is now in more danger than she ever imagined. No longer able to hide among the countless palace ladies, as empress, Daiyu cannot escape the jealousy and scheming of the other women who would do anything to take her place.

But that is not the only danger Daiyu faces.

Foreign enemies besiege Peking, sacking the city and forcing the imperial family to flee for their lives. War changes everything.

With enemies lurking in every corner, Daiyu, the girl from the streets, must step into a role she was never born to play.

All of China depends on it.

ABOUT ZOEY GONG

ZOEY GONG was born and raised in rural Hunan Province, China. She has been studying English and working as a translator since she was sixteen years old. Now in her early twenties, Zoey loves traveling and eating noodles for every meal. She lives in Shenzhen with her cat, Jello, and dreams of one day disappointing her parents by being a Leftover Woman (剩女). Learn more at ZoeyGong.com.

facebook.com/ZoeyGongAuthor

goodreads.com/zoeygong

bookbub.com/authors/zoey-gong

ABOUT AMANDA ROBERTS

 Amanda Roberts is a USA Today bestselling author who has been living in China since 2010. She has an MA in English from the University of Central Missouri and has been published in magazines, newspapers, and anthologies around the world. Amanda can be found all over the Internet, but her home is AmandaRobertsWrites.com.

facebook.com/AmandaRobertsWrites

instagram.com/amandarobertswrites

goodreads.com/Amanda_Roberts

bookbub.com/authors/amanda-roberts-2bfe99dd-ea16-4614-a696-84116326dcd1

ABOUT THE PUBLISHER

RED EMPRESS PUBLISHING

Visit Our Website To See All Of Our Diverse Books
http://www.redempresspublishing.com

Quality trade paperbacks, downloads, audio books, and books
in foreign languages in genres such as historical, romance,
mystery, and fantasy.

www.ingramcontent.com/pod-product-compliance
Lightning Source LLC
Chambersburg PA
CBHW031250160726
47993CB00001B/87